BRANDING HER

SERIES 1, BUNDLE 1

D1737985

BOOK 1

E01: BEGINNINGS
E02: HOLIDAYS

BOOK 2

E03: MUTUAL FUN
E04: BUSINESS TRIP

BOOK 3

E05: EXPLORING
E06: JEALOUSY

By

ALEX B PORTER

GET A FREE STORY
VISIT:

www.ALEXBPORTER.com

CONTENTS

E01: BEGINNINGS

CHAPTER 1

The keys jangled loosely in Kaylee's hand. With a jolt of excitement, she pushed the key into the lock and opened the door to the bright apartment. A rush of cool air met her as she came in from the warm September sun. The bare walls of her new home echoed with potential, a blank canvas awaiting paint. On her heels, a young boy sprinted into the room, stopping to tumble onto the thick carpet.

She laughed at his antics as she swept through the quaint two-bedroom apartment. Ryan would be here; this would be her room; and the desk would go there. Her mind started putting furniture into place as she explored.

"What do you think, Ryan?" she asked her son.

"I love it!"

"Alright kiddo. Once the movers get here we have to go register you for school. You start kindergarten this year. How exciting!" She ruffled his hair affectionately. "Now go play while I get some cleaning done."

The little ball of energy shot towards their bags and searched for his toys.

She pulled out the cleaning supplies and started going over some areas that had been missed. The bathroom mirror needed a bit of a shine and the sink had some water stains. As she cleaned, she caught herself smiling. Being a single mom was more work than she had anticipated, but it finally felt like everything was going to be okay. Pushing tousled red hair from her pixie-like face, Kaylee hummed and whistled as she quickly worked her way through their new home.

A sudden rap at the door brought her from her reverie. She opened it to reveal a large man from the moving company. After giving him a few instructions, she gathered Ryan and her purse and set out towards the next objective. The school was close by, making it easy to walk her son in the mornings and then catch the subway to her promising new job.

They returned home with a deli sandwich and chips in tow. The movers were bringing in the final few things.

There was so much work to do. The mountain of boxes made her feel claustrophobic. Ryan spent most of the evening setting up his Lego while Kaylee started working through the joys of moving. With each empty box came a small victory.

By dinnertime, the not-so-empty apartment seemed much more inviting. Ryan appeared, a blanket cape flowing out from behind him.

"Momma, can we have pizza tonight?" he asked, his tiny voice pleading. Kaylee's stomach grumbled at the thought of food - it was definitely time for dinner. She weighed the options; her budget was tight, but it was a special day. After placing the order Kaylee turned on the television to take a well-deserved break from housework. As soon as she was seated, a bounding Superman launched onto the couch to save her.

At last the doorbell rang and the cuddle monster ran to answer. As soon as the door opened, the realization of hunger overwhelmed her.

Ravenously, she and Ryan tore into the meal. After dinner, it was bath and then bed for Ryan. This had always been the established routine, and it would be no different with school starting in just a few weeks. The apartment was silent as Kaylee worked into the night, unpacking boxes and going over checklists.

Her first week was busy and left little time to enjoy the sights and scenery of her new home. With most of the important stuff unpacked, it was time to turn her attention to the interview. Blaire had walked Kaylee through two phone interviews and had pretty much guaranteed her the job. It was not glamorous, nor well paid, but she would start as an assistant to a clothing designer. She hoped it was finally her break towards her dream job as a top fashion designer.

The in-person interview was meant as a placeholder, just to make sure there were no hiccups. After all, they had paid for her to move up here, and surely that meant something. Still, she fidgeted nervously the entire day before. She went over and over her checklist, making sure her outfit was laid out. The babysitter had been scheduled. Everything was in order; it would all go well. She had to get this job!

The smells and sounds of the subway threatened to overwhelm her as she made her way into the city. As she took in the various sights, she fully realized she was no longer in her rural hometown. The hustle and bustle kept her moving quickly through the streets, landing her squarely in front of the new office building. Gathering her thoughts and portfolio samples, she opened the door to her new life.

"Welcome," a warm voice cheerily said from behind the front desk. "Can I help you?"

After a few small exchanges, Kaylee took a seat while the cute girl paged Blaire. Kaylee looked around in awe, taking in the grandeur of the building's modern design and marbled floors. She had trouble disguising her mix of excitement and nervousness.

A long minute passed before the receptionist stood up and motioned Kaylee over. "Right this way. Blaire is waiting."

The woman's office was quaint, with cute turtles and frogs everywhere. Kaylee let her eyes roam over the office décor while they discussed various aspects of the position. Blaire was extremely knowledgeable on fashion design and company expectations. She was also very friendly. The interview soon switched from technical to personal.

"Do you have any children?" Blaire asked, looking up from her papers and smiling. The sudden change in questioning caught Kaylee off guard; she had only been expecting design and career-oriented questions.

"Yes, my son Ryan is starting Kindergarten this year. I'm very excited. It's going to be a change of pace. I guess I'm a little nervous about it." Her answer roused a chuckle in the older woman.

"I remember when my children left the nest for the first time. You'll do just fine, dearie. Do you have any questions for me about the position?"

The rest of the interview went exceptionally well. Blaire let it slip that she already had an offer drawn up and it would only take a quick signature to seal the deal. For an instant, Kaylee's mind flew through all of the different possibilities that could come from this one moment, and then she took the pen and signed her name.

Beaming from ear to ear, Kaylee walked with Blaire to the front of the building. She explained the best food places, where the parking garage was, and other casual small talk. Suddenly, a woman emerged from a side hall and nearly collided with Kaylee. Kaylee shrank back from the encounter.

"Sorry, I wasn't watching where I was going." Kaylee's gaze met piercing green eyes and shocking bone structure. Strands of dark hair that had escaped from an otherwise neat bun framed the face before her. Lost in the woman's striking facial features, Kaylee stammered out nonsense.

"Alexis, meet Kaylee. She's starting as Rose's new assistant." Alexis took Kaylee's hand in a cordial embrace, their eyes connecting.

"A pleasure. Unfortunately, I've an appointment that I can't be late to." With that, she was gone, down the hall into another part of the building.

"Everyone is always so busy around here. No matter, I'm sure when you start you'll have plenty of time to meet everyone." As they approached the door, Kaylee turned and thanked Blaire, then found herself back on the busy streets of Boston.

Elation washed over her: She had done it. The next chapter of her life was beginning, and she had a firm grasp on the page.

The following days blurred together. Unpacking, preparing for a new school, and starting a new job was hard work. Kaylee and Ryan spent quiet evenings at home, trying to wind down. It had been a long journey, but being so busy meant having no time to dwell on the past. Despite still feeling pangs of loneliness, she knew the best of their lives was yet to come. Before she knew it, Monday morning had arrived. Life had shifted gears and was moving into a fresh new phase.

She promised herself she would not cry, but seeing her little boy all dressed up for his first day of Kindergarten made her go misty-eyed. Armed with a backpack and an Iron Man lunchbox, he made his way into the school building, hardly noticing his mother's distress. He was excited to make new friends and play with everyone. When had he gotten so big?

After a packed subway ride into the city, Rose greeted her at the office lobby. The first day was perpetual confusion and learning. Kaylee met everyone in the office, was assigned her desk, and started her first assignment for Rose before the clock had even struck midday. 'Fast-paced' seemed to be an understatement. By the time lunch came around, her head felt like it could float away. A firm rap on her cubicle wall made her turn with a start.

Kaylee's eyes drifted up the navy dress skirt and white blouse to meet those vibrant green eyes again. Alexis worked in a different department, but frequented her office enough that they would work together on some assignments.

"Grab your things— I'm taking you to lunch."

Kaylee was surprised at the bluntness, but quickly did as she was told. They were soon out the door and walking to a local sandwich shop. Alexis stood a few inches taller than Kaylee, making her stride longer. Kaylee's slight form felt rushed to keep up.

"Welcome to your first day on the job. I'm Alexis, but most everyone calls me Alex. I didn't get the chance to introduce myself before. I hope lunch makes up for it." The conversation flowed smoothly as they walked. Finally, Alex opened the door for her, ushering Kaylee into the tiny shop. The flavors in the air made her mouth water. The Rueben was to die for, but the conversation was even more delectable.

"I swear, it feels like it's been forever since I had a conversation with someone other than my son." The casual remark got a smile from Alex.

"Oh? No husband?" Alex apparently did not have an issue with being forward about her line of questioning.

"No. It was a bad situation." Kaylee fidgeted, feeling a bit uncomfortable. "Let's just say the sperm donor wanted nothing to do with it, so it's just the little guy and me. It hasn't always been easy, but we're making it."

Seeming to sense a dark topic, Alex changed her tone. "I'm sure you're a great mom. I'm not sure I could do it. I've always been fairly career driven."

Kaylee examined all of the evidence she had gathered about Alex. She thought she would be kind and caring, even though she had a straightforward demeanor.

"I bet you would do just great," she told Alex. "You could always have a trial run with my son, if you want."

Alex raised her eyebrow and lightheartedly played at the prospect of babysitting. They both chuckled. As the meal wound down, Alex pulled out her check card and paid.

"You don't have to do that, really," Kaylee insisted.

"I will hear nothing of it. I told you I was taking you to lunch, which means I pay." Despite Kaylee's objections, the transaction went through - she had little choice in the matter. The walk back was just as pleasant as the lunch itself had been. As Kaylee returned to work, she felt that she may have made a new friend, but beneath the pleasant undertones, she felt an ardent desire for something more.

CHAPTER 2

Kaylee established a great routine. Ryan absolutely adored his teacher and the school. She worked hard and fell into her job easily. Rose often complimented her abilities and work ethic. All the while, her friendship with Alex continued to grow. The leaves began to turn myriad hues as the weeks propelled them into autumn. This blossoming new life was demanding, but fulfilling in ways Kaylee had never imagined.

One day, she received notice that the subway would be down for two days. Not thinking much of it, Kaylee dropped Ryan off at school and drove into Boston to the company parking garage. The day progressed as normal until she received a call from the school: Ryan was sick and needed to be picked up right away. After making the necessary arrangements, she headed to her car. As she turned the key, the aged motor sputtered and quit.

A groan escaped her lips. The entire engine looked foreign as she popped the hood. Kaylee did a few checks, but nothing she tried seemed to make a difference. *My baby needs me*, her mind screamed. With the stress of the job and now this, Kaylee felt on the verge of a panic attack. Flustered, she phoned the school, letting them know she would have to take the train and would be a little late.

As she turned to head towards the subway, realization hit. She felt her chest tighten and stomach churn: the trains were down. Kaylee was stranded in the big city and anxiety had truly set in. Flying back into the building, Kaylee looked for the one person she thought could help.

Alexis was just coming out of a meeting when Kaylee found her. "Alex, can I ask a favor?" Kaylee hurriedly explained the situation as she walked to keep up with Alexis. Kaylee was almost in tears. She hated to rely on other people, especially now that she was supposed to be making it on her own.

"Sure, I can take you to pick up your son. Give me a moment to move stuff around."

Kaylee felt a small wave of relief wash through her. While waiting on Alex to finish her work, she phoned the school one last time. Ten minutes later, Kaylee found herself in a tan leather seat of a sleek Mazda 6 speeding down the highway. Career driven, indeed. Kaylee admired the luxury of the car, and felt embarrassed about her own. She gushed with thanks and appreciation.

"It's no trouble," Alex told her. "Besides, I enjoy spending time with you. It's about time you invited me over, even if it is a bit unorthodox." Kaylee was now used to Alex's boldness, but the timeliness and situation made her turn crimson. Faltering for words, Kaylee changed the subject.

"The leaves are gorgeous up here." Kaylee's flush did not go unnoticed by Alex, who smiled but graciously did not comment.

"I forget you're not from around here," Alex said instead. "This is my favorite time of year. The leaves are amazing, the mornings are nice and crisp, and I love the pumpkin spice everywhere." Alex took a slightly different route, cutting through a wealthy neighborhood lined with vibrant trees.

"I love the fall, too. It's a great time to sit around campfires and drink apple cider." Kaylee's mind drifted to the fun times at home, cautioning away from the bad parts. "I remember my dad used to take me to the local harvest festival."

"Really? Well, there's an art festival this weekend in Boston. Would you and Ryan like to go with me?" Another frank question, although this one seemed more like a statement than an invitation. Kaylee could do little more than stammer.

"Alright, it's settled then. How about you meet me at the office around eleven? We can all enjoy the parade, and then we'll drop Ryan off with a babysitter and go to dinner, just the two of us."

Kaylee felt like she had just been told about a date. Her mind fell to turmoil. She hadn't been on a date in years, and her last relationship had been short and fell apart horrendously. Dating a woman with a child was a lot to take on. Kaylee knew the hazards, and she had to consider Ryan's wellbeing alongside her own.

But Kaylee couldn't get ahead of herself— she still wasn't even sure if Alex was gay or not, but she had a hunch. Blushing again, she shyly nodded her head.

"Good." Alex smiled with finality, as if she had been planning for Kaylee's car to break down in order to get her alone. Arriving at the school, Kaylee found Ryan pale and quiet, and not at all like himself. Scooping him up, they quickly made their way home. Alex dropped them by the apartment entrance, said goodbye, and sped off. The rest of the day was spent tending with a sick child, while Kaylee mulled over the coming weekend.

***

Before she knew it, she and Ryan were listening to live music and wandering between the different exhibits. Alex surprised her with a gentle touch on the shoulder. Her fingertips sent shockwaves down Kaylee's spine. Turning, she accepted the extended piece of funnel cake and passed it to Ryan, who dug into the sugary treat before charging off to a kid's area. Alex and Kaylee walked behind him as he explored. The crowd of people made Kaylee a little anxious, but having company made it bearable.

"How do you do it?" Alex's question brought her out of her anxiety. Gathering herself, she watched Ryan enjoying his face being painted like

Spiderman. "I mean look at him, he's a little ball of energy. I wish I had half as much enthusiasm."

"We do what we have to, I guess." Kaylee chuckled at his exuberance but still felt a little overwhelmed.

Alex's demeanor changed subtly, but instantly. Turning to Kaylee, she asked, "What's wrong?"

Those sudden questions always left Kaylee grasping. The anxiety had already started bringing back bad memories. The look across her face must have keyed Alex in.

"It's nothing. I just feel a little overwhelmed with so many people. I'm not used to it." Kaylee shrugged, trying to make light of it and avoid further discussion.

"We can leave if it's bothering you," Alex offered. Kaylee shook her head as she watched Ryan playing to his heart's content.

"He's having a blast here. We can't leave yet." Kaylee fought back the urge to flee. After all, this was supposed to be a fun day for all of them. She felt like she was ruining it. She started to twist nervously, looking for a distraction. With perfect timing, Alex caught her hand and held it tight.

"Well, if you want to stay, I'll be here to help you get through it." The green of Alex's eyes, brighter here in the sun, made her forget the world. The hand holding hers melted the worry away. "And the answer is yes, I *am* gay."

Kaylee's heart fluttered and a wave of warmth surged through her body, causing her to hold breath. Realization hit: Her hopes were not just fantasy. It really was a date. Kaylee was shocked how Alex always seemed to read her mind. Even at work it seemed to happen frequently.

The rest of the afternoon passed with balloons, celebration, and further flutters of anticipation. All too soon, Ryan was complaining of having to leave as they drove back home. The sitter would be there soon, and Kaylee had to get ready for her date.

***

At 7:45 the bell chimed Alex's arrival. Kaylee opened the door in a teal dress, cut to accentuate her curves. A playful whistle from Alex made her turn crimson. Alex lifted her hand, leading Kaylee out into the night. After opening the car door for her, Alex rounded the front and got into the driver's seat.

"Do you like seafood?" The question was more rhetorical than anything. The restaurant Alex had chosen was upscale and offered a beautiful view of Boston harbor. As they drove, they talked about how much they enjoyed the day, how excited Ryan had been, and what their next plans would be.

"I didn't want to ask around so many people earlier, but is there something about crowds that makes you so anxious?" The question was asked benignly, but a flood of emotion brought a lump to Kaylee's throat. Sensing the tension, Alex reached over and rubbed her arm.

"You don't have to share if you don't want to. No judgment."

"It's not that I don't want to," Kaylee responded, shaking her head. "I often feel panicked and anxious in crowds. I've never liked large gatherings, even as a little girl. They sometimes bring back memories of a really messed up time, one that I've tried to put behind me."

Alex's hand brushed down Kaylee's arm and squeezed her hand gently, urging her to continue.

"College was a confusing time. One day my girlfriend and I had a fight, all because of my mother. After the fight a friend offered support. He took me out to relax and have a good time." Kaylee paused. "The party was loud and crowded. I guess I drank a little too much and felt overwhelmed. Nathan eventually found me having a panic attack in the corner. I was a wreck from being lost, and my emotions were all over the place." Kaylee's voice caught as her lips pressed together. She had never uttered this to anyone, and was in no mood to finish the story.

Alex stopped the car and grasped Kaylee's hands, feeling where this was going. Kaylee started to feel like she was destroying the moment again. A squeeze reassured her otherwise.

"With the alcohol swirling through my system, I heard my mom's voice telling me I was an 'abomination' and that I should be 'normal.'" Kaylee paused for a few seconds to draw breath. "That night I lost my girlfriend, my friend and, to a certain extent, myself. My memory of that night is a blur of crowds, darkness and him on top of me. I feel ashamed, but I don't blame him. We were both intoxicated and emotional."

"As horrible of an experience as it was, I have Ryan now, and he's a ray of sunshine in my world." There. She had said it. She had worked through most of the turmoil over the last few years. Still, the memory was an open wound and she twisted away as her eyes began to well up.

"I can't imagine what you were going through." Alex paused, trying to feel out the words. "We should never have to pretend or try to be something we're not."

Fighting back the tears, Kaylee could only nod.

"You have been so strong to overcome it, and all of the anxiety. Plus, Ryan is amazing." Alex reached up to stroke Kaylee's cheek, "I'm right here for you, always."

Alex took Kaylee's chin and turned her head gently, gazing briefly into soft golden eyes. Kaylee's heart swelled by this rare expression of emotion from Alex. In all of their encounters at the office, Alex had come across as quite stern. Kaylee felt like she was melting into the seat.

"Look at me. You're so beautiful." Alex's words seeped into the sadness that had grown in Kaylee's heart. For the first time in many years, she felt a true smile spread across her face. "I say we need a bottle of wine for dinner. Thoughts?"

They entered the restaurant, which was every bit as nice as Kaylee thought it would be. The rustic decor and a view of the bay added to the serene atmosphere. The aromas emanating from the kitchen reminded her how ravenous she was. Walking towards the table, Alex held her arm out for Kaylee to take. Kaylee accepted it with a smile, and once seated, Alex ordered their bottle of wine.

"Would you like something to snack on while we wait?" Alex pointed out some of the appetizers she enjoyed. The waiter went over the evening's specials and brought the wine. Kaylee had never been on a date like this. As the food started to arrive, the conversation was as delicious as the meal.

"So, now you've heard my woes, - let's hear something about you," Kaylee ventured. The plate in front of her was brimming with succulent shrimp, wild rice, and asparagus. She realized how hungry she had been as the aromas hit.

"Well, there's not a ton for me to tell. I'm a workaholic, I stay up too late, and I don't get much sleep. What else would you like to know?" Alex asked, smiling at her lengthy self-description. She speared a scallop while waiting on Kaylee's response.

Kaylee smiled to herself. What *wouldn't* she like to know? "I'm sure there's plenty more to you than your insane work schedule. Why not tell me about your past? How did you end up in Boston?"

"I originally grew up around New York. My father owned his own business; life was grand. As a teenager I discovered fashion and fell in love with it. My parents eventually forgave me for going that route. They actually paid for me to attend one of the top schools here and graduate school in London. I had a great time, some great experiences, and really loved life. Still love life, just work too much. My family has been a real blessing, embracing my career choice and my lifestyle. My brother is still annoying, but my parents are gold." Alex finished her summary and took a sip of wine.

"I wish I could say the same about my mother. She has never liked the idea of me being gay. Even after I had the coveted grandchild. She's a God-fearing woman and I guess with me being an only child, she placed a lot of hope on my being the perfect daughter." The wine had started to kick in and Kaylee relaxed back in the chair. "It was my father who pushed me towards fashion, though. When I was a child, we used to sit and draw together. I would create new work uniforms for his staff. He encouraged creativity right throughout my youth."

"That's wonderful. My dad pushed me to be an architect, the family business. I just didn't feel it though. I wanted to make my own mark on the world. Studying in London gave me a taste of that." Alex smiled, reminiscing. "When I came back, I pretty much walked straight into the office and took over. Been there for five years now."

"That sounds mind-boggling. I've never been outside of the country, let alone to London. There's a lot I haven't had the chance to do yet," Kaylee said, finishing off her glass of wine.

"I think we should change that," Alex said, smiling and draining her glass. The couple shared wine, stories, and a divine array of seafood throughout the evening. The coup de grace was the decadent dessert, a slice of 'death by chocolate' cake. All too soon, they were heading back home.

"Today has been absolutely amazing. Thank you so much for everything." Kaylee giggled, feeling truly happy with where she was in life. Alex parked outside of the apartment, hopped out, and opened the car door for Kaylee. They walked slowly up the path, savoring the crisp night air.

"It was my pleasure. It's not often I meet someone like you." Alex's words echoed through her and a blush started to rise. She turned to mutter a reply but found her lips meeting with Alex's, and the chill of the autumn evening vanished into a single moment. Kaylee could only focus on the soft warmth of Alex pressed against her as she pulled Kaylee into a sweeping embrace. The kiss left her breathless. Smiling, Alex kissed her forehead, saying goodnight as she headed back to her car.

Kaylee paid the babysitter, bid her farewell and sank into the couch. Her mind was racing with the day's activities. The kiss still felt fresh on her lips as waves of mixed emotions spiraled into the night. She had never felt for another person as she did for Alex at this moment. She had laid herself bare to her friend and was not rejected. Despite Kaylee's past, Alex was there for her.

But- What if she wasn't? What if she didn't want children? What if...

The expanding emotions swept down her cheeks. Kaylee's mind recalled events of her past, intermingling them with the day's happiness and her deep-rooted insecurities. She checked in on Ryan, her little angel sent as a gift from past transgressions. Finding him asleep, she pulled off her dress, climbed into a relaxing shower, and began soaping herself. She closed her eyes and let the excitement and emotions of the day overtake her, dreaming of what the future may hold. As she crawled into bed, the dreams faded and were quickly overshadowed with fear and insecurity. Her mind fought sleep, ruminating over every negative thought that entered her mind.

***

Monday posed an interesting dilemma. Alex was making coffee in the break room when Kaylee came in. She flashed a knowing smile, sending a rush of warmth to Kaylee's cheeks. Rose didn't seem to notice anything as she explained an upcoming assignment to Kaylee, but Kaylee's stomach fluttered with excitement and confusion. The what-ifs from the previous night were still at the front of her thoughts, but she smiled back at Alex, hoping to seem nonchalant.

The week seemed to drag by. Kaylee felt unsure of what to think about the situation. She knew that she liked Alex, and that she enjoyed every moment she had spent with her. However, Kaylee's uncertainty, the insecurities from her past, and the contrast of Alex's lifestyle paralyzed her. As Friday approached, Alex cornered Kaylee in the break room.

"Are you avoiding me?" The question stabbed through Kaylee like a knife. The swirl of emotion returned to her gut as Kaylee met those piercing green eyes.

"No, no. Not really. I'm just... confused." Kaylee looked down, feeling shy. "It's complicated."

Alex inched closer, the proximity helping Kaylee relax.

"What if you don't like or want children?" Kaylee asked dejectedly. "What if our lifestyles clash?"

"And what if we live happily ever after? Eh?" Alex returned with a playful smile.

The sudden new 'what if' threw the others out the window. She realized how silly her mind was, running away with the whole ordeal, especially after just one date. However the thought of *that* 'what if' brought a genuine smile of relaxation to her face.

"I might like that," Kaylee smirked back.

The undertone of sarcasm and laughter brought a smile to Alex's face. She wrapped her arms around Kaylee. Her demeanor at work was different, but a trace of tenderness was still there.

"Glad to hear it. Now stop thinking so much and let's just have some fun. It's your turn to entertain me. How about dinner at yours tomorrow night? I'll be there at seven with a bottle of wine." She kissed Kaylee's cheek and turned to leave the room with a smirk across her face, leaving Kaylee dazed. Suddenly, Kaylee felt the need to rush home and start preparing.

***

Asparagus, check. Garlic, check, and lamb chops, check. The shopping seemed to take forever on the hectic Thursday afternoon. As soon as she got home with Ryan, she started tidying her small apartment.

"Momma, what's for dinner?" Shocked, Kaylee looked at the clock, a quarter till eight already. In one quick swoop, she grabbed the keys and a light jacket.

"Let's go get something. What do you feel like, kiddo?"

"Tacos?"

Without a word, Kaylee drove off, mentally going through checklists and preparations. On their way to get food, they talked about school. Ryan had adjusted well. He also seemed to really like Alex.

Finally, in a lull in the conversation Ryan chirped, "Are you and Ms. Alex dating?"

"Well, maybe? Is that okay? Do you like Ms. Alex?" *Kids say the funniest things*, she thought. Of course, he had a right to give his opinion. It was his life, too.

"I like Ms. Alex. Is that why you've been cleaning all day?"

Kaylee chuckled to herself at the innocent line of questions. Why was it so easy for kids to be okay with it all? And why did some people have such a problem with it?

"Yes, darling, that's why I've been cleaning all day." Once they got home, they devoured the tacos and Ryan went to bed. Kaylee worked feverishly trying to prepare for dinner and clean the house.

Around midnight, she had everything clean and the lamb chops were marinating. Exhausted, she whisked herself off to bed.

CHAPTER 3

Friday had never passed so slowly. The minutes marched into hours. A mixture of nervousness and excitement drenched each thought. Finally, she was picking up Ryan and starting dinner at home. The lamb was in the oven with asparagus and potatoes. The doorbell rang just as Kaylee added the final touches to the table.

Ryan answered the door, exuberantly charging past polite rhetoric to ask, "Are you dating my mommy?" A chuckle sounded through the apartment as Kaylee worked her way from the kitchen to the front door.

"Maybe, if she'll let me. Do you think she'll like these?" Alex was leaning over, showing Ryan a bouquet of red striped roses. Kaylee immediately blushed at the gorgeous arrangement. She had never received flowers before. Alex then produced a small set of Hot Wheels.

"I also got these for you, tyke."

Ryan was off like a flash, squealing with glee. Alex brought the flowers up, offering them to Kaylee. Still crimson, she took them and smiled, mouthing a thank you. As she turned to put them in the kitchen, Kaylee was pulled back toward the doorway and into Alex's embrace. The kiss caught Kaylee off guard. After several drawn-out moments in time, she was released to catch her breath.

"I've waited all week to do that," Alex said in a soft, low voice.

Kaylee could only giggle meekly; she had been waiting for that moment too. She returned and busied herself in the kitchen to hide her elation. Soon the roses were on the table, accompanied first by wine glasses and then by a succulent dinner.

"That smells divine. It's been a long time since I had a good home cooked meal." Alex paid the compliment while fawning over the aromas several times. With the table set, all three of them sat down to dinner. The conversation was dotted with five-year-old interjections.

Bath and bedtime had never been so rebelled against. Ryan wanted to stay up and play with Alex, who would race him around the room with the Hot Wheels. Finally, the child collapsed into sleep and Kaylee pulled his door closed. Alex patted the spot next to her on the couch, smiling past the rim of her wine glass, and Kaylee obliged.

A new wave of nervousness washed through her. This was the first time she had had someone in her new apartment, and the first female she had been close to in a very, very long time.

The wine steadily disappeared between the two of them as they chatted about stories of growing up, coming out, and their favorite college regales. It seemed that despite having been with the company for nearly five years, Alex did not have any close friends in Boston.

As Kaylee turned to put her wine glass down, a hand slid up her back, lightly massaging as it went. Time seemed to slow into a heartbeat. Kaylee let out a small sigh and turned back to Alex, who had already leaned in for a kiss. Alex pulled Kaylee towards her gently, leaning down to plant a deep, soft kiss on her upturned face.

Seconds seemed to stretch into minutes as they kissed and explored. Alex opened her mouth and slid her tongue gingerly over Kaylee's lips. Kaylee lost herself to the sensation, kissing back with passionate desire. The hand that was on her back slowly slid around to the front, hooking her waist possessively. Kaylee placed her hand on Alex's cheek as they breathed each other in.

One by one, Alex's hand stealthily undid each button down Kaylee's blouse. Lost in the kiss, Kaylee didn't take heed until she felt Alex press her warm hand against her bare midriff. The hand explored her body, teasing her hips, softly dragging nails across her tummy, and finally cupping her breast through her bra. Kaylee let a soft moan slip into Alex's mouth, which relentlessly pressed on.

Kaylee's blouse was pushed off her shoulder, along with the bra strap. Her bare breasts felt the cool air of exposure and responded to the gentle caress of Alex's hand. With Alex squeezing, teasing, and pinching lightly, Kaylee arched into the ministrations. She realized she was almost bare from the waist up, exposing her feminine curves to her delectable lover. Alex was clearly not satisfied with the clothes still remaining, and started pulling at her hips.

Breaking the kiss, Alex gently pushed against Kaylee's shoulder, laying her back on the couch. With one deft movement, her skirt, panties and remaining clothes were removed, and Kaylee was nude. Blushing, she opened her eyes to see Alex gaze upon her flesh. Then they locked eyes again as Alex leaned down, pushing Kaylee's thighs apart with her knee, and continued to kiss her. After a few moments, Alex left her lips and turned to her neck.

Sucking, kissing, and nibbling, Alex found Kaylee's tender spots, sending bolts of electricity shooting through her. While teasing with her mouth, Alex moved her hands, exploring the length of Kaylee's silky body. Soon she leaned down, taking one of Kaylee's plump nipples into her mouth, and suckled on it lightly. The motion elicited a low, soft moan from Kaylee. The heat of her mouth and twisting tongue caused Kaylee to arch her back, pressing her breasts further into Alex.

Alex responded by sliding a hand in between Kaylee's naked legs and softly exploring. Fueled by carnal desire, a fire erupted throughout Kaylee. She swept a hand up and cupped heavily at Alex's cheek as Alex continued to suckle her nipple. With the other hand, she pulled at the bun on top of Alex's head, allowing her long black hair to cascade down bare flesh. She tugged at Alex's shirt, and Alex paused long enough to let it slip over her head.

Instead of returning to her breasts, Alex kissed Kaylee's stomach down to her hipbone. Using soft kisses and nibbles, Alex worked her way lower, looking up to make eye contact with Kaylee as she moved. Kaylee gazed, hypnotized, into Alex's green eyes as the woman slowly, deliberately, slid her tongue across her womanhood. A surge of heat shot through Kaylee. After the first gentle lick, Alex pressed further, using her tongue to slide among Kaylee's velvety folds.

Inhaling sharply, Kaylee welcomed the thrust of Alex's tongue, gasping and moaning in pleasure. She pushed against the couch cushions while Alex lapped and suckled. Through the haze of desire, Kaylee felt two fingers sink into her, forcing another sigh of ecstasy. Deftly, Alex touched places as nobody had before, sending Kaylee reeling towards the edge of an orgasm. Feeling such a strong response, Alex lessened her intensity and smiled down at Kaylee.

"Would you like me to continue?" The words sliced through the apartment, which was quiet aside from Kaylee's moans. Opening her eyes, Kaylee saw a playful mischief in Alex, who, despite slowing, still kept her close to the edge.

"Ye... ye... yes, please," Kaylee gasped through the teasing. From the look in Alex's eyes she was clearly enjoying the control.

"Good girl, but that doesn't sound very convincing."

Kaylee bit her lip in frustration, at the coy response. Yet she could not keep silent as long as the probing continued. "Please, oh please. I... Please!" Panting and balanced along the edge of a knife, Kaylee began pleading. She needed the release.

"Please, *Ma'am*," she pled.

The last remark did it. Alex felt the submission and leaned down, sliding her tongue along Kaylee's outer lips while continuing to move her fingers inside. Gasping and driven mad, Kaylee mumbled words, begging for release.

Alex's tongue brushed against the bud of Kaylee's womanhood. Unable to contain herself,

Kaylee bucked against Alex, a surge of pleasure tossing her into the storm of an orgasm. Alex teased with her tongue and sucked the nub into her mouth, pushing Kaylee higher, only softening her ministrations when Kaylee returned to earth. Gasping for air, Kaylee blinked her eyes open to see Alex smiling down at her.

"Would you like to go to the bedroom?" The question seemed dumb through Kaylee's clouded mind, and she didn't even quite register when Alex stood up and helped her to her feet. They made their way to the bedroom, arm in arm, kissing and teasing each other the whole way.

As Alex slid her arm around Kaylee, she took notice of the rainbow butterfly tattoo on the small of Kaylee's back. "What a cute little butterfly."

Kaylee started giggling as they got to the bedroom. Not many people had seen her tattoo. Alex lost the rest of her clothing and they stood before each other. Kaylee took in each curve, admiring Alex's hips and breasts, and the way her long hair added to such an exotic allure. A beautiful tribal pattern blossomed from Alex's hipbone and wrapped around to her torso. Alex noticed her admiring and turned to show the wolf tattoo on her back. "These are mine. Not quite so cute, though."

Alex quickly returned to embrace Kaylee, pulling her in for a kiss. Kaylee felt the warmth and softness of Alex's smooth skin pressed against hers. A thigh pushed between her legs, gently nudging Kaylee into a sitting position on the bed. As she sat, Alex straddled Kaylee's leg, grinding her womanhood against Kaylee, who took the opportunity to explore her lover's body with her hands and mouth. She took a hardened nipple between her lips and Alex arched her back, moaning in pleasure. Gently placing her hands on Kaylee's hair, Alex urged her to continue. She did so happily, cupping Alex's other breast, tweaking her nipple, and kneading the bare flesh. Alex panted in approval, grinding her wetness against Kaylee.

"Mmmm, that's it," Alex purred. Alex pushed her body against Kaylee, bringing them both down to the bed, and then shifted forward until she had straddled Kaylee's chest. Kaylee could see the delicate nub in front of her, glistening with excitement and tipped with a small, curved barbell.

"Eat me," Alex panted, lifting her hips and pressing her hands against the wall.

Kaylee needed no further instruction and started lapping at the sweetness in front of her, teasing and toying with everything Alex had to offer. Instantly, Alex arched herself back and moaned. Kaylee wrapped her arms around Alex's hips, pulling her closer. Alex responded by grinding hard against Kaylee's mouth. Kaylee slid her tongue deeply into Alex, working her towards orgasm.

Kaylee focused all of her intent and strength on Alex as she began to buck and moan on top of her until, at last, Alex threw her head back in ecstasy. She gasped for a moment, riding out the bliss before she lay down and drew Kaylee into her embrace. Alex pulled her head up and kissed Kaylee passionately, both tasting themselves on each other's lips.

Alex giggled, kissed her lightly, and then shifted position to lie side by side in a sixty-nine position. Alex started kissing up and down Kaylee's thighs with expertise and deliberation. Cooing, Kaylee mimicked Alex and traced up and down her legs, avoiding sensitive areas. Fingers were added as they traced around tummies and hips, teasing each other's flesh. Sighing and enjoying the attention, Kaylee was first to take the bait, leaning in and planting a kiss upon Alex's inner lips and teasing the small barbell.

Alex dove in too, using her light fingertips to tease while her tongue explored Kaylee's depths. As the energy built, the sighs and moans from the two women filled the tiny room. Alex slipped a few fingers into Kaylee's womanhood, applying a light suction to her nub. The sensation brought a gasp and then a long moan from Kaylee. She felt herself quickly rushing towards release, and redoubled her efforts on Alex. Following the same motion, she plunged into Alex while focusing all energy on the steel-tipped jewel.

They started competing to see who could send the other over the edge first. Intensity built, each using everything and anything they could to push the other further.

Electricity bounced between the two women. At last, Kaylee could take no more and exploded, juices flooding out of her. The release drove Alex over the edge. The two lay panting, still coupled together.

Alex turned herself to lay beside Kaylee again, and they stared into each other's eyes for several moments. Alex leaned in to kiss Kaylee, slow and seductive. Kaylee smiled, and laid her head on Alex's shoulder, trembles still shooting through her body. Alex pulled the covers up, wrapping them together in a cocoon. Kaylee closed her eyes, enjoying the intimacy. Sweet visions sped through her mind as she relived the night.

CHAPTER 4

Kaylee drifted in and out of nirvana, her body humming and feeling more alive than ever. A sudden shift in the bed caused her to jolt awake. Alarmed, she sat up, realizing it was just Alex moving in the dark room. She smiled and laid her head back down, looking sleepily at the beautiful lover standing before her.

"Is everything okay?" Kaylee asked, stifling a yawn. She glanced over at the bedside clock; it was just past two in the morning.

"Of course, but it's getting late and I need to be heading home." Alex leaned down and kissed her, pulling the covers back up over Kaylee's shoulders.

She went around the room, gathering her discarded clothing. "Don't worry though, I'll call you tomorrow."

With that, she made her way to the living room to get dressed. Surprised, Kaylee threw the covers off and found a silk robe to cover herself. By the time she had followed Alex out, Alex was already putting on her shoes.

"Don't you want to stay the night?" The words had a tough time coming. She felt confused about what was going on. Did Alex not feel the magic that she had felt? Kaylee had felt secure and at peace, but now these feelings were stripped away and she felt raw.

"It's not that I don't want to, I just have a busy day tomorrow." Alex seemed unaware of the worries that had exploded in Kaylee's mind. Kaylee desperately tried to rationalize: *It's okay; we didn't agree she would stay over.* Her mind raced. Through thousands of passages, her mind travelled quickly to the darkest tunnels.

"Oh, okay," Kaylee mumbled in meek reply. She followed Alex to the door, not really knowing what else to do.

"Thank you for a wonderful night. I can't wait until next time." With that and a final kiss, Alex went off into the night. Kaylee watched from the window as her Mazda sped off into the darkness. She stumbled back to the bedroom, the musty scent of lovemaking still hanging in the air. Kaylee lay down, her mind flying through different possibilities and her stomach twisting. Sleep came fitfully, but at last her torment faded into darkness.

***

The sunlight streaming through the windows brought a new dawn. She had slept in for the first time in a while. The clock was nearing ten. Soft noises from the other room meant that Ryan was up watching cartoons. Shifting her weight, she rolled out of bed and slipped her robe back on. Making her way into the living room, she saw a loose pile of cereal spilt on the table. Reality was back.

"Momma, why are your clothes out here?" Ryan asked innocently.

A blush blossomed immediately on Kaylee's face. She quickly gathered her discarded clothing, taking them to the laundry basket. After hiding for a few moments, she told Ryan how it had been hot. In true five-year-old fashion, he accepted that answer and went back to his cartoons. Kaylee turned her attention to making a cup of tea and changing into some real clothes. She sat down on the couch, looking at the television but not actually watching it. Her thoughts were elsewhere.

Alex said she would be busy today. Kaylee's mind raced through the night before, reliving the excitement. Her heart melted and fluttered, remembering how she had felt with Alex. She felt a delicious stirring within her, thinking of everything that had happened. Still, her mind remembered the sight of Alex driving away in the middle of the night. Of course, some of her past lovers had left before dawn, too, but that was in college. Who slept through the night with anyone during those days?

Kaylee found herself staring at her phone, as if willing a phone call or text message to come through. What if Alex hadn't really meant everything she had said? Perhaps she didn't feel the same way that Kaylee did.

But how *did* Kaylee feel, anyway? Her mind wandered through the ins and outs of the last few weeks. In the end, she decided that she really did like Alex, and she wanted to explore the potential of dating.

Ryan interrupted her reverie by pushing a toy car at her. "Will you race me like Ms. Alex did?"

Smiling, she took the car and spent the next hour making ramps and highways out of the furniture. On a loop around the table grand prix, her eyes fixed on the flowers that Alex had brought. Kaylee hoped that Alex was just busy, and not put off. Ryan won the race. The rest of the day was spent cuddling, playing, and going shopping.

Throughout the day, Kaylee checked her phone. No call, no email, no text. Her mind continually weighed the possibilities. Sunday passed as well, playing on her anxiety even more. By the time Monday rolled around, she was feeling so overwrought that she nearly called in sick. Yet she had no choice; she followed her normal routine and found herself at work, pushing through the day. About midday, she ran into Alex in the hallway.

"Sorry I didn't call you," Alex told her. "I got a little busier than I expected. I hope you're not upset with me." The words seemed genuine, but after the weekend she had had, Kaylee was unsure of her own judgment.

"It's okay. You said you were busy." The words felt fake, but she had nothing else to offer. She wanted to tell her how she had worried the whole weekend, how she felt like she wasn't good enough. She wanted to tell her how frustrated she had been. Yet all that came out was, "I've been busy too. I'll catch up with you later."

Without waiting for a reply, Kaylee turned and went back to her desk, leaving Alex mystified. The next few days ended up equally as awkward. Kaylee was miserable, but felt that the issue wasn't an office-appropriate discussion. Alex, although cool, seemed distressed. Finally on Thursday, Alex popped her head into Kaylee's office with her arms full of papers.

"I need your assistance this afternoon. I've already cleared it with Rose. You'll help me with a presentation downtown. We're leaving in about twenty and will grab some lunch after." Kaylee turned to reply, but Alex was gone. Soon after, they were in the car, heading north on the highway. Kaylee sat in silence for the first few minutes, watching out the window at the passing scenery.

"Look, I wanted to apologize for my behavior last weekend. I should not have blown you off when

I said I would call." Kaylee listened but had no words to offer. Alex followed up with a probing question, "Is anything else on your mind?"

Kaylee reflected for a few more moments, not exactly sure how to approach the subject. Fidgeting only made the car ride stretch out. Finally, she resolved herself and turned to Alex.

"I guess my feelings were first hurt when you didn't want to spend the night. I know that we hadn't planned on it, and that you said you were busy. Rationally, I know that, but my mind just runs away with things sometimes. I tried to reason it out, but every attempt ended back at suspicion and worry." The words burst from her mouth like water rushing from a broken dam.

"But truly, I think it upset me more that I didn't hear from you when you said you'd call. I knew there would be a logical reason for it, but I couldn't convince myself." Kaylee stared blindly into space as she spoke. "I felt abandoned, frustrated and full of uncertainty. Then, every time I tried to bring it up at work, I lost my nerve. I feel so pitiful. I was worried that my feelings for you had been totally misplaced and you didn't feel the same. Maybe everything I felt that night was just in my head. And now I just feel stupid."

Why was she acting this way? She felt like an idiot. Like she was falling and out of control. It had been less than two weeks since their first 'date' and they'd only been together once. *What the hell is wrong with me?* Kaylee felt caught in the past again, always feeling abandoned by the people who had left her life. How could she already fear that Alex would do the same?

The car ride fell quiet, and Kaylee felt herself slipping towards the edge of a panic attack. The stillness in the air felt thick and suffocating. Kaylee returned her attention to the window, hoping to mask the emotions threatening to spill down her cheek.

"How do you feel about me?" Alex asked. "Be honest."

The last punctuated remark held Kaylee in check. Had she not listened? Was Alex disregarding everything she had just said? How would she even begin? She had barely known Alex two months, yet over the past couple of weeks she seemed to be the most important person she had ever met. She made the sun shine brighter.

"Alex, I feel safe in your arms. You make me laugh and smile like nobody ever has. I want to explore what we have together." Kaylee started to blush as uncertainty knotted up inside her. Alex reached over to hold her hand, warm and comforting against Kaylee's skin. The touch gave her the courage to press on. "I just don't want to lose this feeling."

"I don't want to lose this, either. You give me balance, and that is a nice thing to have." Alex's words rang through the car, cascading through Kaylee. Hand in hand, they rode for a moment in silence, letting the emotions seep through. "Besides, I like your kid, he seems fun." The last words made Kaylee laugh; he *was* a great son.

"Although," Alex continued, "there *are* a few things we need to get straight. Things will never work if we can't communicate openly. It's not going to be perfect, but I'll work hard to always be there for you. I'll try to be more receptive of how my actions can affect you; I realize I can be somewhat lacking in that department. And I'm sorry for not staying with you last week, or at least calling afterwards." Alex paused in thought. "Perhaps it was rude on my part not to warn you in advance that I had to leave." Alex looked over at Kaylee, smiling. "But the night just took us over."

"Apology accepted. Thank you." Kaylee leaned over for a quick kiss. They pulled into an office complex and put on their professional faces. The meeting went well, resulting in a new client. Alex could have easily handled this one alone, and Kaylee realized that Alex had only invited her so they could finally talk; the thought sent a wave of warmth through her. Afterwards, they got a leisurely lunch and relaxed at a park. By the time they made it back to the office, it was time to leave and pick Ryan up. Parting ways, Kaylee felt better than before, and looked forward to Friday more than ever.

CHAPTER 5

Kaylee found work difficult to concentrate on while thinking of Alex. When Friday finally rolled around, Kaylee rushed home to tidy up before Alex arrived. A little after seven, Alex showed up carrying a pizza and breadsticks. Ryan answered the door, not expecting the gourmet dinner. He was ecstatic that Ms. Alex brought his favorite food. The perfect blend of toppings made the apartment smell like a small Italian restaurant. Afterwards, Alex played with Ryan, racing around the living room.

Bedtime came quickly, again with avid objection from Ryan. Alex took a moment to find something in her car while Ryan was reading his bedtime story. Soon, the house was quiet and the two were sitting on the couch, a small duffle bag by the door. After Ryan was fully asleep, Alex cupped Kaylee's cheek in her hand and pulled her in for a deep, passionate kiss.

"I want you," Alex whispered into Kaylee's ear. The words sent a shiver of excitement dashing down Kaylee's spine. After a few more kisses, she pulled back, staring intently into Alex's eyes.

"I do too, but this time let's go to the bedroom first. Ryan asked why my underwear was on the living room floor last time." Chuckling, they both went into the bedroom, duffel bag in tow. Once the door shut, Kaylee found herself wrapped in Alex's arms, their breasts pushing together in the embrace. Alex pulled her in for another deep kiss, exploring her mouth with her tongue.

Feverishly, her hands roamed over Kaylee, pulling at clothes and tossing them away until Kaylee stood in just her underwear, her luscious curves on full display. Smiling, Kaylee turned to pull the bedcovers down and teasingly exposed her lacey backside. Alex stripped quickly, wrapping her arms around Kaylee again, her hard nipples sliding against Kaylee's bare back. Alex made quick work of the bra hooks, allowing her hands to freely explore the tender flesh, tweaking and kneading, her total focus on Kaylee's breasts.

The action forced a gasp and a moan from Kaylee, who arched her back and pushed into her lover. Alex started suckling Kaylee's neck, letting her free hand trail lower, cupping Kaylee's womanhood. Pushing aside her panties, Alex slid a finger into Kaylee, feeling her wetness. As she withdrew the soaking finger, she teased Kaylee's nub.

After a few moments of exploration, Alex gently pushed Kaylee forward into a kneeling position on the bed. Kaylee was on all fours, her cherry rump exposed to Alex. Alex wasted no time taking advantage of her upturned tail and slid a finger deep into Kaylee. Kaylee gasped at the sudden intrusion, but moaned as Alex started to push in and out of her, her dew coating Alex's teasing fingers. Kaylee arched her back, granting her lover more access.

Second and third fingers joined in while Alex took her free hand and tweaked Kaylee's nipples from underneath. The assault quickly overwhelmed Kaylee, who squirmed and moaned and turned herself over onto her back. The ember that had been inside her all week was now a raging inferno.

Her passion and desire threw all caution to the wind as Alex grabbed Kaylee's hips and pulled them towards her. Alex knelt at the foot of the bed, kissing the back of Kaylee's thighs as she went. Her tongue glided into Kaylee, tasting her honey and causing a ripple of pleasure to wash over her. Alex was not being soft and gentle, but ate her with intent, pushing Kaylee closer and closer to the edge. Her tongue dove deep, darting in and out, teetering Kaylee on the brink of orgasm.

In one movement, Alex slipped three fingers into Kaylee, while simultaneously twirling her tongue around Kaylee's clit. Muffling her screams with her hand and bed sheets, Kaylee plunged over the edge, juices flooding Alex's waiting mouth. Alex continued to suckle and push against Kaylee, holding her down as she rode the waves of bliss. The world finally returned to focus and the caresses relented.

"I want you, Kaylee, in every possible way. I brought something with me, but I'm not sure if you'd be up for it." Alex reached into her duffle bag and brought out a leather harness and large phallic dildo. Kaylee chuckled out of nervousness. She didn't have much experience in that realm of sex.

"If you aren't okay with it, please say so, but I want to make you mine." Alex waited patiently for Kaylee's response.

Kaylee smiled after a moment. "Just be gentle with me," she said, swallowing her nerves. Kaylee wanted this, wanted to be Alex's. Alex quickly stepped into the harness and attached the silicone cock to the front, her feminine curves offset by the protruding object. She moved behind Kaylee, running her hands down her back and legs. She moved to slide a finger into Kaylee, then coated the cock with her juices.

"Are you ready?" A small nod made Kaylee's red waves bob. Kaylee felt the large, bulbous head at her entrance. Slowly, Alex inched forward, pushing into her dripping pussy. Kaylee felt like she was being impaled by God herself. She grunted and gasped with pleasure, gripping the sheets as Alex pulled out slowly.

"Good girl, take my cock," Alex instructed through gritted teeth.

The dirty language was punctuated with Alex thrusting into Kaylee whilst firmly holding her hips. As she did so, Kaylee felt as though she would burst, as if she had never felt so full. Alex quickly pulled out and pushed into her again, building up a momentum. Kaylee gasped and groaned, clutching the sheets from the bed. With each thrust she felt another orgasmic wave building inside of her. Each thrust pushed the cock deeper into Kaylee, sending electric jolts through both of them. Soon, both women were panting and moaning, their cries of pleasure building off one another. Alex would thrust, and Kaylee would push back against her. The phallic intrusion became too much to handle, and Kaylee started to buck in orgasm. Alex grabbed Kaylee's hips, pulling her back onto the silicone cock. The force pushed Kaylee even higher.

"Come for me now," Alex demanded.

Kaylee had no choice in the matter. She pulsed around the intrusion, feeling wave after wave wash through her. Alex kept going, quickening her rhythm, building towards her own orgasm. Kaylee had no reprieve, shaking and shuddering, the orgasm threatening never to subside. Moaning into the sheets, lost to euphoria, her body trembled as Alex thrust harder and faster.

"I'm coming," Alex gasped as she shuddered with her own release. She continued thrusting until her tightened muscles relaxed and her own orgasm started to subside. Pushed to her limits, Alex collapsed forward on the bed, the silicone cock squelching as it left Kaylee empty.

Alex pulled the sweat-drenched harness off, positioning herself so she could hold Kaylee. Kaylee hummed with delight as the world finally started to come back into focus. Her limbs still trembled, entirely overwhelmed. Sticky and sweaty, they laid together, basking in the afterglow of each other. Content, Kaylee leaned her head on Alex's shoulder. Alex pulled the covers over them, arms and legs entangled. Soon, both were fast asleep.

CHAPTER 6

The next morning rang with songbirds, the scent of their lovemaking heavy in the air. Alex was the first to stir, neither having moved all night. She brushed Kaylee's hair softly, pushing it off her face. Kaylee's lashes fluttered sleepily open, and found those startling green eyes staring at her. She smiled and stretched her body, aching from their passion.

"Good morning, beautiful."

Kaylee blushed at the compliment, sure that her hair was an absolute mess. Alex leaned down and kissed her, pressing her hard against the sheets, the sensations from last night still fresh in their minds.

"Mmmm, good morning to you, too," Kaylee smirked.

Slowly, they stretched and got out of bed. Soft noises floated through the door; Ryan was watching cartoons again. Alex held Kaylee tight against her once more, kissing her deeply. Then they dressed and made themselves presentable, at least to the eyes of a five-year-old. Together, they walked into the living room.

"Ms. Alex? Did you have a sleepover?" The child's innocence brought a chuckle from Alex, who nodded. Kaylee stepped into the kitchen, starting some tea for the two of them. Soon breakfast was in full swing: Cereal, milk and hot tea.

Ryan chimed from his bowl, "What are we going to do today?"

"Well, anything you want to do. My schedule's clear." Alex's words made Kaylee smile. She would enjoy having someone to spend the day with. After breakfast they tidied the dishes while Ryan continued his Saturday ritual, oblivious to the flirtatious sparks.

"What would you like to do today?" Kaylee asked as she put away the last of the dishes.

Alex had busied herself, wiping things down and tidying the kitchen. "Like I said, my schedule is clear for you. We can do whatever you like." She paused. "You know, I really could get used to playing housewife," teased Alex, whipping Kaylee's behind with the towel.

Her last comment made Kaylee blush. Laughing, Alex leaned in and kissed her softly, placing a hand on Kaylee's hip.

"So should we say we're officially a couple, then?" Alex asked playfully.

Kaylee went crimson, nodding her head until her curls bounced vigorously. As she answered, Alex pulled her into a full embrace.

"Yes, I would like that very much."

Alex leaned in and kissed her again, this time with more passion. A tiny blur entered the kitchen, looking for a snack.

"Momma, what's a couple?" Laughing, the two looked down at the little scamp. "Are you going to stay around, Ms. Alex?"

"Only if your momma lets me," Alex said, smiling. Ryan raced forward, joining the hug.

"I would like that. You bring me fun cars."

Ryan missed everything else, including the look exchanged between Alex and Kaylee. They all ended up laughing in the kitchen. After the dishes were cleaned up, they decided to go for a picnic in a nearby park. The Mazda roared to life in the cool October day.

The park was quiet, the playground empty and the pond perfectly smooth. Ryan ran and played on the swings, leaving Alex and Kaylee on the blanket, watching the festivities of nature. Alex reached over and took Kaylee's hand, smiling at her. Kaylee returned the smile, feeling happier than she ever had. Her mind relived the last few months and she felt a wave of relief. She had made the right choice in coming to Boston.

"What are you thinking about?" Alex asked.

The sudden question brought Kaylee out of her thoughts. She considered the move, the job, Ryan loving school, and her newfound romance. What to say first?

"Just about how happy I am, and how happy you make me," Kaylee breathed. The answer seemed to please Alex, who leaned in for a kiss. "I want to see where this goes."

"I think it can go a long way. You've made me a very happy woman." Alex paused, reflecting on her words. "You tame me and I can think of nowhere else I'd rather be."

Kaylee's heart swelled at the prospect. They beamed at each other, both reflecting on the path forward. Hand in hand, they watched as Ryan came over from the playground.

"Ms. Alex, come push me on the swing."

Together, they headed to the swings, Ryan walking happily between them.

E02: HOLIDAYS

CHAPTER 1

The rustling of the sheets brought Kaylee gently out of sleep. It was Saturday. No work, no pressing meetings, and no fighting the subway. She took a few moments to relish the heat of Alex's body spooned against her back, one arm draped protectively around her. She smiled to herself. It had only been a couple of weeks since they started dating, but Kaylee felt more secure than ever before. Memories of the previous night flooded through her mind, making her smile broader.

A tiny pitter-patter scurried past the door — Ryan was up now. Kaylee let herself relax as the television buzzed on. She could afford a few more moments wrapped in her cocoon of covers and Alex. Subconsciously, she wriggled her bottom back against Alex as she slipped into light sleep again. Her muscles rippled, reminiscent of the passion from the night before. Suddenly, the hand wrapped around her clamped onto Kaylee's hip.

"Good morning, sexy," Alex's smooth voice whispered behind Kaylee. The hand started to glide over Kaylee's hips, thighs, and tummy. Kaylee purred with the attention, rolling her hips teasingly against Alex. The two stirred together for a few moments, reigniting embers. "I know what you're doing, missy. And I like it."

"I have no idea what you're talking about," Kaylee teased, giggling into the pillow. Without warning, the roaming hand latched back onto her hipbone. This time it was not meant to be sexy. The writhing and tickling fingers quickly brought a squeal of laughter from Kaylee who jumped from the bed. "That was evil!"

A mischievous grin spread across Alex's face. "I have no idea what you're talking about." The coy echo caught Kaylee off guard. Alex rolled off the bed to join her and kissed her sweetly. "So, what's on the agenda today?"

"Well, I was thinking of taking the tyke shopping for Halloween and a few other things. Do you want to come?"

Alex nodded and kissed her again, and then started to get dressed. Kaylee followed suit; she would take a shower after breakfast. For now, they both threw on lazy pajamas and made for tea. Alex mostly played with Ryan as Kaylee set the table up and cooked pancakes.

"Momma, Alex says we get to go shopping today. Is it true? Do we get to go shopping for Halloween?" Kaylee cut a glance at Alex as if to say, *Way to let the cat out of the bag!* Alex simply smiled and shrugged. "Can I be Batman this year? Or no, Iron Man!"

Ryan busied himself rushing around the rooms, pretending to be various superheroes. The two adults laughed as they finished their breakfast. Alex jumped in the shower as Kaylee cleaned up from the meal. Afterwards, Kaylee got Ryan ready, and then herself. The three set out for the day in Alex's Mazda. Ryan always loved the little sports car, despite the cramped backseat. Alex showed off by zooming about for him.

"What are you going to be, momma?" Ryan asked from the back seat. It was a normal tradition that she matched whatever he was going to be. However, she was stumped when he said he wanted to be a superhero. A lesbian Wonder Woman seemed a bit too cliché. She thought she might just do something simple, yet in the style of a superhero; it was for him, after all.

"How about I'll be Catwoman, since you're going to be Iron Man." Ryan laughed at her remark. Kaylee turned to Alex as she sped along the highway. "What about you, Alex?"

"What? You want me to dress up?" Alex seemed taken by surprise. She scrambled for a few minutes trying to come up with an excuse. "I don't know Kay, I haven't done anything like that in at least ten years. In fact, I'm fairly certain it *was* ten years ago."

"Come on, Ms. Alex, don't you want to go trick or treating with us?" Again the questions started to get heated. Alex fumbled to find her response. "So what are you going as Ms. Alex? Tell us!"

"I tell you what kiddo, I'll show up in something. I'm just not sure what yet." Alex sounded relieved as they pulled into the Halloween store parking lot. The attention quickly turned from her as the group headed into Scare City. "I felt like I was about to get the third degree from a five-year-old," Alex said, bemused, as Ryan charged ahead.

They spent a good portion of the morning wandering through the store. Kaylee chuckled as Ryan darted in and out of aisles, rushing back with dozens of props, masks, and costume ideas. Alex even joined in on his hijinks: sword fighting, shooting each other with blasters, and trying to scare one another. Kaylee could do nothing but watch and laugh at their antics. The thought struck her that Alex was a completely different person outside of the office.

"So what are you going to choose, kiddo?" Kaylee asked at last. Ryan stopped his galloping and shrugged his shoulders. "I was actually talking to the other kiddo," Kaylee said, and directed her attention towards Alex.

Alex stopped dead in her tracks at the comment. Then, she laughed and continued rampaging after Ryan. A few minutes later, Alex approached Kaylee and handed her a costume. The image showed a very sexy kitten on the packaging with a bared midriff, cleavage bursting at the seams, and rips up the side of skintight pants. As soon as she saw it, Kaylee felt the skin on her face rise to a full blush.

"I want to see you in this," Alex teased back for the earlier comment. "Although maybe, not during trick-or-treating. Maybe for a private demonstration?"

Kaylee had no words to offer. Ryan came screeching around the corner, causing Kaylee to fumble the package and rush to put it back.

"Momma, are you going to wear that?" Kaylee wanted to hide her face; Ryan's shrill tone had caused people to look over at them from across the aisles. "It would show off your boobies!"

Alex laughed out loud at the child's exclamation. Kaylee could hear other people chuckling to themselves as well. With crimson heat burning her cheeks, Kaylee did her best to divert the five-year-old away from the adult costume. As they found the superhero section, Kaylee finally started to laugh about it. Alex relished making her blush, especially in public. The rest of the day and weekend was spent discussing plans for the hectic months ahead.

***

'Hectic' was an understatement on the following Monday. First, Kaylee was brought into a meeting at the last minute. Twelve of her colleagues across various teams peered at the whiteboard with a sense of nervous anticipation. Rose stood up and approached the board as Alex took control of the slideshow from her seat.

"I'm sure some of you are wondering exactly what is going on at 10 am on a Monday morning. I assure you, we are not having a case of the Mondays — Not today. I've gathered you all here to make an announcement that will make the next six months of work in this office very critical. We have started a potential merger deal that will unfold over the next few months. The details are all still very shaky, but we have a monumental opportunity on our hands.

"Now I know we're in a very critical time of year for the fashion industry. Our fall and winter lines are doing well. That being said, the new work is in *addition* to our normal workload. This means a few of you may get the opportunity for some overtime. I'm anticipating that the extra workload will come after the New Year, for the most part. Closely connected to the merger is a new business opportunity. It's a big project for a prestigious client in LA and, if successful, will add a new level of credibility to our profile. Both Alexis and I will be heading this project. Remember, we are *all* a team here, so everyone please help each other out.

"The holidays are going to be hectic; they always are. Please submit your time-off requests by the end of the week. For the members in this room, I see an intensely busy new year, so relax and enjoy the time off while you can." Rose trailed on about various aspects of the project. Hands shot up now and again to ask questions or comments. Alex spoke in her normal business tone, addressing a few individuals with tasks and reiterating the team mentality.

The rest of the week passed in a blur, and the next week followed in the same manner. Kaylee felt that all she had done was work, eat, and sleep. Rose kept pointing out that with these projects, the hardest parts were the beginning and the end. Kaylee pushed herself to the limit, working late into the evening several nights. Her designs had to be flawless, she told herself every hour or so. After almost a month of grueling work, it was Halloween night. Kaylee had requested to leave at noon so she could spend extra time with Ryan.

***

Ryan bounced from the walls as Kaylee started getting his costume set up. In the end, he had decided to be Captain America. He had a red, white, and blue shield and he seemed to toss it around whenever Kaylee wasn't looking. Kaylee just finished putting on her cat ears and mask when she heard the door close, followed by a boisterous "Arrrrr." Ryan ran to the door laughing. Kaylee peered around the corner to find a sexy pirate in her living room.

Alex was dressed to kill in tight black leggings covered with knee-high, heeled black leather boots. She wore a blouse covered partially by a corset under a long leather overcoat. The hat even had a feather sticking up from the side of it. She brandished a rapier at Ryan who playfully deflected with his shield. They were both laughing and giggling until Alex spotted Kaylee and let out a low whistle.

Kaylee had been thrifty with her shopping. She wore black stretch yoga pants and a tight black top that hugged and accentuated her curves. She also had knee-high leather boots, but not high-heeled; keeping up with Ryan made heels impractical. Kaylee knew Alex wasn't used to trick-or-treating and hoped she would be okay in her heeled boots. The three of them piled into the car and started towards several neighborhoods around Alex's condo. Ryan was a little ball of energy the entire trip.

The trio walked for what seemed like miles, visiting house after house. Captain America got a lot of attention and a ton of loot. After a while Kaylee noticed Alex was losing stride, so they began to let Ryan go to each door while they remained on the sidewalk, watching.

"My feet are killing me," Alex griped as they passed towards the next house. "I should have thought ahead about this."

Kaylee chuckled, holding the loot and watching Ryan bounce around. "I suppose I could have warned you. I thought you'd know. At least you look like a sexy pirate."

Alex smiled at her despite the obvious pain in her feet.

"We can head back after this block and I'll give you a foot massage. How about that?"

"Mmm," Alex hummed, taking Kaylee's hands. "That sounds amazing. I had a thought, though. You know, you're looking rather sexy in that cat outfit. I was thinking you could leave it on tonight. I might even be able to find you a collar and leash."

The implications made Kaylee turn red. Thankfully, it was dark and nobody noticed in the limelight of the street. Soon the pair made it back to the car with a tired tyke in tow. By the time they made it home, Ryan was fast asleep in the backseat.

CHAPTER 2

The next Monday started right back into the hectic fray of work and holidays. The pace only seemed to intensify as the days went by. Before Kaylee knew it, it was Friday again. The next week came and went with little hesitation to the amount of work she put in. On Tuesday, she found herself wearing thin, but she was unable to do anything more than push forward. Six thirty rolled around and she decided to get a cup of tea to relax.

Alex was also in the kitchen. Kaylee had thought she was the only one left in the office. She smiled as she entered and went over to cuddle Alex for a moment. Alex slowly rubbed Kaylee's back, helping her temporarily forget about the stress.

"What are you doing for Thanksgiving, Alex?" Kaylee asked, not really keen on her own current plans.

"Oh, well, I usually end up going to see mum and dad. They take Thanksgiving and the whole month of December for themselves and spend it in a cozy cottage in New Castle, Delaware." Alex started to follow Kaylee back to her desk. "What about you?"

"I'm going to go see my mother, I guess. Yay..." Kaylee's sarcasm was blatant. "Sorry, I'm just not really thrilled about the holidays. They've been lonely ever since my dad passed. I still go to see my mum, but it gets harder every year, listening to her spew crap about my 'lifestyle'."

"Well, why don't you come to New Castle with me? We'll spend Thanksgiving with my family. I'm sure they'd love to meet you."

"Shhh. What if someone overhears you?" Kaylee whispered, a tinge of alarm in her voice. "I mean, I'd love to go, but I would hate to intrude."

"Intrude? What do you mean? We're dating, of course you're welcome at my parents' house." Again,

Alex did nothing to keep her voice down. Kaylee set her tea on her desk and grabbed Alex's arms in alarm; she didn't want to find out what the repercussions of dating a coworker could be. Alex smiled at the gesture and wrapped her arms around Kaylee. "So, will you come with me?"

"I'll have to check with my mother and make sure it's okay." Alex shocked Kaylee by smacking a cheeky powerful kiss right on the lips. Kaylee found her arms pinned so she could not struggle away. She whispered, "Are you crazy? What if someone walks by?"

Alex merely chuckled at her predicament and continued to shower her face with a rain of kisses, despite the protest. Finally, Kaylee opened her mouth once more to protest, but was instantly swept up in heated passion. Even her worries about being caught couldn't keep her from melting against Alex's lips. Alex cupped a hand over Kaylee's butt cheek and squeezed, making Kaylee squirm even more.

A cough from the hallway made Alex release her. Kaylee flew to her seat trying to look busy. Her cheeks were crimson and she was trying not to hyperventilate. Alex only smiled down at her. After a few moments the hall went silent again, and Kaylee turned to face Alex, a scolding look in her eye.

"What happens if we get caught?" Kaylee hissed at Alex. Alex leaned in close to her chair.

"We weren't, though. Besides, aside from one or two people, this office is empty right now. Nobody has any reason to come into this area. I think you need to lighten up," Alex teased playfully. "In fact, I have an idea. You need to live a little. Tomorrow is my birthday – I want you to come to dinner with me, and then we're going to go buy something special."

"Wait, what?!" Kaylee said out loud as Alex started to go.

"Be ready. Leave here tomorrow at five. I'll pick you up at seven." With that, Alex was gone, disappearing down the hallway.

Kaylee was speechless. She hadn't known that tomorrow was Alex's birthday, but of course she was excited about the date. What did she mean about the shopping trip, though? She tried to clear her head and get back to work.

CHAPTER 3

Friday flew by and before Kaylee knew it Alex was there to pick her up. Kaylee paid the sitter for an overnight stay, and then Alex whisked her off into the night. Kaylee found herself in front of a five star restaurant a few minutes later. Alex confessed she spends however much she wants on her birthday; it was her splurge for the year. The maître d' greeted them as they walked through the door and showed them to a private room. Low-lit candlelight filled the air as soft music chimed through the hallways.

"What is all this?" Kaylee asked once they were both seated and alone. She was in awe of the restaurant's grandeur.

"This is my birthday dinner, and you are my birthday date. So we're going to enjoy ourselves." The explanation was simple and straightforward. It was also the only one she was going to get. The server came in, offering a variety of appetizers and wines to start off the evening. They decided to share a bottle of Riesling while they dined.

"You mentioned you want to go shopping after this? I can't imagine any place that will be open once we leave here. Where are we going?" Kaylee decided to try some of the tender calamari Alex had ordered.

"Well, it's a secret, so you'll just have to wait." The coy response made Kaylee burn with curiosity.

They continued through the appetizer, enjoying each other's company and trying to avoid office talk. The main course was served: a delectable rack of lamb chops laid over newly roasted red potatoes and bacon-wrapped, grilled asparagus. The first bite melted in Kaylee's mouth.

"Have you thought about going to my parents with me?" Alex asked.

"I'd love to," Kaylee said, taking a sip of her wine. "But I haven't requested it off work yet – and didn't you say you were flying? I'm really not good with flying."

"I did say that, but it's such a pretty drive down the coast this time of year. I was hoping you might enjoy it with me. I also took the liberty of putting you down to have the week off work. We can leave next Saturday and come back the following weekend." Alex said all this as if it was absolute and Kaylee was already going.

"What about Ryan's school?" Kaylee started pouring over ideas and what to wear and meeting Alex's parents. She'd never had a relationship where she met the other person's parents in such a manner. Nervousness washed through her. "What do you mean, you already requested time off for me? How did you know I'd say yes?"

"I didn't know for sure. I just hoped that you'd go with me. My family will adore you and Ryan. Plus, my mother has been giving me grief for years about when she'll be getting grandchildren." Alex's words were as smooth as the wine. The thought made Kaylee blush; they had hardly been dating a month and she was already hinting about a long-term relationship.

"Alright fine, you've twisted my arm. I'll go with you. On Monday I'll call Ryan's school and my mother to let them know."

With that, a chef walked in pushing a cart. He introduced himself and made fresh bananas foster in front of them. The whole meal was unlike anything Kaylee had ever experienced before. They left the restaurant hand in hand. "Now please, tell me where we're going."

Alex simply smiled as the Mazda sped across the highway. Despite all of Kaylee's efforts, Alex refused to spill the beans. At last, they pulled up at a nondescript building with a small sign on the front entrance. Kaylee tried to look inside, but the storefront was bare.

"Now, remember the other day? When I said you needed to live a little?" Kaylee could only nod at the question, confused now more than ever. "Well, I wanted to do some personal shopping with you, but I don't want you to freak out, okay? This is a sex shop. For women."

"What?" Kaylee was stunned. She knew this type of place existed, but she had certainly never been to one. The few toys she had acquired were online purchases. The good part was that the shop was for women only. "Um, I guess we're here now... although I'm not really too sure."

Alex opened her car door and walked around to open Kaylee's. Kaylee paused for a long moment before taking the extended hand and climbing out of the car. Once inside she was met with rows upon rows of toys, lingerie, and movies. Kaylee blushed and tried not to stare at anything for too long as she followed closely behind Alex. They browsed several different sections. Alex held some lingerie up to Kaylee and asked if she would feel comfortable wearing something sexy for her.

"I wouldn't mind, if it was for you," murmured Kaylee. "Do I get to pick something out, or do you want to?"

Alex busied herself for a moment and then held up a flowing turquoise two-piece set that would leave nothing to the imagination.

"*That*?" asked Kaylee.

Alex nodded, smiling.

"All right, if that's what you want. It is your birthday, after all!"

"Can I help you ladies find anything today?" The clerk had come up behind them. For a split second, Kaylee almost felt like she was in a shoe store. Before she could open her mouth to say no, Alex interjected.

"Actually, I do have a few questions," Alex said with a smirk. Kaylee froze, mortified that Alex was bringing attention to them in the middle of a sex store. "I was hoping to find something that could please both me and the missus at the same time."

Alex must've known exactly what she was doing to her. Kaylee wanted to curl up and disappear, but all she could do was meekly hide behind Alex. Here was Alex, having a casual conversation about a sex toy. And not only that, but she gave a description of what she wanted to a complete stranger.

The clerk nodded and went off in a different direction, much like a clerk in any other store would do. Alex took Kaylee's hand and followed the clerk, and soon they came face-to-face with a wall of strap-on style toys. Kaylee knew she was bright red, but at this point, there was really nothing she could do about it.

"If you're looking for a standard double dildo, there's a huge selection here. However, I would direct your attention to this premium section." The clerk pointed to three different toys. "These two are nice, they have good sturdy straps, offer penetration for both of you, and are reasonably priced. Alternatively, you could go with this strapless model. It's extremely intimate, lots of skin on skin, but does make some positions virtually impossible. With a bit of practice, it can really do wonders for your orgasm. If you have the budget, 100% silicone is the way to go for any rubberized toy."

Alex stood there, discussing the pros and cons of each item as if they were talking about a formal dress, clearly enjoying Kaylee's glowing cheeks. In the end, they made a few purchases and left for Alex's condo.

CHAPTER 4

Alex sent Kaylee to change while she poured some wine. Once Alex was in the bedroom, Kaylee slipped out of the bathroom wearing the sheer turquoise lingerie, her pert nipples exposed and outlined by the fabric.

Alex let out a wolf whistle as soon as she saw her, making Kaylee blush into her hands. Alex turned her finger in the air for Kaylee to do a twirl. Alex quickly removed her dress and pulled Kaylee into her arms, kissing her deeply and caressing her silky curves. She slipped a hand between Kaylee's legs and rubbed her through the sheer fabric while directing Kaylee's attention to suck on one of her hardened nipples.

Kaylee elicited soft moans against Alex's bosom, circling her tongue around the tender flesh as they moved towards the bed. Alex positioned herself on the edge, leaned back, lifted her heels to the mattress and spread her legs. Kaylee needed no encouragement; she fell to her knees and brushed her tongue across Alex's wetness. Alex sighed with pleasure as Kaylee began to glide her tongue over and around her lover's womanhood.

Kaylee paused to take in the moment, juices glistening on her lips. "Mmmm, birthday girl tastes good." Her gaze lingered on the perfection laid out in front of her before delving back in.

As Alex became heated, Kaylee got more and more into it. With each groan Kaylee increased her pace, pushing her tongue deeper into Alex. Alex started to gyrate her hips, pressing into the motion of Kaylee's tongue. She raked her hands through Kaylee's hair, pulling her mouth even closer. Kaylee lapped at her lover, driven to bring her to orgasm. She pulled her tongue in an upward motion, encircling the shiny metal piercing and suckling hungrily.

In the same upward stroke, Kaylee pushed two fingers into Alex. Alex moaned in the low-lit room. Kaylee tugged on the metallic jewel lightly with her teeth, then snaked her tongue against the tender nerve center behind it. With a few more flicks of her tongue and pulsing of fingers, Alex gasped and pulled Kaylee hard against her. Alex started to ride her face, hips thrusting with the waves of orgasm. As the electrical storm subsided, Kaylee slowed and eventually stopped her suckling.

Alex was not ready to stop. Spasms and splinters of electricity were still raging through her rigid body. Sensitivity heightened and feeling dazed, Alex pleaded, "I want more. Fuck me, Kay."

Kaylee did as she was told, thrusting a third digit into her lover and driving Alex deeper into lust. Alex started to gyrate against Kaylee's hand, bringing herself close to the edge again. "*Fuck*!" Alex's hips and back arched sharply as another explosion quickly rippled through her body.

Taking barely a second to savor the bliss and catch her breath, Alex reached under the pillow and pulled out their newest purchase. "What do you think? Are you ready to try out our new toy?"

Kaylee blushed, remembering her embarrassment as Alex handed the toy to her. It was a double-ended model with straps. Kaylee examined the dual phallic heads protruding at different angles and looked back at Alex questioningly.

"Would you like to do the honors?" Alex asked.

Kaylee got the hint and placed one of the bulbous heads at Alex's entrance. She watched in fascination as half the toy entered Alex to the hilt. Once the half was fully inside, Alex stood and secured the harness around her hips. Kaylee was still on her knees. The pronounced silicone dildo bobbed just a few inches from her face.

"My turn, my love." Alex pulled Kaylee to her feet and laid her back on the bed, knees raised. She leaned down and kissed Kaylee, letting her hands roam over soft curves. The toy pressed between them, its tip gently teasing Kaylee. After a few moments, Alex broke the kiss and stood up.

From Kaylee's angle, she could see the engorged purple phallus sliding against her. She was a touch nervous with the new toy. It not only looked bigger than the one from before, this was now hers and Alex's. To her it was a special moment. Kaylee watched in fascination as Alex applied a squirt of lube to the tip and let the moist bulb slide around Kaylee's opening.

"Are you ready?"

Kaylee nodded, still reeling at the size of the beast before her. Alex shifted her hips slightly, causing the head to push forward, stretching Kaylee wider than she had ever felt. She watched as the shimmery purple material disappeared into her body, inch by inch. Kaylee let out a deep moan. Finally, she felt Alex's hips press against her. The toy connected both of them in its entirety. As full as she felt, she was sure Alex felt the same.

Alex remained still for a few moments, letting Kaylee adjust to the large object inside her. She leaned down and kissed her once more. The minute shift in weight caused the piece to push deeper into their conjoined bodies. Gasping, Kaylee opened her eyes to see Alex smiling a few inches from her face.

"What do you think of your purchase now? Are you still embarrassed by it?" Kaylee opened her mouth to say something, but at the very moment, Alex thrust her hips. The resulting movement sent small electrical jolts cascading through Kaylee. The words came out as a moan. "I'll take that as a good thing."

Alex gently pulled out of Kaylee as she leaned down to kiss, only to pump back into her with a rock of the hips, eliciting another groan, and another. Alex took the noise as her cue; she gripped Kaylee's hips and pumped into her, as deep as she could go. The slow, deliberate thrusts quickly had Kaylee panting for release.

Alex found a rhythm their bodies could dance to. With each push into Kaylee, it surged through Alex. Soon, the two women gyrated against each other, using each other's bodies to drive themselves to ecstasy. The bulbous head hit all the right spots in Kaylee; she gripped the sheets as Alex started to thrust harder and faster. The two women moaned together and moved as one. Kaylee felt the world tremble as her orgasm built.

Thrust after thrust, Alex pushed into Kaylee and moaned her name, driven by her own burning desire for release. In an echo, Kaylee cried out Alex's name and started thrashing wildly on the sheets. Her taut muscles clenched the phallic beast as it drove into her core. Gripping her hips harder, Alex rode against Kaylee until her third orgasm of the night ripped through her. The two women collapsed against each other, panting and breathless. The intensity of their lovemaking had drained them both.

Alex lay down next to Kaylee, drawing her into her arms. As they cuddled, Kaylee could still feel their newfound friend slick against her thigh. She could feel her own juices drying where the object lay. After recovering for a moment, Kaylee looked up at Alex. To her surprise, Alex was staring intently at her with vixenish green eyes.

"What did you think? Worth the investment?" Kaylee could do little but smile and nod. Alex smirked. "Was it worth the embarrassment of shopping for it?"

"Definitely," Kaylee said with a giggle. "Happy Birthday, Alex." The two women cuddled for a while, not saying much. Finally, Kaylee broke the silence. "I'm really glad we bought that; it was amazing. One question, though: Are you ready for round two?"

CHAPTER 5

Kaylee would be taking an additional three days off for Thanksgiving, which meant she needed to work double hard to make up for the lost time. She made arrangements with Ryan's school and called her mother. As Friday night quickly rolled around, she realized she had yet to pack for the trip, and spent the evening frantically doing laundry. Saturday arrived before she had time to breathe.

The three of them piled into the Mazda and started on their trek toward Delaware. The map said the trip would take about 6 hours; Alex planned to take a scenic route to see some of the beautiful sights along the coast and liven up the journey. The drive was stunning; even Ryan enjoyed the view. The three played games and enjoyed each other's company the whole trip.

At last the group arrived in New Castle, Delaware. The place was several times the size of Kaylee's entire apartment, but cozy nonetheless. The Tudor-style architecture stood tall against a small inlet, a sailboat tied to a quaint jetty nearby. The Mazda pulled to a stop outside the three-car garage. The wonderful trip suddenly washed away in a storm of nerves. *This* was their summerhouse?

Alex stepped out of the car as a man walked towards them from the garage. She embraced him warmly; Kaylee assumed it was her father until he turned around. They truly looked nothing alike.

"Ms. Alexis, so wonderful to see you again. It's been too long." The elderly man smiled at her. He then took notice of Kaylee and Ryan, who were standing sheepishly to the side. "And who do we have here?"

"Max, this is my girlfriend, Kaylee, and her son, Ryan. Kaylee, this is Max, my father's trusted advisor and old family friend." Kaylee smiled and curtsied a little. The elderly gentleman took her hand and kissed it. He then took Ryan's small hand and shook it resolutely.

"A pleasure to meet you both. Will you join us out back? Your father was regaling us with a tale from our youth back on the veranda."

The four of them started through the house. Kaylee and Ryan were astounded by the elegance; the extravagant furniture, granite counter tops, gorgeous paintings, and the exquisite tile work. Nerves wracked her body, but at least Kaylee could still function. They walked out onto the veranda where a few people were gathered.

Max called to everyone, interrupting their conversation. Alex walked through the door, followed closely by Ryan and Kaylee. The door swung shut behind her and she was faced with several glowing faces. Kaylee swallowed hard as another older man came forward. This time she was sure it was Alex's father.

"Alexis, we were starting to get worried. It's not that long of a drive from Boston." The older man held her tight in a warm embrace. "Knowing you and that sporty little car you drive, you probably took the scenic route. Always worrying your mother and I."

"Dad, you know I'd never do anything to purposely worry you. I'd like you to meet my girlfriend Kaylee, and her son, Ryan." Kaylee felt the world spin. She'd felt nervous before, but Alex had just called her 'my girlfriend' in front of her parents and a small audience. If Kaylee said that to her mom, her mom would flip. Expecting the worst, Kaylee could only muster a meek smile. But Alex's father only returned the smile, walked over to Kaylee, and gave her a big hug.

"Welcome to our home! It's very nice to meet you. We've heard nothing but good things about you." Alex's father seemed very pleasant. In the meantime, Alex had hugged a regal-looking woman who seemingly had aged beautifully. After Alex's father moved away, the woman also gave Kaylee a warm embrace.

"A pleasure to meet you, Kaylee." Alex's mother's voice was as smooth as silk. The couple looked ravishing together.

"Kaylee, this is my father, Robert, and my mother, Julia," Alex said. Kaylee again smiled and nodded in nervous acknowledgement.

"Truly an honor to meet you both." Kaylee tried to keep a calm appearance. The rest of the party was introduced, but Kaylee could hardly keep up with the names and occupations. The entire group seemed very welcoming and at ease with a lesbian couple in their midst. The rest of the afternoon was spent touring the house, reliving stories of the past, and enjoying their time off work. Kaylee felt this was as good of a vacation as any, considering she hadn't had one in years.

Ryan was also a huge hit at the party, lapping up the attention at every opportunity. Kaylee could see where Alex got her exuberance for children. It made her heart happy to see Robert playing with Ryan as she imagined her own father would, had he still been alive. As the afternoon wore on, she realized that there was no judgment; she was as much a part of the family as Alex. Kaylee relaxed after her revelation and started enjoying the cozy winter home.

After such a hectic few months, Kaylee savored the languor of the house. Days were spent playing games, talking with friends and family, and enjoying delicious food. Over the week Kaylee grew fond of Alex's parents, despite having only known them a few days. She felt like they were more of a family than her mom ever would be. The thought made her a little sad, but the atmosphere of the house made it impossible to dwell on such things.

***

On Thanksgiving morning, Kaylee shifted out of bed softly as not to wake Alex. She plodded down the hall to the restroom before returning to bed. Once back, she snuggled in for a good morning kiss. It felt so liberating to be able to do such a simple act in a house full of people who accepted it. They spent a few minutes in bed, warm and snug together under the sheets, before showering and getting ready for the day. At the breakfast table, Ryan was mesmerized by Robert demonstrating *real* magic.

"Good morning, girls," Robert said as he produced another quarter from Ryan's ear. "Did you two sleep well?"

"Getting to lie in for the first time in two months? Yes, I would think that constitutes sleeping well," Alex said, moving to grab a bowl of cereal for her and Kaylee. "What's on the agenda for today, Dad?"

"Well, your mother and I are going to sail round to the cove, then around lunch time we'll return and help the staff finish preparations. Most guests should arrive by one. Then we stuff ourselves silly and complain about it for the rest of the day." Robert excused himself from Ryan, tousling his hair lightly. "Would you care to join us on the boat?"

"What do you think, Kay? Would you and Ryan like to go?" Ryan squealed and ran off at the mention of going on the boat; he had been eyeing it up all week. Alex laughed. "I guess that's a yes."

A few hours later, they were all gathered on the deck of the sailboat, watching the shore roll by. It was Ryan's first time on a boat and he had a blast. Kaylee spent most of the time nestled blissfully with Alex under a blanket. Once back on shore, the cooking was in full swing and the family took to the kitchen in earnest. Despite the hired help, Julia was adamant about contributing to the Thanksgiving meal. It also meant that Alex and Kaylee joined in, making pies and side dishes.

The men of the household made it a habit to steal and pick at the food when they had the opportunity, at least until Julia ran them from the kitchen with the aid of a large rolling pin. All too soon, guests started to arrive. Kaylee felt overwhelmed by the amount of people, names, and faces to remember. Ryan, on the other hand, immediately found some playmates, and they all ran through the yard playing tag.

"Bradley, I'd like you to meet Kaylee," Alex said to a dark-haired guest who had appeared in the kitchen. "Kaylee, this is my brother, Bradley." Bradley was taller than Alex and shared a strong family resemblance. He had the same dark hair as Alex, although his was cut short and business-like.

"Pleasure," he said, nodding at Kaylee. Then, to Alex: "Have you seen Pops? I've something to discuss with him." With that, he was off.

Alex apologized for his behavior, but Kaylee paid little heed to it. There were over thirty people milling about in various groups, all of whom she had met in such a short time. In fact, she felt a little relieved that Bradley had left so quickly; she finally had a moment with just Alex.

"What do you think of my crazy family so far?" Alex asked as they took a break.

"I love them. Everything's been amazing. I've never experienced a Thanksgiving quite like this." Kaylee took the moment to get close with Alex, snuggling into her arms. "I really couldn't have asked for a better way to spend the holidays."

***

At last, they were all seated. Alex, Kaylee, and Ryan all sat around the head of the table, near Robert and Julia. The large table hummed with excitement and stories. Robert stood to carve the bird and propose a toast. The meal was divine.

Afterwards, everyone sat in the great room talking about various things from business to sports to family. Kaylee had never experienced anything like this; everyone was so warm and welcoming to her and Alex. It was a nice change to be recognized and accepted openly as a couple, especially in the hearts of family. As the afternoon wore on, the group started to dwindle until only immediate family remained.

***

Kaylee felt exhausted, although it was a serene kind of fatigue, very different to the end of a busy workday. After all was said and done, Thanksgiving had been a major success.

"I'm exhausted, but that was a lot of fun. Is your family always like this?" Kaylee asked sleepily.

"Always have been, always will be. Dad likes to make sure his business partners and friends feel like family. He loves throwing extravagant parties." Alex rubbed Kaylee's back as they cuddled in bed. "I'm really glad you came with me, it's made my Thanksgiving. And it's pretty clear my family have taken a shine to you and Ryan.

"Really? You think? That's great. I really like them, too. Your dad has some amazing stories." Kaylee yawned. She wanted their time here to last forever, but she knew there were only a few more days before the chaos of real life returned. They fell asleep shortly after.

The last few days with Alex's family made Kaylee long for that sense of belonging all the time. When it came time to say goodbye, Kaylee felt the warmth of their hearts, and looked forward to the next visit with them.

CHAPTER 6

The following Monday Kaylee felt like she had been tossed in the ocean with an anchor tied to her feet. Kaylee knew she had a mountain of work to finish, but it seemed daunting to consider it all at once and she struggled to even begin. Rose and Kaylee spent several hours in a meeting trying to get plans sorted out. By the time five o'clock rolled around, Kaylee felt taxed and stressed again, all pleasantness from the previous week forgotten.

On top of it all, that Monday was the first of December. She only had a few more weeks to get holiday decorations, do her shopping, and make plans. Her head was torn in a hundred directions at once.

The grueling workweek passed quickly. That Saturday was spent decorating the small apartment. Alex came over and spent the day helping Kaylee get the tree up. Alex confessed she normally didn't put up a tree; she didn't see the point when it was just her. Kaylee told her that this could be the beginning of a new tradition for them. Saturday and Sunday together passed quicker than any one day of work, and soon it was Monday again.

The drudgery of overtime and the stress of holiday preparations were in full effect now. Traffic seemed worse, people were rushed and rude, and shops were packed every hour of the day. Everyone in the office was on edge; even Alex, who was normally cool, calm, and collected, seemed keyed up and snappy. Kaylee wanted to think that January would be better, but it was only going to get busier after New Year's.

The following Saturday mercifully rolled around, giving Kaylee a small reprieve from work. It was two weeks before Christmas and she had done absolutely no shopping. Kaylee confessed to Alex how stressed she felt and how the shopping had made no progress. Alex's solution was to hire a babysitter and take Kaylee out for the day. They hit the streets looking for presents, fighting crowds, and enjoying solace in each other.

"What do you think about this?" Alex held up a huge Lego set that consisted of over a thousand separate pieces. Kaylee's eyes bulged at the price tag.

"C'mon Alex, I can't afford stuff like that. I don't have my own office yet!" Kaylee meant the jibe in jest, until Alex put the huge toy in the buggy. "What are you doing?"

"I'll get it. It's as simple as that."

Kaylee shook her head at Alex. She moved to put the toy back, but Alex wouldn't let her.

"Alex, please," Kaylee said. "You've already finished your shopping – You told me as much! I can't let you keep buying toys for Ryan, especially stuff like this. I feel bad about not being able to afford this stuff myself."

"Listen, one day you'll have that office of your own. One day you'll be a top designer and make more money than I do. Until then, let me spend my money how I want to spend it. It's just money, and Ryan will be so excited. I've never really had a

Christmas with someone. Let me spoil you both. Please?"

Kaylee was not used to being spoiled, nor was she used to the extravagance of what Alex offered at every turn of the hat, and Alex's gesture overwhelmed her. Kaylee had only budgeted for one big present and a few small toys, and with this gift Alex had already well exceeded that price range. However, Kaylee could think of little argument against Alex's generosity and started down the next aisle, secretly fluttering with happiness.

Over the next few hours, Alex loaded up on gifts and spent more money than Kaylee could dream of. To top it all off, she even took the presents home where she could wrap and store them, so Ryan wouldn't know what to expect. Once they dropped off the loot, Alex told Kaylee she was taking her out to dinner. This came as another surprise to Kaylee, who was still feeling frazzled over holiday pressures.

Dinner was at a wonderful German restaurant where the delicious and overwhelming aroma made Kaylee hungry as soon as they walked in. They chatted and enjoyed a glass of wine while waiting on the food to arrive.

Alex seemed to be enjoying the spirit of the holidays, even if Kaylee was stressed. "This has been an eye-opening experience for me," Alex told Kaylee, taking her hand over the table. "Normally my holidays are spent sending gifts to my parents and enjoying some peace and quiet at home. It's so much more hectic with children. It's fun though – I can't wait to see Ryan light up like the tree when he sees all the gifts!"

"He's going to be ecstatic. I'm excited for him. I can't believe how much money you've spent." Kaylee shook her head, digging into the scrumptious plate that had just been placed in front of her.

"It's nothing compared to what I spent on you." Alex smirked for a second before taking a bite.

"Wait – What did you say?" Kaylee glared at Alex. "You don't need to spend money on me. I'm used to not getting much for Christmas. I don't need anything. I'm a single mom, remember?"

Alex chuckled at her. "Well, fortunately, you aren't my accountant, and I can spend my money how I please."

"Alex, that's not fair." Kaylee was genuinely concerned. She had wanted to get something for Alex that was thoughtful and meaningful. She had been struggling for weeks to think of something. She knew Alex could – and did – buy anything she wanted, so she didn't need something materialistic; and Kaylee couldn't afford the trips and excursions Alex was always getting for them anyway.

After dinner, Alex took Kaylee to see one of the blockbuster movies that had come out recently. It had been ages since Kaylee sat through a movie in the theatre. It was nice to sit and watch the film without having to make sure Ryan behaved. She sat through most of the film cuddled against Alex in the stadium seats. They drove home discussing the movie and their plans for Christmas Day.

"I think my mother will be over around mid-morning," Kaylee said as they neared her apartment. "So if you want to stay the night, I'd love that. We can be up and respectable before she gets here. When she arrives, we'll open the presents, have a short meal, and then she'll be on her way. It's not much of a tradition, but it's all we do since dad passed."

"That sounds wonderful. I haven't really spent Christmas doing much more than watching movie marathons the past few years. I'm excited to get out there and do something, even if it means coming face to face with your scary mother." The last words dripped with playful sarcasm. When the two walked inside, Ryan was already sound asleep, and the sitter was quickly out the door.

"My mother's not exactly scary, just a bitter old woman who doesn't seem to care if I'm happy." Kaylee felt flustered thinking about her mother and her attitudes.

"Shh. I'm sure it will all work out in the end," Alex promised. They went to the bedroom, undressing before they crawled into bed together. "If it makes it easier on you, I can just be your 'friend' for now."

Kaylee wrapped herself in Alex's arms, relaxing as Alex caressed her back. "I don't want you to just be my friend. I'm proud to be your girlfriend. I just don't want the drama from my mother."

"I know you are, and I'm so happy to have you in my life. It's just one little white lie to get us through the day. We can tell her at a later date. Deal?"

"Deal. We'll tell her after the holidays are over." Kaylee leaned in for a goodnight kiss. She was not expecting the tongue that lashed over her lips. When she opened her eyes, Alex was staring at her intently. Kaylee felt a rush of tingling across her skin. She knew they were not about to go to sleep, despite being exhausted. Alex kissed her deeply once more, pressing her hand down on Kaylee's hips and rolling to position herself over Kaylee. Kaylee could feel Alex's piercing against her thigh as they kissed.

Their lips pressed together, tongues danced, and bodies writhed. The embers within Kaylee quickly burst into flame. Alex started to grind her pelvis against Kaylee's thigh. She reached up and grasped Kaylee's hands, stretching them above her head. Alex paused there, smiling down at the beautiful sight of her lover sprawled below. She leaned down to kiss and nuzzle Kaylee's neck. Kaylee could feel Alex's hardened nipples brushing across her breasts, sending jolts of electricity through her.

For what seemed like an eternity, Alex teased, kissed, and nipped at Kaylee's neck and collarbone. The light tickle of Alex's long hair across her skin made Kaylee shiver. Alex moved her knee up to press against Kaylee's womanhood, continuing to gyrate her own hips. Kaylee could tell the piercing was doing its intended job from Alex's ragged breathing. Alex let out a long moan, dismounted, and twisted her body to a 69 position, her hips spread across Kaylee's chest.

Kaylee licked her lips with anticipation as she watched Alex's nub descend towards her waiting mouth. Kaylee slowly slid her tongue around the outer lips. Once in position, Alex leaned down to do the same. Soon the two women were lapping at each other, each striving to push the other over the edge. Kaylee gulped as she felt two fingers push into her.

Kaylee pushed her tongue up into Alex, tasting her sweet nectar, then with deft movement she slid her tongue down over the small metal tip and back. She gripped Alex's thighs, bringing Alex closer to her as she repeated the same motion over and around the piercing. Alex shuddered, which only pushed Kaylee to move faster. Alex moaned into her lover's velvety folds at the circular motion that was driving her wild. Kaylee could feel Alex tensing and knew she wouldn't be able to last much longer at this rate.

Responding to Kaylee's teasing, Alex pushed a third finger into Kaylee. She circled her tongue around the nub, sucking lightly. Both women bucked and writhed against each other, climbing toward their own release. Taking the opportunity,

Alex slowly snaked her little finger against Kaylee's opening. Without warning, she pulled her fingers out just enough to line up the fourth and drove them deep inside Kaylee.

Kaylee gasped and moaned into her lover as she felt the searing force fill her. The surprise made Kaylee falter for a moment before she could focus again. To get even, she reached up and spread Alex open, driving her tongue deep into Alex's folds. With her thumb, she started making circles around Alex's clit. The added stimulation caused Alex to buck, riding Kaylee's tongue with the gyration of her hips. Both continued to build each other towards orgasm, neither wanting to give in first.

Alex pushed further into Kaylee, twisting and contorting her hand to get deep into her lover. Kaylee gasped. Full and overwhelmed, she struggled to contain herself. She desperately wanted to get Alex off first. Both women worked each other into a frenzy, refusing to yield. Each minute seemed to stretch into eternity.

At last, Kaylee buckled. Alex's fingers, coupled with her gentle sucking, sent Kaylee careering over the edge. Her muscles clenched around Alex's knuckles, each wave of pleasure making a gush flood Alex's mouth, hand, and the bed sheets.

As Kaylee's wave crashed, Alex felt herself exploding, her muscles clenching. Electricity ripped through her body as she withdrew and rode her lover. Both women rode the cascade of passion, slowly bringing each other off the edge. They embraced and their bodies entwined, falling into a deep, satisfying sleep.

CHAPTER 7

Monday morning marked ten days until Christmas. Kaylee tried to concentrate on the tasks at hand, but it was taking a monumental effort. Her thoughts were once again split between finding a meaningful gift for Alex, how she would deal with her mother, and the large contract she was supposed to be working on.

As she browsed through webpage after webpage, an idea suddenly blossomed in her head. The thought developed and Kaylee smiled to herself; she had found what she hoped would be the perfect gift for Alex.

Each day at work felt rushed, and yet each day felt like a year had passed, too. The traffic and shops became even more insane, and people hustled without heed of others. *'Tis the season*, she thought wryly as she came home on Friday.

The babysitter who sat through the day with Ryan bid her farewell. This was the last weekend to really pull it all together. She had arranged for Alex to come over after Ryan went to bed to finish wrapping presents. Kaylee managed to get Alex's gift wrapped as well and placed it on the pile.

The five days before Christmas disappeared in the blink of an eye. Ryan bounced from the walls on Christmas Eve, fully wired. At last, Kaylee managed to calm him down by offering to put out milk and cookies for Santa Claus.

Kaylee collapsed onto the sofa. The last step was to wait until Alex arrived with all of the gifts. Kaylee waited in the stillness, appreciating the long-deserved silence, and eventually she drifted off.

She was awoken by Alex kissing her lightly on the forehead. She smiled up at her, realizing she had fallen asleep on the couch. Alex brushed the loose hair out of her face as Kaylee stretched.

"Do you want to go on to bed? I'm sure I can handle putting the gifts out."

Kaylee thought about it briefly, but decided against. "Not on your life," she told Alex. "This is our first Christmas together. Do you really think I'd sleep through it?"

The two of them snuck out to bring in the bags and boxes of presents from the car. The tree had looked barren with no presents beneath, but now it really felt like Christmas. The sudden appearance of the gifts would make Christmas morning that much more magical for Ryan. Alex really got into it, making sure the gifts were stacked beautifully. Kaylee packed four little stockings, one for each of them and one for her mother.

By midnight, the little apartment looked inviting and cozy. Alex pulled out a bag of fake snow and glittered it around the room. She also ate most of the cookies. In the end, they were both content with the job they had done. They spent some time cuddling in bed and talking about the excitement of the morning. It would surely be an early start. Lying together, they both drifted into sleep.

There was no need for an alarm on Christmas morning. Ryan bounded into the room shouting with youthful glee, unable to wait any longer. The two adults gradually woke, surprised they had slept until nine, and even more surprised that Ryan had done the same.

As they stumbled toward the kitchen for tea and coffee, a pounding on the door signified Kaylee's mother had arrived. Before either of them could stop him, Ryan jerked open the door and yelled, "Grandma, look!"

"Hey Mom, glad you could make it." Everyone was still in their pajamas as they came from the kitchen. Kaylee's mother was a shorter, older version of Kaylee who had a permanent scowl on her face. She did almost smile at Ryan, though, handing him a gift to put under the tree. Kaylee grabbed the other box of gifts and took it to the couch. "Mom, I'd like you to meet my friend, Alexis. She helped me get all of this ready."

"Nice to meet you, ma'am," Alex said cheerfully, not exactly sure what to say or do. She excused herself back to the tea as the kettle keened from the kitchen. "Would you care for a cup of tea?"

"Sure, I'll take one. I'll be right back, I have bagels in the car."

Breakfast commenced as the three adults sat around the small table, making idle chit chat. Ryan could hardly contain his excitement when they finally started to open presents. He chose the large present containing the Lego set to open first, causing Kaylee's mother to raise an eyebrow.

"My, you must be making pretty good money at that new job of yours!" she said, at which Kaylee only smiled.

Gifts large and small were exchanged. Kaylee gave her mother a candle set. Ryan got some action figures. Finally, Alex came to her big gift. Kaylee had paid extra attention on the wrapping. Alex pulled the ribbon loose and opened the tiny box, revealing a golden ornament engraved with their names and the date. It signified their first Christmas together. Below that was a small piece of paper. Careful not to reveal the ornament, Alex pulled up the paper to reveal a gift receipt to a wine and painting club.

"This is an absolutely amazing gift. How did you know I liked to paint?"

Kaylee's heart swelled at the compliment, ignoring the scowl on her mother's face.

It was Ryan's turn to open a few more presents: small toys, some much-needed clothing, and a few favorite candies. Alex brought out a small gift for Kaylee and handed it to her. With fidgeting hands, Kaylee opened the box to reveal diamond earrings.

"Alex!" Kaylee exclaimed. "I told you not to spend this kind of money on me! These probably cost a fortune."

Then she froze, remembering suddenly that her mother was present and watching them. Kaylee shifted the attention back to Ryan immediately, telling him to open the last of his gifts. Her mother said nothing.

As soon as they were done, Kaylee's mother gathered her stuff into a box and prepared to leave. "I think it's time I got going," she told them. Without looking at Alex, she said, "Nice to meet you." Then she headed for the door without another word. Ryan ran up to her as she left. "Goodbye, sweet thing. Merry Christmas."

As the door shut, Kaylee said nothing. Alex put her arms around Kaylee to comfort her. They watched as the small car zoomed away in a flurry of snow. Kaylee turned back to watch Ryan, who was blissfully unaware of his grandmother's negativity. Alex moved to offer her apologies.

"No," Kaylee said, "don't. Look around. Ryan is happy, I'm happy. I certainly hope you're happy, too. If she doesn't want to be a part of this wonderful holiday, then that's her choice. I'm not going to let her ruin this special day." Kaylee nudged Alex, giving her a small smile. "But you really shouldn't have spent that much money on those earrings."

Alex laughed, taken aback. "Are you kidding me? I feel like my gift is inferior. You spent the time to find out I enjoy painting, and now we can go do it together. Not to mention that lovely ornament commemorating our first Christmas together. *I'm* the jealous one."

Alex seemed to have tears in her eyes. Kaylee kissed her, happy to have her here, happy to know that she loved the gifts.

Ryan came rushing up to Alex a minute later. "Will you please help me build this?" The thousand-piece Lego set was calling everyone's name. Ryan had already started a pile in the middle of the floor while waiting on the adults to help. As Alex followed Ryan to the middle of the room, she turned to Kaylee.

"By the way, those earrings are nothing compared to what my parents sent you. Those presents are still in the car." Before Kaylee could protest, Alex went on, gesturing at the pile of Lego. "But for now, I think we have an intergalactic spaceship to build."

The two adults sat down and cuddled close as they spent the rest of the afternoon trying to piece together the massive project. Kaylee and Alex laughed together while struggling to find the pieces. Despite the frustration of trying to find miniature plastic parts, their blossoming family had a wonderful time.

Between hot cocoa, the joy of sharing time together, and watching each other be happy, both of them felt it was truly a magical holiday.

TEN YEARS EARLIER

TEN YEARS EARLIER

Alex moved on the dance floor with Sara, their bodies bumping and grinding to the music in rhythmic trance. They had only been dating for a few weeks, but this was the most intense she had felt about anyone in a long time. Sara was almost three years older, hot, confident, and out of college. Their first kiss had been explosive and driven them into immediate wild abandon.

As their bodies gyrated to the pulsing beat, Alex admired Sara's fit yet curvy body, her full bosom and flowing hips. Sara locked eyes with Alex, smiling. That look made Alex weak in the knees. Her cascading blond hair twisted as they bounced to the song. Alex felt the music surging through them. This is what life was all about.

As the song ended and something slower came on, Alex took the opportunity to pull Sara in and give her a passionate kiss, trying to hold her on the dance floor; but Sara had no time for slow songs. They ended up back at a small table, drinking an assortment of alcoholic concoctions. At just 20 years old, Alex was slightly underage and very much a fledgling on the New York party scene. At that moment, nothing could beat downing cocktails and dancing all night with the lovely Sara.

A siren echoed through the room, signaling it was time for the drag show. Everyone whistled and hooted as drag queens filtered out onto the stage to strut their stuff. The music ranged from rowdy and rough to cheesy and soppy. As they laughed and kissed, Alex couldn't remember a time when she felt so free. Her parents had been sticklers growing up; being well off, they thought she should be more of a lady to suit her status. But with her new found freedom and experiences, Alex was loving college life; she loved life, period.

Sara leaned in close as they shared a drink and watched the show, expressing jealousy on how well some of the queens could move and the length of their legs. The evening passed in liquid reverie and the show ended after several rounds of enthusiastic applause and encores. The atmosphere of acceptance was unlike anything Alex had ever experienced. Sara leaned in for a kiss as they rejoined the dance floor for a few more upbeat songs. As the evening wound down, they made their way out of the club.

"That was an amazing night," Alex said as they walked arm in arm towards the exit. "What's next? I'm up for an adventure."

Sara looked at her and smiled, the neon glow of the evening still in her eyes. "How about we go back to my place for some fun?" Alex could only giggle at the question as the cool air hit. "My roommate might be there. Will that make it awkward?"

"How about I take you down that ally and fuck you up against the trash?" Alex responded with a playful cheeky grin and pouted lips. "Your roommate can come watch if she wants."

"Very funny. How about we head back to mine and see what happens? The walk will do you good."

Soon they were prancing down the road, arms swinging, hand in hand. Alex started giggling at the thought of Sara's roommate pressing her ear against the wall to hear them going at it.

"When did you decide you were gay?" Alex suddenly asked.

Sara looked over with a sly grin. "Well, firstly I'd still probably identify as bi, even if I haven't been with a guy for a long time. Anyway, a few years ago my boyfriend had been going on about being in bed with two women. We'd been pretty adventurous, but at the time I was still that perfect little straight girl who didn't really know any better. After months of begging, I finally told him I'd do it; I'd go with a girl. The condition was that I got to explore with her first, alone. Then, if I liked it, I'd let him know and he could come join in. He jumped at the opportunity."

"Really? You have to tell me the details now." Alex was a little turned on by the concept, even if she had only been with one man and vowed it would never happen again. She wasn't sure about the guy being involved in the sex, but it seemed like a hot scene nonetheless. Besides, any first-time-with-a-woman story was always hot.

"Well, I made arrangements to meet this girl, Jade, through a friend of a friend. The plan was to meet in a hotel and I'd call Scott once we were ready. She was about 30 and bisexual. I was your age. We met in the hotel bar, had a few drinks and she told me she'd been shopping at a high end sex store. It was really hot – my heart was racing the whole time. Until then, I'd never thought of girls in *that* way. This entire situation was all purely to appease and impress Scott, but I found myself really turned on. When we got up to the room Jade had an array of movies and toys, including a double dildo. I realize now of course, this was all part of her foreplay plan to get me heated up."

Alex felt her mind exploding. Evidently she had not lived at all. She knew stores like that existed, but school work had made her a bit of a homebody. Well, until Sara had happened into her life.

"I've never been to one of those stores," Alex said. She was intoxicated with excitement as they meandered through the streets.

"No kidding?" Sara seemed to contemplate something before continuing with her tale. "Anyway, we got up to the room and she was all over me; kissing, sucking. I'd never been with a woman, but evidently she had. Lots. She made me see the light. I hate to say it, but we kind of forgot about Scott and the entire reason I was there. We put on a movie but never touched the toys until the early hours of the morning. Having only ever been with a bloke, the female touch really blew me away."

The pair came to a stop in front of a nondescript building, black tape over the windows and doors. Alex took one look, remembered what district they were in, and realized Sara had nefarious plans. Laughing, they rushed into the sex shop. Guys turned their heads as the two women entered, but Alex was too buzzed to care. They made their way back to the girl-on-girl section to see a wide arrangement of toys, lubes, and novelty items. Alex immediately laid eyes on the only toy she wanted: a leather strap-on harness.

She moved to pick up the box, looking at the description. Sara came over to her, laughing and holding a new movie, a vibrator, and some lube. She took a glance at the toy Alex was holding and smirked.

"And what do you intend to do with that, young lady?" Sara peered over Alex's shoulder as she read. "The last time someone tried one of those on me, it failed miserably. Almost made me go back to guys. Get it if you want though. I'm happy to explore anything and everything."

Alex stood quiet for a few moments, considering. Her rational side did not want to make a mess of things or embarrass herself, but the buzz of alcohol kept screaming that it was an amazing idea. A slow, sinister grin finally spread across Alex's face. They grabbed an appropriate-sized dildo and a few accessories to go with the strap-on and went to the counter. The girl on the other side lit up when she saw the product.

"Ooh, lovely choice, ladies. Have you ever tried one of these before?" The girl was loud enough that the male patrons looked around, tripping over themselves at the girl-on-girl action. Alex shook her head, oblivious to the stares she was getting. "Just make sure you use plenty of lube, and a tad bit of cornstarch after a few uses to keep the texture up. Oh, and it's all in the hip motion." She winked.

The two girls left the store with a bag full of goodies and raced towards Sara's apartment. On their way, they told more tales of their experiences and got heated up. Alex pulled the rubber dildo out of the packaging and began thrusting and twerking at Sara. They laughed and teased each other all the way to the front door.

"So what ended up happening with the whole threesome thing?" Alex was curious to the point of bursting at the seams. She also realized she was soaking wet.

"Well, that particular threesome never happened. Jade and I ended up being so into each other that we forgot to call Scott. Our phones were on silent and she had booked the room under a fake name, so he had no way of getting in touch. By the time I realized, I didn't even really care." Sara sighed. "I vividly remember how her tongue kept lapping away at me while her fingers touched places I never knew existed. It was an awakening and I've never looked back."

The lights were off as they entered the apartment. They made it to Sara's bedroom without a sound. As soon as the door closed, their bag dropped to the ground and clothing was stripped away. The two girls attacked each other with the fervor of their youth. Hands roamed over bared flesh, tongues locked, bodies writhed. Alex was glad to finally have this sexy Sara all to herself.

The bed rose up to catch them as they tumbled onto the sheets. Alex ended up on the bottom, pinned beneath Sara as she licked and sucked on her breasts. Alex bit her lip to be quiet, not sure if Sara's roommate was home or not. But Sara was determined to elicit some noise. She sucked one of Alex's nipples into her mouth while two fingers pushed against her wetness. Alex gasped as they drove deep inside.

The pumping, twisting fingers and sucking tongue had Alex panting at the edge in minutes. Her body pulsed with pleasure as heady rushes surged through her core. Sara kissed her way down Alex's smooth stomach while sliding down the bed. The first stroke of Sara's tongue across Alex's clit made her gasp. Sara seemed to enjoy the reaction she was getting and removed her fingers to lap at Alex's silky folds. Alex was not used to such intense attention and soon found herself closing in on the edge of an intense orgasm.

Sara felt the change in tempo and became determined to toss her off the edge. She drew her tongue up Alex's slit and swirled her tongue around the nub while plunging three fingers into Alex's depths. Alex moaned loudly, unable to contain herself anymore. Her hips started to buck and writhe against Sara's skilled tongue. Alex panted as she rode the waves of her orgasm, pushing against Sara's deeply embedded digits to extract every last drop of pleasure.

Sara smiled triumphantly as she withdrew. "You were so hot to watch," she told Alex. "I bet you woke my roommate up." Sara lay next to Alex while she recovered. "So, are you ready to try out your new toy? I have to admit, it's been a while since I've been fucked by a cock and I miss it."

Alex smiled devilishly, rolling to retrieve the bag of goodies. She studied the harness and accessories for a few minutes. A small protrusion stuck out where the dildo connected. There was also a smaller part that went inside Alex. Alex slid the harness up her legs, securing the small dildo within herself. She locked the larger dildo on, tightened the harness' straps, and looked over at Sara.

"How do I look?" Alex asked as sexily as she could. The large phallus dangled straight outward with a slight curve to its shape. The bulbous head glistened with lube.

Sara giggled. "Like you're about to get revenge on me for making you cum so hard!"

Alex walked flirtatiously back over to the bed, kneeling between Sara's open legs. She leaned down and kissed Sara's wetness before guiding the head to her entrance. With a slow, deliberate push, the dildo spread Sara open.

Sara gasped. "That's... That's a lot bigger than I thought it was going to be."

Alex watched in amazement as her new appendage sank into her lover's depths. She was mesmerized at the feeling of their union, as if this silicone toy had connected them on a deeper level. She experimented, pulling the cock slowly back out. As she pulled, it applied suction to the smaller one inside her. When she pushed in, it pushed the one in her deeper.

After a few experimental thrusts, Alex started to get the hang of the toy. Building up pace, she eventually buried the toy deep inside Sara, causing them both to moan.

"Fuuuck! God! I may... I might have to change—" Sara struggled to find words as she panted. Meanwhile Alex had found her rhythm. Sara cried out as the silicone phallus found spots in her that had never been hit by a girl before. She began to writhe and gyrate her hips to match Alex's pace. "Oh, *fuck*, Alex."

Sara uttering those words echoed into Alex. She felt further passion awake within her. If there was one thing Alex knew got her going, it was the sound of a woman moaning her name. Alex began thrusting her hips back and forth, increasing the pace. She made sure to keep it focused; measured and controlled. She watched, poised over Sara, as her lover writhed in pleasure.

"Please, Alex, give it to me," Sara pleaded urgently, the need and fire burning within her screaming to cum. Alex started thrusting faster. Sara wrapped her arms around Alex as the toy pounded into her. "Oh, god, fuck me."

The smaller dildo pushed in and out of Alex as she rode Sara. Sara knew Alex was going to cum and tried holding back so they could finish together, but the large phallus was too much. Sara bucked and moaned into the night, her body convulsing with electricity. Alex smiled and felt sweet release wash through her body as well. Both women collapsed, the silicone toy still joining them together.

***

Alex slowly became aware of her surroundings. A small hangover reminded her of the bar from the night before, and the soreness of her loins reminded her of what had happened after they left. Her new toy was still strapped to her, sticking straight into the air. She could feel the small part jutting into her. She realized she must have fallen asleep without taking it off. Before she could roll over to remove it, Sara opened her eyes and looked at her.

"That was amazing. I may have to change my mind about strap-ons if you keep this up! I swear, that was ten times better than the real thing. And no sticky mess!" She eyeballed Alex's naked body greedily. "Looks like you're ready for round two?" The two girls laughed. Sara brought herself to her knees, kissing Alex deeply. "You're hot as hell and I'm still soaking wet."

With that last word, Sara swung her leg over Alex, positioning herself above the appendage. Alex again watched in fascination as the silicone shaft disappeared into her lover. She could feel Sara's weight press down on her hips. Alex raised her knees slightly and grabbed Sara's curves as she began rocking back and forth. She loved the sight of her naked lover gyrating above her, intent on getting herself off.

Sara swayed and bucked, slowly grinding on the silicone cock, oblivious to the world around her. Her intent was solely on the fire burning between her legs. Alex could feel the smaller member driving into her each time Sara came down. The two girls started writhing together once again, the roles slightly changed this time. Sara controlled the pace and depth, rocking back and forth on her knees, grinding her clit against the harness. She picked up the pace, focused on her building orgasm.

Sara panted as her tempo increased. Alex leaned up and took one of Sara's plump nipples into her mouth, suckling as Sara rode her. Alex was feeling a sense of power she had never experienced before. Sara responded by leaning down further, changing the angle of their lovemaking. Alex brought her hands up to caress and squeeze Sara's nipples. The action drove Sara over the edge.

Sara bucked and moaned into the otherwise quiet bedroom. Her body writhed with pleasure as waves of orgasm cascaded through her. After a few moments, her gyrating stopped and Sara repositioned herself next to Alex.

"You have definitely renewed my faith in those things," Sara told her, rubbing Alex's hip affectionately. "That was unreal. Are you happy with your purchase?"

"Are you kidding? That was amazing." Alex smiled. "I'm just mad I never discovered it sooner!"

The two of them fell back into light sleep. After a few hours, Sara stirred and kissed Alex. "What plans do you have for the rest of the weekend, missy?" she asked.

Alex shrugged and smirked in response. "The sofa? The kitchen? Doggy style? I'm all yours."

"Mmmm. Sounds perfect. Let's see how much more my roommate can take before she kicks off." Sara gave Alex a quick kiss before throwing back the bed sheets. "But first, let's grab some food. You're gonna need the energy!"

E03: MUTUAL FUN

CHAPTER 1

Kaylee pinched the bridge of her nose, trying to stave off the headache that was building. Only one more day before a nice relaxing weekend. Kaylee sighed; she was definitely excited to be working on such a large-scale project, but she had not realized how much time and effort it was going to require.

"Meeting in ten," Rose said, popping her head around the corner. Kaylee turned to say something, but Rose was gone. Rose and Alex were under considerably more pressure than her. The whole team felt the crunch, but what could be done? Kaylee shuffled some papers, mock-ups, and a folder together and took off for the conference room. By the time she got there, Rose and Alex were busy setting everything up.

"So, Kaylee, any fun plans this weekend?" Rose asked, trying to make small talk before the meeting started. Kaylee briefly thought about what the weekend would hold.

"Nothing really. Just celebrating another year older, yay." Kaylee was not exactly happy with her birthday being right around the corner. It had been almost five years since she had really celebrated it; it was just one of those days that reminded her of the passing time. "Maybe I'll do a small dinner."

Before anything else could be said, the rest of the team started filtering in. Kaylee caught Alex watching her from across the table, an odd look in her eyes. She didn't give it much thought as the meeting started. After almost two hours of number crunching and going over designs, the group broke for lunch. Since it was Friday, Kaylee and Alex walked down to one of the sandwich shops. It felt good to be out of the office, even if it was frigid outside.

"Why didn't you tell me it was your birthday?" The look on Alex's face as she spoke seemed a bit dejected. Kaylee realized that she hadn't said a word, despite Alex's exuberance for her own birthday a few months before.

"I guess it slipped my mind, to be honest. For the last five years, it's just been me and Ryan. I get the Facebook feed stuff, and my mom usually sends me a card, but it just sort of slips by. It wasn't much different before Ryan, really. After my dad passed, birthdays started just being another day." They walked in silence after Kaylee's confession, got to the shop, and ordered their lunch. "I wasn't trying to keep it from you; it's just not something I hold in high regard. And besides, you didn't exactly give me much warning about *your* birthday!"

They ate in silence for a moment. Kaylee was contemplating how the news was affecting Alex. Alex seemed to be chewing the revelation as much as her food. Kaylee still did not think much of her birthday; after all, it was just another day.

"I'm sorry, I guess birthdays were always seen as important events for my family, days to celebrate. My parents always made a big deal about it, so it carried over into my adult life. I shouldn't be upset that you didn't tell me. However, I definitely think we need to do something about it." Alex started to get that glint in her eye. Kaylee looked at her questioningly. "If you're going to be my girlfriend, then you're going to have to get used to being a little spoiled on your birthday."

"Alex, I appreciate that, but it's really not a big deal. We can have a small cake with Ryan at home." Kaylee said with a tone of finality.

"You're absolutely right, we can do a small cake with Ryan. I'll be at your place tomorrow so we can celebrate. You just let me take care of everything, okay?" Alex smiled sweetly as she spoke. The two finished up their lunch and trudged back through the bitter cold to the office. The lunch had offered a great break from the tense environment, but the rest of the day was spent working hard in the conference room. Alex slipped out of the office about an hour early. *Lucky her*, Kaylee thought as she sat going over designs.

***

Saturday started slowly. Kaylee felt a little odd not having Alex cuddled up behind her. She twisted over and stretched. It felt amazing just to lay in the bed and not have to do anything. A clank from the kitchen, followed by a yelp from Ryan, reminded her that she still had work to do. She dressed and found Ryan frantically trying to clean up milk with an old towel. She chuckled to herself and got busy.

Soon the mess was cleaned, they were both dressed for the day, and finally sat eating cereal together. By mid-morning, Kaylee had caught up on the laundry, tidied the house, and sat down to read a book while Ryan played with Lego.

Around eleven, Kaylee got a text saying to be ready at noon. Puzzled, she pushed herself up off the couch. There wasn't much to do; she got shoes and socks for Ryan, and then made herself more presentable.

The doorbell rang and Ryan bolted to answer. Alex waltzed in carrying a small cake and a bouquet of flowers. Kaylee was excited to see flowers; she was still getting used to the whole concept of getting small gifts like that. Alex embraced her warmly, giving her a kiss.

"Happy birthday, beautiful. See, small cake and flowers, just like you ordered. Although I was thinking, perhaps we could all go out for the afternoon before coming back to have the cake. Sound good?" Alex looked innocent enough, but Kaylee wasn't exactly sure how much she bought it.

She nodded reluctantly and then started grabbing coats to travel outside.

Once everyone was in, Alex started the car. Ryan bounced around the backseat, wailing for the hot air to start. Despite the frigid weather and the snow-covered ground, the Mazda was still warm from Alex driving over. Alex smiled at Kaylee and shifted the car into reverse. The gears changed and the three of them took off through the city. Kaylee had no idea where they were going.

"So exactly where are you taking us?" Kaylee finally asked after ten minutes on the interstate. Ryan was busy entertaining himself with a pocket full of Hot Wheels, pretending to drive along with Alex.

"Oh, just a little place I know. You said you weren't used to doing much. I didn't want to overwhelm you the first year, so we're just going to do a few small things." Alex smiled elusively. Kaylee felt her ears heating, blushing at the gesture.

"Can I at least get a hint?" Kaylee smiled, coyly. Alex looked thoughtful for a second, then shook her head. "Oh please, Alex? That's not fair. It's my birthday! I should get to know what's going on."

"Hmm, well it is your birthday..." Alex said nodding her head. Then she trailed off and pretended to be paying close attention to the road.

"Well?" Kaylee quizzed. Alex chuckled and kept smiling.

"You're so cute when you get pouty," she cheerfully replied. "You'll see shortly. We're almost at our first stop."

"First stop? I thought you said this was going to be a simple celebration." Kaylee's thunder lost its boom as she contemplated what else Alex had in store.

"Oh, it will be simple... ish. Just wait and see, relax and enjoy the day." With the final remark, Alex pulled into a small parking lot.

CHAPTER 2

The storefront had several pieces of pottery on display, from vases to trinkets to plates and bowls. They were painted with all the different hues of the rainbow. "I thought the first thing we could do is make some pottery together. Have you ever been to one of these places before?"

"No, what is it?" The group got out of the vehicle and went inside. Several tables and chairs were sat out in the middle of the room with a ton of white clay items around the edges.

"Essentially, we're going to pick out a piece of pottery and paint it, then they'll fire it for us and we can pick it up in a few days," Alex explained. Kaylee smiled; it seemed like a fun little activity.

Ryan could barely contain his excitement looking at the vast choice of shapes and models. The group came back to their table after choosing their clay pieces.

Ryan held up his dinosaur piece, an angry T-Rex. Alex and Kaylee had chosen a set together, a matching pair of medallions. One depicted the sun, the other a moon and a few stars. The attendant came over and set out brushes and paper towels and gave each of them a small paint plate. Kaylee took Ryan to get his colors first.

"Make sure you don't get any on your shirt," Kaylee warned as she hung an apron over Ryan's head.

Ryan took off with the exuberance of youth, painting zig-zags and polka dots all over his fearsome beast. Kaylee and Alex took a little more time gathering their paints and choosing colors before joining the tyke. Alex had an array of orange, red, yellow, and blue for her sun. Kaylee chose a mix of grey, dark blue, and a dab of yellow for the stars.

"Now remember, Ryan, you'll need to put on two or three coats of the paint for it to show up properly. The darker the paint, the better it will come through. Watch this." Alex coached Ryan through part of the process. It warmed Kaylee's heart to see the two of them enjoying themselves. Alex started on the sun and went over it with yellow. "Now, once this dries, I can go back and add a second coat of paint. See?"

The three of them knuckled down, decorating their pieces. Kaylee's moon had a smiling face emblazoned in the clay. She spent time making the base coat perfect and added tiny details to make it unique. Kaylee worked intently for the next hour, adding various tones and depth to her stars and moon. When she looked over at Alex's, she saw a vibrant sun with several hues emanating from the smiling orb.

"That looks amazing, Kaylee. I love how you made the sky." Kaylee blushed at Alex's compliment. They sat their pieces side by side to dry on some newspaper. "These are going to look amazing once they are done."

"Yours looks a lot better than mine. You're so talented at painting," Kaylee said smiling. She had really enjoyed the activity; it had been the first time she had done something like it. "Ryan, that's a great little dinosaur. What are you going to call it?"

"This is going to be Fred!" Ryan placed his green, purple, and blue T-Rex model onto the newspaper. The lady on duty came over with a tray to gather up the works of art, paying special attention to Fred. Ryan beamed with pride as they exited the building.

"That was a lot of fun. Thanks, Alex." They kissed sweetly before climbing back into the Mazda. The afternoon was still young though. Alex pulled out of the parking lot and took a different direction than where she was supposed to be going. "Uh, where are we going now?"

"What did I say before we got to the pottery place? Just relax and let it unfold. This is your birthday and you don't have to worry about a thing." Alex smiled through Kaylee's faux exasperation. Kaylee was lavishing the attention, even if she was still getting used to it. Alex took an exit and sped along as best as traffic would allow.

The next venue happened to be the Institute of Contemporary Art on the Boston waterfront. The three of them walked into the modern art museum hand in hand. Kaylee was taken aback by some of the works, whilst others made her laugh. The two of them strolled through the exhibits, keeping Ryan close. The artwork ranged from ultra-modern, to bright colors, to downright creepy. Kaylee enjoyed the time with Alex, discussing what certain pieces meant, or poking fun.

"Are you sure you can call *that* art? I mean even I could paint a bunch of lines on a sheet and call it art." Kaylee chuckled. Alex laughed with her as they moved to the next piece. "This one looks like it could be one of Ryan's drawings from Kindergarten."

The group moved on to a more interesting exhibit that showed humanesque statues in various positions. They were posed to represent different emotions. The love statue showed two of the creatures intertwined together in ways that would not be humanly possible. Ryan was out of earshot, looking at the deformed humanoids that represented fear and anger.

"This looks like the next Kamasutra pose we should try." Alex's comment caught Kaylee completely off guard. Alex smirked over to Kaylee, who blushed and boiled over with laughter. As time wore on the group made it through several further exhibits before starting to get hungry. "It's getting close to five. What would you think about grabbing some dinner and then heading home?"

"Sounds great to me – what did you have in mind?" Kaylee questioned as they made their way to the car.

"It's *your* birthday, so what do you feel like?" Alex asked as they all climbed in and buckled seat belts.

"How about Italian? Or even fish? I could do anything really. I'm starving."

Alex put the car back in park, unbuckled her seat belt and got out. Kaylee was confused but followed suit. Ryan leapt from the back seat and the three started walking up the street. "Where are we going?"

"Well you said that you were in the mood for seafood or Italian, so why not do a bit of both? There's an excellent Sicilian restaurant just up here that specializes in seafood," Alex said as they walked. Kaylee shrugged and fell in with Alex for the short jaunt. A few minutes later, the group was sitting at a table looking at the menu. Ryan wanted popcorn shrimp. Kaylee could not decide between a number of tantalizing entrees.

"What are you thinking about getting? The calamari and black ink pasta sounds really good, but then again, so does the surf and turf." Kaylee wavered back and forth through several dishes. The waiter stopped by and greeted them warmly. After taking drink orders, Alex ordered a half dozen oysters and a bottle of wine. With that, he was off and left the three of them to contemplate the menu.

"I normally get the monkfish. It's excellent here. If you want, you could order the pasta, I'll get the monkfish, and we can split it." Kaylee smiled at Alex's proposal and it was settled. They placed their order and sat back enjoying the cozy little restaurant. Alex played tic-tac-toe with Ryan until the appetizer arrived.

"Ryan, would you like to try an oyster?" Kaylee inquired as the two adults slathered sauce on the morsels. Ryan wrinkled his nose at the sight and went back to coloring. His reaction caused a chuckle from them both. "This has been a really nice day, Alex. I can't remember having had such a wonderful birthday before."

"I'm glad I could make this one extra special for you then. I still find it hard to believe you've never really done anything, not even for yourself," Alex commented, digging out another oyster.

"Well, the last few years have been a bit of a struggle financially speaking. Being a single parent is not a cheap or easy endeavor. Most of the time, in order to work I had to pay huge amounts to daycare. Now that he's in school, it makes things a lot easier. Not to mention a girlfriend who's hell-bent on spoiling me every chance she gets." Kaylee chuckled, preparing for another bite.

"Yeah well, I like spoiling you. I think that everyone needs to be spoiled once in a while. Speaking of which, I forgot to give you your present earlier." Alex made a smug maneuver. Ryan looked up at the mention of presents.

"Alex? This day has been a wonderful present – the flowers and this meal, not to mention the museum or the pottery. What more could I ask for?" Kaylee looked concerned as Alex fished something from her purse. The gift at least appeared small.

"You didn't ask for anything, which means I had the luxury of getting you whatever I wanted. I've had a wonderful day and think this will cap it off nicely." Alex smiled and handed the gift across the table. Kaylee pushed the small plate away as they finished up the appetizer. "Happy birthday, gorgeous."

Kaylee opened the exquisitely wrapped paper to reveal a small jewelry box. Kaylee's mind raced as she opened the gift. The reflection from the jewelry captured the myriad of overhead lights and sparkled with each twist and turn. A small pair of princess cut earrings and a pendant necklace glimmered before her.

"Alex... These are gorgeous. I can't accept such a lavish gift. These are... Wow." Kaylee stumbled over her words, not exactly sure what to say or how to react. She found herself fighting back emotions, not wanting them to spill down her face. "Thank you Alex, *really*, but why? Why such a huge gift?"

"Because you're worth it. I've worked hard for the last ten years to get to where I am. Recently I realized I was becoming lonely with my life. You changed that. You've made me a very happy woman over that last few months. To me, that's worth all the money in the world. I'm glad you like them."

Alex reached out and took Kaylee's hand across the table. They smiled in contentment. Ryan realized the presents did not include Lego and quickly lost interest, going back to his drawing. The waiter announced his presence with a large tray of food. The succulent aromas made their mouths water. The plates were placed while Kaylee put the gift in her bag. The black pasta stood out against the white sauce and chunks of calamari.

After the waiter set everything down, he left the three of them to dig in. Ryan all but attacked his plate, not having eaten since their early lunch. The two adults chuckled and divided out portions to share. The seafood was fresh and everything tasted wonderful. The two laughed while talking between bites. As the last of the meal was being finished, the waiter stopped by to box up the leftovers. He then disappeared to grab the check for them.

"Ma'am, I hate to say this, but I overheard a bit of your conversation earlier." The waiter said, placing a plate in front of Kaylee. It was a dessert, a piece of decadent chocolate pie with whipped topping and caramel sauce. It had a single glowing candle. "Happy birthday!"

The waiter then dropped the check and left the three to pick over the piece of pie. Alex swept the check up as Kaylee started to reach for it. She glanced at it, placed her card inside, and put it at the edge of the table. The waiter collected the payment after a moment and the three of them finished up the meal. Kaylee felt stuffed as they made their way back to the car. The car ride home seemed to pass quickly, with Ryan almost falling asleep in the back seat.

CHAPTER 3

Kaylee closed the door to Ryan's room after she put him to bed. Alex had a glass of wine ready for her return. Kaylee sank down on the couch, grabbing the glass and taking a small sip. They spent a few moments snuggling and unwinding from the day.

"Happy birthday. I hope that it's one you'll remember," Alex said, sipping her wine. Kaylee inhaled the faint scent of her perfume as they sat together. Alex lifted her arm so Kaylee could lay on her, then wrapped it around Kaylee protectively.

"Are you kidding? Today was amazing. I can't recall a better birthday – not in my adult life, anyways. You must have spent a small fortune."

Kaylee cooed as she got comfortable. She ran her hands up and down Alex's thighs slowly. Alex in turn started stroking her nails gently across Kaylee's back.

"Like I said, I wanted to spend it, so I did. You're worth all of it and a whole lot more." Alex finished her glass of wine and put it on the side table. Kaylee took another sip before Alex gingerly took it from her. Once it was safely on the table, Alex cupped Kaylee's face in her hand and kissed her. Their tongues entwined and circled together, dancing with each other.

Kaylee felt lightheaded, but Alex continued her assault by kissing down Kaylee's neck. Enjoying the sweet attention, Kaylee laid her head back against Alex's arm. Alex ventured a small nibble, and softly kissed up to the tender area behind Kaylee's earlobe. The sudden breath and heat on flesh sent shivers racing down Kaylee's spine. Alex latched on and started gently sucking, careful not to leave a mark.

Alex started to explore Kaylee's body through her clothing, rubbing her hip, back, and thighs. Kaylee sighed into the silence of the room. Alex didn't seem to be content with just suckling and kissing her neck, and soon she started working her way down. She pushed the thin sweater off Kaylee's shoulder and nibbled at her collarbone. Alex's hands then found their way under the sweater, quickly pulling it off and over Kaylee's head.

Alex savored the sight of Kaylee's soft skin in the dim light of the living room. Her hand returned to Kaylee's back and snapped the bra loose with ease. Alex gently pushed, guiding Kaylee to lay on back the couch, kissing her on the way down. Alex straddled Kaylee's thigh as their tongues dueled slowly. A growing passion swirled within Kaylee, igniting her need for Alex. The two women writhed together on the couch, hands exploring each other.

"Is this another one of those birthday surprises?" Kaylee murmured, voice low and sensual. Alex slid her hand up Kaylee's exposed flesh, cupping her breast and kneading it. Alex took her time mindfully exploring and teasing, in no rush to have the night end quickly. The best part about doing stuff all day was an early bedtime for Ryan, and lots of adult time after. The night was still young, and the fires of passion burning between them would last until morning.

"I think we'd be more comfortable in the bedroom. What do you think?" Alex said after a few moments of suckling Kaylee's breasts. Kaylee nodded breathlessly and moved from her spot on the couch. This time they made sure to gather discarded clothing to avoid any awkward conversations with Ryan the following morning. Once in the bedroom, Alex wrapped her arms around Kaylee from behind. The sudden embrace caught Kaylee off guard. Alex started kissing the back of Kaylee's neck sweetly, breathing in her ear. "How tired are you?"

Kaylee danced away from Alex's grasp, turned and smiled coyly at her would-be captor. She wiggled her hips while pushing the skirt from them. Alex followed suit, stripping her top and jeans down. In seconds, the women were nude, standing just a few feet apart.

"Oh, I don't know. What did you have in mind?" Kaylee teased. Alex quickly closed the distance and they bounced onto the bed together, Alex pinning Kaylee's arms above her head.

"How about we tie you up and give you tongue lashes until the wee hours of the morning?" Alex was half-serious, but Kaylee didn't catch it. Instead, she leaned up and kissed Alex teasingly. "Or we can just do that?"

Alex quickly dropped her kinky pretense and twisted her body into the bed with Kaylee, cradling her head as they kissed. Once again they started exploring each other's bodies with tongue and fingers. Kaylee ran her hands down Alex's back as Alex turned to take Kaylee's nipple into her mouth. Alex continued to roll her body so that she was poised above Kaylee. The fire within Kaylee had built all night, and showed no sign of dying any time soon, yet Alex seemed to be avoiding contact with Kaylee's sex on purpose.

As if reading her mind, Alex ran a hand down Kaylee's stomach and over her mound. Just before touching Kaylee's womanhood, Alex adjusted course to stroke her thigh instead. Kaylee let out an exasperated grunt, the urge for release building. Again the tracing finger circled back, but again it continued up her other thigh. The whole time, Alex had Kaylee's nipple in her mouth, driving her insane. After a few more passes, Alex stroked Kaylee's outer lips tenderly, sending shockwaves through her. The finger trailed off again, down her leg.

"Gah, you are evil! What a tease," Kaylee bemoaned, half aroused, half frustrated.

Alex chuckled, releasing Kaylee's tender flesh from her mouth. She leaned up for a sensual kiss before looking Kaylee in the eyes. For a long moment they locked gaze and said nothing. No movement, no breathing, just each other.

"Do you want something, love?" Alex whispered into Kaylee's ear as she leaned down to tease her neck some more. Kaylee wrapped her arms around Alex's neck as she nuzzled the spot behind Kaylee's ear lobe.

"I want you..." Kaylee seemed to lose the words. Alex chose that moment to start suckling Kaylee's neck and tracing fingers close to her nub. "...I don't want you to stop. *Please.*"

"Oh, I have no intention of stopping," Alex said seductively, running a single finger up the velvety slit. After so much teasing, the smallest touch seemed to cascade through Kaylee, making her moan. "I have absolutely no intention to stop teasing you."

The finger danced away, leaving Kaylee frustrated again. Alex continued the game for a few more moments before kissing her way down Kaylee's neck, then her breasts, then her tummy. Alex rocked her body back until she was kneeling between Kaylee's legs. She leaned down and slowly slid her tongue across Kaylee's sex. The gentle lapping soon turned into long strokes of Alex's tongue. The dam broke for Kaylee as she realized the teasing was finally over.

Kaylee's voice raised in soft moans, echoing through the room. Alex slowly lapped at the outer lips, taking care not to touch the sensitive nub at the top. It was only a matter of seconds before Kaylee would become impatient with the inferno raging inside her and calling for release. Alex teased and suckled, snaking her tongue into Kaylee briefly before returning to the light strokes.

"Please, Alex. You're driving me crazy," Kaylee panted. The heat began to rise and Alex became bolder, edging closer and closer to Kaylee's button. *She knows exactly what she's doing*, Kaylee thought to herself in a brief moment of clarity. With one more upstroke, the thought shattered as Alex switched from teasing to assault. The suckling on Kaylee's nub threatened to overwhelm her instantly. Kaylee found herself gripping the sheets and trying to hold back the flood of pleasure.

As suddenly as it started, Alex paused, leaving Kaylee teetering on the brink of ecstasy. Kaylee groaned, frustrated, throwing her eyes open. Alex leaned up and kissed her. As they kissed, Alex straddled Kaylee's thigh. Kaylee could feel the familiar steel of Alex's piercing and the heat emanating from her womanhood. She did not notice that Alex's knee was poised just a few inches from her opening.

As the kiss broke, Alex wrapped her arm around Kaylee's neck and gazed piercingly into her soul. Kaylee smiled, despite the torment. A flood of emotion surged through her; she felt like utter jelly when Alex looked at her like that. Alex smiled back and then leaned down to kiss her once more. As their tongues entwined, Kaylee wrapped her arms around Alex. She had never felt so connected to anyone before.

Alex slid her free hand between them, slowly pushing two fingers into Kaylee. Kaylee gasped, breaking the kiss for a moment. She quickly recovered and continued dueling with their tongues. Alex started to gently rock her body, her fingers driving deep in and out of Kaylee whilst her palm grinded against Kaylee's sweet spot. Feeling the movement, Kaylee started to writhe to the rhythm, driving her thigh upwards while Alex pushed into her.

The two women rocked together, each keeping pace with the other. There was no need to rush, each content to enjoy the slow build of anticipation. Kaylee could feel the heat on her leg, knowing full well the raging inferno within Alex. The slow rocking was building towards an earth-shattering release. As the passion intensified, Alex broke the kiss and started nuzzling and suckling Kaylee's neck once more. Both women started to push each other harder, the softness melting away into pure need.

Alex started to thrust her knee harder, pushing the fingers deeper with each stroke. The hours that had been building up to this moment started to crack. Their writhing bodies became as one, working off of each other. With one final, passionate kiss, Kaylee let out a long moan, her body convulsing and the tide flowing forth. Her body churned with bliss as the slow deluge engulfed her. Alex ground her body hard onto Kaylee's thigh, reaching her own orgasm in the process.

Alex collapsed next to Kaylee, drawing her into an embrace. As the world came back into focus, the two stared longingly into each other's eyes. Kaylee nuzzled into Alex's breasts and yawned sleepily; Alex responded with one of her own.

It had been a wonderful day. As the two started to drift into sleep, Alex reached down and pulled the cover up over them.

"Happy birthday, beautiful."

CHAPTER 4

The echoes of the wonderful birthday faded all too quickly as January plowed onward. The Monday following Kaylee's birthday started with a change in the project schedule. The new deadline was at the beginning of March. This shortened the entire project and meant that both teams had a mere six weeks to complete their designs and branding concepts. Kaylee had never felt so rushed before on a project. The new workload kept her busy, mentally and physically.

Rose and Kaylee were the mastermind duo behind the designs. While they did have people they could bring in for small tasks, the bulk of the work was squarely on their shoulders. This left both of them crammed, day in and day out, in a tiny conference room. They had taken it over for themselves, hanging designs on various walls, leaving notes and timelines on the white board. It was their domain. One of the few positives to come from this change was that Kaylee had the chance to get to know Rose better.

Another plus side was that Alex needed to work very closely with Rose in several aspects of the project, so Kaylee would see Alex more often in the office, even if their interactions could only be subtle. Every so often, Kaylee cursed the 'no employee dating' policy, and this was one of those times. Most of the week, lunch was ordered or brought into the office so the team could continue working together through their scheduled break. Alex made sure they got away every Friday, though, regardless of the looming deadline.

"How would you feel about pulling some overtime again, Kaylee?" Rose sat pouring over a template as she spoke. Kaylee knew Rose was frustrated with their progress and the new deadline.

"I hate to do it – I know you have Ryan – but I think it would really help move us along."

"How much overtime are we talking? Five or ten hours a week?" Kaylee inquired, the wheels in her head turning. The extra work would make her look professional and dedicated to the job, though she did feel bad about leaving Ryan in the care of others so much. But her neighbor probably wouldn't mind, especially for a little extra money.

"For now, probably an extra hour or two every night. Maybe a couple of Saturdays over the next month. I know that that'll take away from personal and family time, but it would mean a lot to me, and it would push us farther forward. You're just about the only one I can count on to get this kind of stuff done."

Rose was laying it on thick; she must really need help. Kaylee felt conflicted. "I'll do what I can to make sure we meet our deadline," Kaylee said resolutely. Just then, Alex came through the door. The two of them locked eyes and smiled before Alex went back to her stoic, business-first self.

"Rose, how are the designs coming along? We'll need some finalized products fairly soon for the marketing campaign." Alex seemed a bit stressed although her cool exterior hid it well. Alex walked over to the wall of images and mock-ups. "Were these here yesterday?"

"No, those are new. Kaylee finished them this morning," Rose said, fiddling through some folders. Rose was generally a fairly collected person, but the frantic work schedule was getting too much for her. The entire team seemed to be struggling with the workload in some form or another.

"I thought you were going with a different color scheme? Can I borrow these for a minute?" Alex said furrowing her eyebrows. Alex sighed as she looked over the sketches. She turned to the wall that was covered with a variety of other clothing options and pointed to another. "Is that one new too?"

Rose went to stand, but caught the corner of her folders. Papers and sketches tumbled to the ground in a heap. Frustrated, Rose started gathering her work. Kaylee and Alex bent down to lend a hand. Alex pulled a sheet from the stack.

"Rose, this is also completely different than what you originally gave us to work with. When were you going to tell so much had changed?" Alex seemed to be losing her cool as she gathered up papers, glancing at each one.

"Well, we were happy with the originals, but Joseph determined that these work better with the latest trend data, so we changed direction. I should have told you sooner. I'm sorry, Alex." Rose stumbled over her words. This was not the first goof-up Kaylee and Rose had gone through, but it was a significant one.

Rose was struggling to answer the first question, let alone the follow-ups. At last everything was in order and back on the conference table. Rose looked disheveled, the stress etched across her face. She stared at the floor, downcast like a scorned puppy. Alex appeared to be in contemplative thought.

"Yes, you should have. I'll be right back." Alex pulled the drawings from the wall and left. Kaylee could feel the tension between the two. Normally, they got along swimmingly. The stress was starting to wear them down.

Twenty minutes passed before Alex came back in with the set. "I think we need to have a meeting on Monday, Rose, so we're all on the same page. Kaylee, are you ready for lunch?"

Rose nodded at Kaylee, waving a hand toward the door. "Go ahead, Kaylee."

Kaylee almost objected until she realized that Rose wanted to be alone. Gathering her purse, she started for the door.

"Do you want me to pick anything up for you? We're going to Chipotle," Kaylee offered. Rose nodded and gave her a quick order. With that, Kaylee left, reaching the door just as Alex was coming out of her office. "Shall we?"

"Absolutely," Alex said. "What a headache." Alex was referring to the changes in plans that hadn't been discussed. The chilly air at least reminded Kaylee that a world existed outside the four walls of the conference room. "Rose knows better than that. This could really throw a wrench into things, especially this late in the game."

"I understand, I'm sorry. Rose asked me to start working late again. I guess it's crunch time." Kaylee wrapped her arms around Alex once they were a safe distance from the office. Normally, she wouldn't be so bold, but the extra hours and stress had made personal time very scarce. As much overtime as Kaylee had already put in, Alex had been working more. In fact, Kaylee's birthday was the last time they had been able to find alone time in any measure.

"I know, and I hate that it will take you away from Ryan. I know I'm certainly missing you. Rose appreciates the help more than you realize, though. I don't think this project would be where it's at without your involvement."

Kaylee smiled, flattered by the compliment. They arrived at the small Tex-Mex place and got out of the cold. After getting their food, they sat down to enjoy the break.

"Speaking of which, are you doing anything this weekend?" Kaylee asked, hoping the answer would be 'I'm coming over to see you.'

That hope must have shown in her expression, because Alex's shoulders dropped and she looked suddenly apologetic. "I'm sorry, babe. If I don't work tomorrow and probably on Sunday, we're going to be too far behind to finish on time, especially with this color thing. In a few more weeks, I promise I'll make it up to you." Alex smiled wryly, and Kaylee understood that it was duty first. Alex hadn't gotten to her position by taking days off. Kaylee was learning that she would need to have that level of dedication sometimes, too.

The lunch, at least, was a pleasant break. They spent the lone hour making each other laugh and forgetting about the stress. Kaylee went to order Rose's food and the two of them started back through the cold. As the office building came closer, Kaylee could feel the stress building again.

"Do you really think that we're going to pull this project off?" Kaylee asked as they approached the building. Alex's posture and expression had changed as well, stoic and professional.

"Oh yeah, we'll make the deadline. I just hope it's good enough to win the contract. First things first though, we need to buckle down and nail the designs." Kaylee felt bad about Alex's last statement. She knew that the comment was made in frustration and not aimed at her, but she was a core part of the design team and the words hit home. "Listen, in a few weeks we can have a date night," Alex told her. "I promise."

The words alleviated some of the stress building in Kaylee's mind. Without another word, they parted ways. Alex headed for her office, leaving Kaylee to trudge back to the conference room. The four walls seemed to be padded; she felt like she was going mad. Rose thanked her for the lunch and ate in silence. Kaylee bent over one of her designs and started fresh.

***

Days started to pass very quickly. Get up, take Ryan to school, work all day, come home. Eat dinner, bathe, bed, collapse.

Kaylee knew that she couldn't be the only one in that boat, but the pace was definitely not anything like she was used to. The team members really started coming together after Alex addressed the interdepartmental issue. With only a couple of months to crank everything out, everyone was expected to give it their all.

As February came to a close, Kaylee started to feel lonely again. She saw Alex often enough, but given their workload, it was always in a professional setting. She managed to become good friends with Rose, despite their lifestyle and age differences. Kaylee truly felt part of the team, wanting to make sure they did an amazing job. Aside from Valentine's Day, Alex and Kaylee hadn't managed any date nights since her birthday in January. Both of them were feeling the effects of being close but separated by the office law.

The project was still in full swing as the month turned. Only two weeks left before the deadline, and

Kaylee was unsure if they would make it. She busied herself over the finalized work, swiping a loose strand of hair back over her ear. Rose sat on the other side of the conference table, preparing for the Friday meeting. The rough designs that had adorned the wall over the last month now stood polished. Alex's team filtered into the tiny space, each looking strained.

"I want to thank everyone who has poured so much of themselves into this project," Rose began. "It was something larger than we have ever attempted before and I realize it has taken a lot of effort from everyone. However, looking around this room, I'm proud of the work we have put together. Alex, you and your team have done amazing work in such little time." Rose paused, letting a soft round of applause subside. "We aren't out of the woods yet, though; we have two more weeks. It's crunch time to get everything finalized. Alex?"

"Rose, Kaylee, and the rest of your team have been the backbone of this project," came Alex's even response. "I think we have definitely seen what great minds can do when they work together. You're right though: We're not finished yet. Up on the board is the timeline for the next two weeks..." Alex's smooth voice carried on in her professional tone, assigning tasks to groups and individuals. Kaylee and everyone else watched intently as their schedules were laid out. As the meeting drew to a close, Kaylee looked forward to their usual Friday lunch date.

The two women made a clean getaway. Once they were clear of the office, Alex took Kaylee's hand in hers as they walked. The Indian restaurant ended up being a great retreat from the hectic day. The aromas reminded Kaylee of just how hungry she was. A small buffet was located near the kitchen, and in short order the two women were enjoying a delicious selection of perfectly spiced dishes.

"Will you be coming over tonight?" Kaylee ventured. She felt like she was going through Alex-withdrawal. With the exception of Valentines, they had gone almost two months with very little cuddling or intimacy, let alone sex. Feeling moody and irritable, it was the closeness she wanted more than anything else. A surge of hormones had her a bit on-edge and restless.

"I want to come over, babe, I really do. The plus side is that we're almost done. I tell you what – I need to work tonight, but I'll try and stop by after, if it's not too late. How does that sound?" Alex spoke as if she was still in the meeting.

Kaylee struggled to understand. Her rational mind told her that this was Alex's job, and that it sometimes required long hours. The irrational part just wanted to be selfish and lay in bed with Alex wrapped around her.

"Okay," Kaylee murmured. She did not want to get her hopes up; there had been a number of times over the last few weeks where Alex had dropped the same line and hadn't followed through. She always texted that it was too late, and usually that she would be working Saturday as well. "Part of me can't wait for this project to be over so we can have some *us* time again."

"I hear you. It definitely hasn't been easy, and it's not because I don't want to spend time with you. This is an important stepping-stone for both our careers. It's hard, but I think it'll work out great for both of us. Chin up, love, we can do this. Together." Alex's words were soothing, and put Kaylee at ease a little. She was still not happy about missing the snuggles and intimacy, but managed to resist the urge to sigh. In the end she blamed her feelings on premenstrual moodiness.

After they finished their meal, they walked hand in hand towards the office. At one point, Alex stopped in her tracks and pulled Kaylee to face her. Puzzled, Kaylee looked at Alex and smiled. Suddenly, Alex was kissing her, slow but unyielding, in the middle of the street and in broad daylight. Kaylee closed her eyes, the rest of the world fading away until there were only Alex's lips brushing against hers. She responded fervently, moving closer so that their bodies pressed together. When at last she broke the kiss, Alex smiled sweetly and continued walking, as if nothing at all had happened.

"I've been wanting to do that for too long. I couldn't resist anymore." Alex sounded smug as they turned the corner towards their building. Kaylee was flustered and had no time to digest what just happened. Now she would have to face the afternoon hopelessly aroused, and in a tiny box with her coworker.

"That was evil," Kaylee said under her breath as they ascended the stairs.

Alex opened the door for Kaylee. "Yeah, well, now we'll both have to suffer in silence. I've been wanting you for weeks now." Kaylee flushed crimson as she walked through the door into the foyer. She felt that every person in the building knew what Alex had just said. "I'll see you tonight. Bye for now."

Flustered and throbbing, Kaylee made her way back to her makeshift prison. Thankfully, it was Friday. A few more hours and then she'd have the weekend to recuperate. It took every ounce of energy to get through the final hours of the week and, just before five o'clock, Kaylee was reminded it was that time of the month again. Groaning internally, she hit the restroom before heading home. *Why couldn't it wait one more day?* Kaylee grumbled to herself. *There goes any remote chance for tonight.*

CHAPTER 5

On the way home, Kaylee grabbed fast food, no longer in the mood to cook. She felt bad that this had been occurring more often than it should have, but she was just so physically and emotionally drained. Ryan was happy to see her as she picked him up from the afterschool program. The two of them made their way back to the apartment. After dinner, they read books and played games until bedtime.

Just as she was about to run a bath, Kaylee received the expected text: *Sorry, working later than I thought. I'll try to be out there before it's too late. xx*

The respite of lunch now seemed so far away. The stress and emotional turmoil had worn Kaylee down. Once Ryan was in bed, she sat in the tub and soaked for a while. The warmth felt great on her tired muscles and eased away some of her cramps. In the silence of the bathroom, she let frustrated tears roll down her cheeks. After nearly an hour of soaking, she told herself that it would do no good to sit and wallow in the tub. Unfortunately, she didn't feel like doing much of anything else at the moment.

She went to lay in bed, thoughts tumbling through her mind. Her body ached and the faintest tinge of a headache had formed at the edges of her skull. She turned on her lamp and tried to read, but she kept reading the same lines over and over again.

Her mind kept wandering back to the kiss that Alex had planted on her earlier. It had screamed with need and desire. Kaylee reflected on the last time she'd felt that desire. The more her mind wandered, the more aroused she became.

She felt a little dirty even contemplating what she was thinking. Her mind was conflicted, but her body pleaded for release. In the end, she tossed caution to the wind and grabbed her small bullet vibrator from the drawer. If she wasn't going to get any for the next week, she could at least do something herself. She imagined the lovemaking from her birthday, and the heated passion of all the previous times Alex had seduced her. Kaylee's blood boiled as she worked herself into a frenzy.

The hum of the small machine and faint moans echoed through her bedroom. The world started to drift away as the electric pulses raced through her. Kaylee squeezed her knees together, holding the vibrator firmly against her flesh. The need for release pushed her on, the stress and loneliness melting away. All that mattered was the singular need to get off. While it was no match for the real thing, after the dry spell, any pleasure was welcome.

In the living room, Alex let herself in. She felt bad for coming over this late, but she had wanted to see Kaylee so badly. She had even brought flowers to offer a peace treaty for working so much. The apartment was fairly silent as Alex walked through the empty kitchen, thinking Kaylee must be in the bath. With the flowers safely in a vase, Alex started towards the bathroom. The door was wide open, and

Kaylee wasn't there. Just then, a faint moan came from the bedroom.

She crept to the door, slowly opening it. The view took her breath away. Kaylee lay nude on the bed, the vibrator pulsing at the top of her slit. Kaylee's eyes were screwed shut; Alex could tell she was close to orgasm. Without thinking, Alex's hand drifted into her skirt, pulling her panties to the side. She was instantly on fire - not that she needed much goading after such a hard month. She slowly unbuttoned her white dress shirt and leaned against the door for support.

The doorframe creaked suddenly. Kaylee's eyes flew open to see Alex standing there. Embarrassed, she moved to cover herself. Alex's mind shot through the haze and back to reality as the beautiful sight before her was lost to the covers. Dazed, she shook her head and eventually locked eyes with Kaylee from across the room.

"I.... I'm sorry babe. I didn't mean to barge in.... I was just coming to surprise you. You know, I told you I would be here. Uh, but... Wow. Please, don't stop." Alex steadied herself and closed the door. "You look so fucking hot." The words dripped with deliberation as she slowly crossed the room, stripping off her remaining clothing. "Please?"

"Uh…" Kaylee was frozen, not exactly sure how to proceed. "I can't, uh…"

"Yes, you can. Please, keep going. You've got me all hot and bothered. It really turned me on, watching you." Alex pulled back the cover, exposing Kaylee's nude body, the vibrator still buzzing away. "What if I join you?"

"Alex… uh, I'm sorry, I wasn't… I… I don't know, Alex." Kaylee squirmed and pulled her knees together. Alex moved up on the bed and knelt next to her. She positioned herself so Kaylee would have a clear view of everything.

"You can watch me, and if you let me, I would like to watch you." Alex resisted the urge to lean down and kiss Kaylee. Instead, she looked at her intently. Kaylee bit into her bottom lip as she shifted back and forth from arousal to outright embarrassment. "C'mon Kay. You know, I really can't get off unless you do. So what do you say? Do it for me?"

Alex let one hand slip between her legs, watching as Kaylee's eyes followed. Alex slowly stroked her outer lips in hopes of coaxing Kaylee to join in. Her sudden shyness turned Alex on even more. "Okay. How about you just watch me? I won't watch you. I'll look away."

Alex remained on her knees and stretched her body back, arching her neck towards the ceiling. Kaylee was mesmerized by what was unfolding in front of her. Her breathing and heart rate started rising again. She studied the length of Alex's body: her sweeping tattoos, her lithe form, her hardened nipples, her supple breasts. Kaylee's vision finally settled on the small metal ring protruding from the nub of Alex's womanhood. She could not see Alex's eyes, but knew she must be studying herself as well. The only thing she could focus on was the hand and fingers slowly caressing the flesh before her.

As Kaylee loosened up, her hand began to echo Alex's movements. Alex spread herself open just slightly and teased her piercing. Kaylee could hear a soft moan escape from Alex. The heated passion spurred her to action – After all, she had been so close. Kaylee retrieved the vibrator and slid it against herself. The electric vibes once again shot through her body. This time, she no longer thought of the past, but instead riveted her vision up to the woman pleasuring herself before her.

Alex could feel Kaylee getting into it, the need for release overpowering the shyness. She spurred her on with a display of slow, rhythmic hip movements and soft moans. Alex could feel her own orgasm building as she sensed her girlfriend working herself into a frenzy. She leaned forward and watched as Kaylee's hand twitched and drove the toy against herself. Kaylee's body writhed as the heat built between them. The two women moved together, the waves of release mere moments away.

With a gasp, Kaylee moaned deeply, the pulsing vibrator pushing her body over the edge. Her eyes met with Alex's as the waves of climax echoed through her body. That one moment was all it took, and Alex too felt herself plunge over the edge. The two women crashed for a moment in satisfaction.

"Fuck, that was good." Alex recovered her breath first, not quite so shy about pleasuring herself as Kaylee. She pulled her body down, placing herself between Kaylee's legs. Alex kissed Kaylee's knee and then started on a swift trail down her thigh. Kaylee clamped her legs shut before Alex could get too far between them.

"There's no need to be shy, babe," Alex said, placing her hands gently on Kaylee's knees. She trailed her fingertips up and down Kaylee's outer thighs. "I've got lots more to give."

"It isn't shyness, it's... Well, it just isn't a good time." Kaylee frowned, trying to explain herself. "I'm sorry. I was hoping nature would wait." To her surprise, Alex smiled.

"Yeah, you've been a right moody bitch all week." Alex chuckled softly, trying to ease the tension. She leaned down and kissed Kaylee's knees once again, pushing her hands more firmly.

"No Alex, you don't underst..."

"Kay, I understand perfectly. You think this kind of thing is new to me? I get one every month too, y'know." Alex's logic was flawless. Alex leaned down and grabbed the towel from Kaylee's bath earlier. "Here, roll onto your side."

"I'm really not sure I'm comfortable with this, Alex," Kaylee pleaded, though she reluctantly did what she was told.

"And now back over." Alex leaned down and kissed Kaylee hard on the lips, raking her fingers through Kaylee's wavy locks, still damp from the bath before. She deftly grabbed a handful of tissues and snaked her way down Kaylee's naked body. "Look babe, I know you're all fired up. We've both been super stressed." Alex returned her attention to Kaylee's soft flesh. "I can hear your heart pounding. It's faster than your fucking vibrator. And after just watching you, I can't resist. Relax and let me take care of you." Alex continued to stroke her lips slowly across Kaylee's navel. "Let me fuck you."

"I'm really not sure about this, Alex," Kaylee started again. This time though, she allowed her legs to be pushed apart. Alex knelt between her knees and kissed down her abdomen. Kaylee could feel Alex's hot breath inches from her womanhood. She was torn: On the one hand, she was extremely turned on; on the other, she was mortified.

"Just like you weren't really sure about touching yourself in front of me?" Alex's finished her statement by running her tongue across Kaylee's womanhood. Her long hair cascaded down Kaylee's thighs. The after-tingles of Kaylee's orgasm had left her extremely sensitive. The moment Alex's tongue touched Kaylee's swollen nub, electricity raced through her. Kaylee was torn but could no longer deny the fact that she really, desperately wanted it.

Kaylee's mind boiled over as Alex suckled the sensitive clit. Alex moved her hand between Kaylee's legs, pushing two fingers deep into her. Kaylee gasped at the sudden fullness, still feeling slightly conflicted. Alex took advantage of Kaylee's swollen state, gliding and twisting her fingers to hit all of the right spots. The intensity took Kaylee by surprise. Her moans echoed off the walls as she rushed towards a second orgasm.

Alex shifted her body to lay next to Kaylee, pushing her palm down against Kaylee's clit. She pushed a third finger into Kaylee while rocking her hand back and forth. Kaylee panted and gripped at the sheets. Alex propped herself up on an elbow, reveling in her focus and the control she held over getting her girl off. Alex watched Kaylee's face as her lover tumbled off the cliff of another orgasm. Alex could feel the swollen muscles grip her fingers as they tightened.

Instead of letting up, Alex pushed the envelope further. Pulsing her hand into Kaylee as quickly as possible, Alex could feel the suction of Kaylee's womanhood around her. She shifted one more time to kiss Kaylee, her hand thrusting faster and faster. Kaylee came again, hard, in Alex's arms. Alex held Kaylee as her body jolted and the earth shattered around her. She slowed her pace as the world came back into focus. With a deft movement, Alex discarded the tissues and laid back beside her lover, cradling her as she floated in bliss.

Kaylee's eyes finally fluttered open, exhaustion weighing them down. Alex smiled at her, getting a smile in return.

Kaylee snuggled into Alex; everything felt right in the world. The stress of work was gone, and even the cramping didn't bother her as much. Kaylee still felt a flush of embarrassment, but Alex just seemed bemused.

"It is only a bit of blood, Kay," Alex said. "Don't buy into all that male-media bullshit. There's no reason why we can't enjoy each other all the time. I'll happily strap up and give you the works no matter what time of the month it is." Alex's last line and smirking wink made Kaylee chuckle. The two drifted serenely into slumber, cradling each other.

CHAPTER 6

Monday morning started a little brighter, despite the cramps. Kaylee felt like a brand new woman walking into the conference room. She arrived before Rose and started in on finalizing one of the designs that they were almost finished with. Rose arrived thirty minutes later, carrying a steaming coffee and a hot tea for Kaylee.

"Hope you had a relaxing weekend," Rose said as she came in from the cold. Kaylee's mind drifted over the weekend events and smiled.

"It was really good," Kaylee said, exuberant. "I'm fully charged and ready to tackle the week. How was yours?"

"That's the spirit. Here, I brought you a tea, since I know you're not a big fan of coffee." Rose handed her the cup. "Mine was not nearly as relaxing, but I did manage to catch up to your work. I swear, you've been keeping me in line this entire project."

Kaylee smiled as she took a sip of the hot drink. The hard work of the last few months had caused some of the most stressful days in her life, but she was not about to give up. She was in a great position, doing the work she loved, and she had the most amazing girlfriend. The thoughts made her giddy and warm.

"I think we've worked together to create a stellar product," Kaylee replied, not wanting to take any of Rose's credit. "I couldn't have come up with this on my own." The women had worked exceedingly hard to create a strong design line.

Rose nodded at the compromise. "Well, either way, there's good news on the horizon. With that piece you're working on, and this one here – I think between the two of us, we only have about six more to finish up. After such hard work, we're almost done," Rose said proudly.

Kaylee slumped back in her chair. After hundreds of design iterations and do-overs, the end was near.

"That's great to hear. That means we should be ahead of schedule, right?" Kaylee asked, looking over the beautiful works of art hanging around the conference room. It wasn't all hers, but she had a strong tie to most of it.

"Well, *we* are. We'll still need to help Alex and her team finish up, and then we start building our presentations. All in all, we've done a great job. Thank you for all the hard work, truly. I assure you it has not gone unnoticed." Rose turned back to the piece she was working on, getting into the thick of it again.

Kaylee turned back to her own piece, sipping her tea. Her mind started to wander about Rose's comments. It had been a long, hard road, but she was finally living the dream. Her stress level had receded a few hundred yards. Despite the normal monthly stuff, she felt really good about the week. She started in on the piece, wondering what the future would hold.

VALENTINE'S DAY

VALENTINE'S DAY

The aroma of coffee hung heavy in the air. Friday held promise of a small getaway, with only eight hours left until work ended. Kaylee focused on her tea in the breakroom, talking herself into seizing the day. Alex strolled in, her normal business mask on as she headed toward the coffee pot. She smiled at Kaylee, sharing a private moment despite being surrounded by coworkers. As the group filtered out of the small kitchen, Alex sat down momentarily.

"Do you know what tomorrow is?" Alex's piercing gaze held Kaylee's as she talked. Kaylee nodded, but didn't know what to say. "It's

Valentine's Day, our first. And I want to make it memorable. Do you trust me?"

"Trust you? Absolutely. Uh, why though?" Kaylee was a bit taken aback by the odd question. She sipped the tea as it cooled off, still trying to move through the fog in her mind. The overtime they had been putting in kept her eternally exhausted, it seemed.

"Because I want to spoil you, and I don't want you to question it." Alex was in business mode; Kaylee was not.

"I trust you, but seriously, a simple night out is just fine. We don't have to do anything fancy."

That answer seemed to work on Alex, who nodded. "You're absolutely right. I was thinking about just doing dinner and then an evening together at my place. I'll pay for an overnight babysitter. What do you think?" Alex was never this quick to agree. Suspicions stirred in the back of Kaylee's mind.

"What's the catch?" Kaylee asked, starting to wake up, the gears of her mind creaking into motion.

"No catch. Well, maybe a small one." Alex smiled, a little more coy than her usual stoic persona. "I want you to wear the diamond set I got you for your birthday. I think they'll look great with your outfit."

Kaylee found herself playing the game. "Okay, but how do you know what outfit I'll wear?"

"Oh, I got you a dress that I thought would look amazing on you. I hope you don't mind. It was something I've been designing for a while, so I had it made up. Would you do me the honors of modeling it for me tomorrow?"

Alex may have headed up the marketing department, but Kaylee knew she had the skills and creative mindset to come up with the most spectacular designs. Kaylee was a bit speechless, but excited at the prospect.

"Of course I will, and of course I'll wear the diamonds." Kaylee smiled at the thought of being spoiled. This was going to be the fourth month in a row that they'd had a full night to spoil each other.

"Excellent. I'll pick you up at 6:15 sharp. That way we can get to our reservation in time." Alex stood up as she said the last line, heading for the door.

"Wait, where are we going?" Kaylee was too late; Alex was already down the hall, power-walking to her next meeting. Chagrinned, Kaylee walked back to her desk with her tea, imagining what tomorrow would hold.

***

Kaylee felt rushed the next day as she was getting herself and Ryan ready. The doorbell rang at around four; a courier from an upscale dry cleaning service handed her a hanger before heading off. She took the bagged dress inside, unzipped the hanger, and was stunned by the exquisite dress. It was teal with a cinched hip, imperial waist, and an elegant laced V-neck. Coupled with the diamond jewelry, Kaylee felt dressed for the ball. She was showered and ready with thirty minutes to spare.

The babysitter arrived, followed soon after by Alex. She wore a black tailored suit with opals, her long black hair done in a graceful updo. Kaylee grabbed her purse and climbed into Alex's car.

"You look absolutely stunning," Alex commented as they started across the city.

"Thank you, but *you* did this. The dress is amazing," Kaylee retorted. The city zipped past as the two women chatted. "So, where exactly are we going?"

"We're going to a great little restaurant. It may be a bit busy, but you'll definitely be the best looking woman there."

Kaylee turned pink at the compliment.

The car entered a historic downtown district where Alex found a parking spot. As they exited the vehicle, Kaylee looked up and down the street for signs of a busy eatery, but there was nothing. A small plaque on the nearby wall said Menton, other than that, there was little evidence it was actually a restaurant, or anything for that matter.

Alex offered her arm to Kaylee as they entered the now-intriguing building. They were greeted warmly by professional staff who sat them at a table with plenty of privacy. The French-style restaurant was buzzing with people, and Kaylee could feel the heads turning to look at her. The attention put her a bit on edge. Napkins were placed in their laps and menus opened for them. They found themselves alone, finally.

"Alex, this place is really lovely. I think my menu has a few too many zeroes on it, though." Kaylee voiced her concern in a low tone. She looked over the menu: Veal, lobster, monkfish... Everything sounded amazing.

"Don't worry about it," Alex said, nonchalant. "Get what you want. Remember, you said I get to spoil you. You agreed to this."

Kaylee blinked. She had indeed said yes to being spoiled, but she had never thought it would include such an exclusive and prestigious restaurant.

The waiter introduced himself, explained the menu, and took their order before disappearing into the back. The low lighting and gentle music created a wonderful ambience. Kaylee felt like she and Alex were the only two in the entire restaurant. After such a hectic work schedule, it was the perfect opportunity to catch up with each other while they worked through a light salad and a bottle of wine.

"So, you've been in Boston for almost six months now. What do you think of everything so far?" Alex's question made Kaylee reflect on all that had happened to date.

"I love it. My entire life has changed. I have started out on what could be a great career in the field I've always dreamed of. I have a solid home environment and a good school system for Ryan.

Plus, I've met this amazing, crazy woman who seems to love spoiling me."

Truth be told, Kaylee was feeling madly in love with Alex, but couldn't find the courage to express herself. She didn't want to sound like a cliché, having only been in the relationship a few months, and she feared scaring Alex off. Yet she found herself thinking of Alex at every turn, finding ways that they could be together or do things together.

"I do love to spoil you every chance I get." Alex smiled across the cozy table at Kaylee. "I consider it a small repayment for all of the happiness you've brought me over the past few months."

"Aww, do I detect someone being a bit of a sap?" Kaylee gently teased, feeling an emotional surge at the thought. She was worried at times about Alex being emotionally closed off, but Alex's little comments always made things better.

"Oh, hush, you. You know you make me happy. You've reminded me that there's more to life than just conquering the corporate world." Alex smiled again.

The waiter interjected into the conversation to place succulent-looking plates in front of the two women. Kaylee's plate consisted of perfectly seared filet mignon and lobster tail, while Alex had chosen pheasant. Alex raised her wine glass. "Happy Valentine's Day, my love."

The two women clinked their wine glasses before diving into the meal. Between shared bites, the wine, and the conversation, the evening was enchanting. As they dined, Kaylee struggled with her emotions slightly. She wanted to confess her love to Alex, but she wasn't sure how Alex would take it. The setting was perfect: A date with just the two of them, no worries, no work piling up. By the same token, she didn't want to come across too strong, too soon.

"Is everything alright?" Alex asked, picking up on Kaylee's inner turmoil.

Kaylee quickly smiled to cover up everything she was battling herself over. "This is just so perfect, that's all."

After the plates were cleared away, the server brought a silky crème brûlée with the shape of a heart toasted into it. Before they dug into the dessert, Kaylee grabbed her purse. "I um, I actually got you something. It isn't a new dress, or dinner at the most glamourous place in town, but it is something. A little token."

She handed Alex a small, stuffed Snoopy dressed up in a faux tuxedo and holding a rose. The small chocolate box it held also had an envelope stuffed into it. The envelope contained tickets to the LGBT Film Festival in April. As Alex examined the gift, Kaylee could see her normal rigid appearance cave a little from the cuteness.

"You got this for me? I'm the one supposed to be spoiling *you* here. This is truly very cute. Nobody has ever gotten me anything like this before." Alex held it close to her chest. "I will cherish it always."

Kaylee wanted to scream her feelings for Alex to the world. Alex reached across the table to hold hands, making Kaylee forget everything but the moment. "Thank you so much. Happy Valentine's Day."

"Happy Valentine's Day," Kaylee echoed, too afraid to say the words she wanted to spill forth.

The two of them attacked the crème brûlée, eating it slowly around the edges to leave the heart intact. As they closed in, they started feeding each other bites. Laughing and smiling, they finished off the dessert and started toward Alex's place.

***

The dim lighting in the hallways and bedroom shadowed their way through Alex's condo. Once they reached the bedroom, Alex crossed the room to turn on the bedside lamp. She placed her Snoopy on a shelf near the bed, and then pulled the four small chocolates from the heart-shaped box, placing them on the table.

"Come share one with me?" Alex said before biting into the decadent treat. Kaylee was stuffed but made room for one more morsel. She joined Alex on the bed, where Alex fed her the remaining bite. Before Kaylee could finish, Alex leaned over and kissed her, making her giggle. Alex stood and took off her jacket, watching Kaylee watch her. "You know, you look absolutely stunning in that dress. Too bad I want you out of it."

Kaylee smiled at the sentiment and stood. She turned to undo the zipper, but Alex caught her in her arms instead. Alex's lips found their way to Kaylee's neck, planting several soft kisses in lieu of her normal nips and bites. The moment felt tender and it made Kaylee weak in the knees to know that Alex would catch her. Alex held her, arms wrapped around Kaylee's slight form.

Kaylee turned while Alex kissed her softly. When they were facing each other, Kaylee placed her arms on Alex's shoulders and tilted her head slightly to gaze into Alex's eyes. Alex leaned in close, her lips parting to caress Kaylee's, their tongues entwined as they embraced. They stood together for several moments as time seemed to melt away. At some point, Kaylee felt the zipper slide down her back and the dress fall from her shoulders.

Alex broke the embrace after what felt like several minutes and moved toward the bed, holding Kaylee's hand. Once at the bed, they both finished undressing before lying down together. The room seemed enchanted. Passionate desire thrummed through the space, but there was no rush; in fact, time seemed to stand still. Alex took Kaylee into her arms once more, planting soft kisses all over her face. Kaylee felt the tenderness emanating from Alex.

Kaylee felt secure in Alex's arms, with one wrapped protectively around her shoulders while the other traced up and down the length of her body. Kaylee felt another surge of emotion: The moment felt right, so why couldn't she just let it out? Perhaps she was waiting for Alex to make the first move, as always.

Their lips parted once more as their tongues danced. The low lighting of the room made everything else feel distant. The only thing that existed was the kiss.

Kaylee could feel Alex's hands roaming over her body. Shivers raced up and down her spine. Alex twisted towards Kaylee, kissing her neck and shoulder. Again, they were loving and soft instead of her normal nips. Alex slowly moved all over her body, kissing here and teasing there. The slow and steady pace only heightened the tension. Kaylee felt ablaze with passion, despite Alex not pressing any of her buttons.

The gears suddenly shifted as Alex traced a fingertip slowly across the hardened peak of Kaylee's breast. She gasped aloud, electricity crackling through her skin. Alex followed the trail with kisses, sucking Kaylee's nipple into her mouth lightly. The soft warmth of Alex's mouth made Kaylee moan.

"Oh, *Alex*—" Kaylee gasped. She suddenly became aware she had spoken out loud and held back the words that nearly followed. She felt self-conscious for saying something, still rather shy in the bedroom.

"Don't be embarrassed, Kay, I love it when you called my name." Alex must have thought she had caught Kaylee's thought process and attempted to quash it. Alex readily returned to what she was doing, hoping to get the same reaction. This time, Alex's fingers trailed lower on Kaylee's body.

"That's okay with you?" Kaylee asked, trying not to sound too naïve. In response, Alex kissed her.

"You are so cute sometimes. It's more than okay. In fact, I encourage it," Alex cooed back. As if to punctuate the statement, Alex's fingers found Kaylee's inner folds and embedded themselves in her. Kaylee gasped at the intrusion, twisting her body to give Alex more room to maneuver. As Alex started rhythmically pushing in and out of Kaylee, Kaylee started to moan louder.

"Alex," Kaylee panted, still not allowing herself to fully let go. Alex maneuvered to hold Kaylee close. The tension had been building for hours now, and Kaylee felt like a dam about to burst. Alex kissed her deeply, savoring the intimacy. Their bodies slid against each other, Alex cradling Kaylee. Alex ran her free hand through Kaylee's chin-length hair, pulling her into a loving kiss.

Kaylee bucked against the intruding digits, forcing three fingers as deep as they could go. Alex had one leg draped across Kaylee's thigh, grinding herself against Kaylee. Kaylee's head spun, the intimacy and emotion spilling over. Their kisses became fervent; Kaylee needed Alex. Despite the aching desire, Alex refused to quicken her pace. Kaylee could feel her body thrumming to Alex's beat, but it wasn't enough to send her over the edge.

"Alex, you're driving me crazy," Kaylee moaned.

Alex knew exactly what she was doing, and she was in no rush to finish. Instead, she put her head against Kaylee's, kissing her on the nose. Kaylee opened her eyes to meet Alex's affectionate gaze. She could see that Alex was just as heated as she was but kept it controlled.

The electrical storm pulsing through Kaylee's body intensified as Alex quickened her fingers. Their eyes were locked as their bodies writhed together. Alex could feel Kaylee's body responding and leaned down to slowly kiss her. Kaylee reached the eye of the storm within that emotionally charged embrace. Her body twisted with intense need for release and her mind screamed with desire, yet her soul felt complete. The kiss brought time to a standstill.

Kaylee's emotions threatened to overwhelm her in that brief moment. She moaned into Alex as their mouths became one. Alex pulled back, smiling, watching the dam begin to burst in Kaylee's eyes. A small string of saliva still connected the two as they parted. Alex leaned in for one last peck, and then thrust her fingers as far as they could go into Kaylee. Kaylee felt love, lust, and happiness explode from her as her body threatened to rip apart. Cascades of electricity raced through her.

Kaylee cried out through gritted teeth as a powerful orgasm echoed through her body. Kaylee's eyes slammed shut as her body convulsed. Alex refused to let up, causing wave after wave to crash upon the shores. At long last, time resumed. Kaylee's eyes flickered open, her mind still floating in the sea of desire. She wrapped her arms around Alex, kissing her over and over.

"That was so beautiful to watch, and hear," Alex teased lightly, meaning every word of it. Alex still held three fingers deep in Kaylee, twisting and twitching them at intervals, making Kaylee shudder with aftershocks. "In fact, I want to hear more of it from now on. Understood?"

Kaylee still felt a bit embarrassed about the whole ordeal. She chuckled and nodded, laying her head on Alex's shoulder. She closed her eyes, floating in bliss.

Alex pulled Kaylee into a cuddle. She stroked her fingers along Kaylee's hair, cheek and neck, caressing every wonderful part of her. They lay in silence for a few moments, enjoying heated intensity and contentment.

Kaylee opened her eyes again to see Alex's intense green gaze staring back at her. "What?" Kaylee asked, smiling. Her mind reeled from the night's events.

"Just thinking about how much you mean to me, and how happy you make me," Alex smiled back.

"Aww, you make me happier than I've ever been. I'm so glad you're in my life." Kaylee spoke the truth, but still could not find the courage to say those three words.

Alex watched as Kaylee's eyes settled again. "I hope you're not tired, my love... The night is still but young..."

E04: BUSINESS TRIP

CHAPTER 1

Kaylee gradually drifted into consciousness, realizing the alarm had not yet blared. Why was she awake? Inwardly sighing, she fought to slip back into her dream. A slight movement made her aware of the hand loosely holding her hipbone. The pleasant memories of the night before drifted through her mind. Darkness started enveloping her once again, drawing her back into slumber.

Suddenly the room filled with a cacophony of sirens, dashing any hopes of more sleep. Alex stirred next to Kaylee, giving her hip a loving pat. Kaylee in turn swatted at the intruding alarm clock and snuggled back against Alex. In her half-conscious mind, she wondered how she had ever gotten along without her. They had been dating nearly six months and it seemed like life was complete now they were together.

"Come on, sleeping beauty. You know what day it is." Career-driven 'Alexis' took all the joy out of Monday morning. Grunting in disapproval, Kaylee protested the disturbance. Alex leaned down and nibbled Kaylee's neck.

"Don't make me resort to more drastic actions, missy," she warned.

Alex started to dress. She needed to pop home before heading into work. Kaylee threw on a simple robe and headed to the kitchen to make tea. Alex joined her and they discussed their plans for the day.

"We've a meeting at nine sharp, don't be late. You know how Rose gets."

Kaylee nodded in agreement, still pushing the fog of sleep from her mind. After a quick breakfast and a farewell kiss, Alex headed out, leaving Kaylee to get Ryan and herself ready for another Monday. The shower finally got her moving and she left soon after with Ryan in tow.

The morning commute was another humdrum of loud noises, lights, and what seemed like millions of people. At the office, Kaylee prepared her tea and went into the meeting room. Most people were already sitting around the circular table, including Alex, who had saved her a spot. It was against company policy for two employees to date, but nobody had figured it out yet.

"Good morning, ladies and gentlemen," Rose began in her typical fashion. "I'm sure it's no surprise to any of you that we're moving along very well with *Tobi* as a new client. This partnership could mean the start of a new line of products, elevated status in the design world, and a nice advancement for all of us, especially if the merger goes ahead."

The news was great. Kaylee was excited. If this deal went well, she would be promoted to a designer position and would have her own assistant. The thought had her daydreaming and paying little attention to the meeting.

"Kaylee? Will that be a problem?"

Kaylee jolted back to reality, and looked around the table at staring faces. Fumbling, she tried to remember the last thing she heard. Nothing was coming to her.

"No, it shouldn't be, but if anything comes up, I'll let you know." Kaylee tried to give the most vague answer possible. To her relief everyone moved on and stopped staring. Alex threw her an odd, questioning look. Kaylee was determined to pay attention for the rest of the meeting, although it seemed there was nothing else of importance.

Kaylee felt flustered. She had a ton to do this week already, and now she had no idea what she had just agreed to add to her plate. Soon after she returned to her desk, Alex came by, tracing her fingers along the length of Kaylee's back as she slipped silently into the cubicle.

"What were you thinking about, young lady?" Alex still had no penchant for chewing the fat and could now easily read when Kaylee was in lala land.

"I was daydreaming about what happens when we win this contract. I'll be bumped up to a designer status; you know it's something I've dreamed about my whole life." Kaylee fidgeted, knowing she had been caught not paying attention.

"That's all fine and good. So what are you going to do about next week, then?" Alex smirked mischievously and watched Kaylee with intent as she drew a blank. "I knew you weren't paying attention."

"You got me. What did I miss?" Kaylee smiled with chagrin. Even though they were dating, Alex was still her superior and had a very career-minded goal set. Kaylee hated the idea of disappointing anyone, especially Rose or Alex.

"Well, the fact that you'll be getting on a plane next Monday was probably something you missed," Alex commented almost nonchalantly, sarcasm dripping from her tongue. Kaylee felt the information land in her stomach like a dead weight.

"*What*?" Kaylee exclaimed, her mind suddenly racing at ninety miles an hour. She was going to be part of the team to win the bid. She would be part of this. She could prove her worth. She might get a promotion and a raise. She could get a better apartment, or car. Ryan would be so excited.

Wait... Ryan, who would watch Ryan? That finally struck home.

"So what are you going to do with Ryan?" Alex asked, as if reading her thoughts. Kaylee focused solely on that problem. She *had* to go on this trip. It would be a great boost upwards for her career. A list of babysitters shot through her head.

"How many days is the trip?" Kaylee asked as the list started diminishing rapidly to who could stay overnight.

"You really were off in the woods, weren't you?" Alex chided, squeezing her shoulder affectionately. "It'll be all week. We leave Monday morning for L.A., have an afternoon meeting to schmooze the client, and then we head to dinner. Tuesday and Wednesday will be all sorts of boring meetings and presentations. Thursday will be a half-day, hopefully. Almost everyone will be flying home on Thursday afternoon."

"That isn't quite *all* week, you know," Kaylee teased in a feeble attempt to dampen her noisy thoughts. As further news of the trip unfolded, the list of known baby sitters who could possibly stay an entire week dropped to just one: her mother.

"I know, Kay, but you and I will be returning Friday afternoon." Alex caught Kaylee off guard using her pet name in the open office. Shooting a questioning glare at Alex made her continue. "You're going to stay behind in the afternoon and work on a 'special project' with me. Make sure you pack something a bit more formal, too," Alex added flirtatiously.

Kaylee blushed a little, thinking of all the mischief that could mean. She knew company policy would make things rather difficult to find personal time during the trip, but a date night, out on the town with no danger of being caught, sounded beyond perfect. It also dawned on her that they would have every evening alone with no Ryan. As much as she loved the little guy, adult time was few and far between. The more she thought about it, the more she wanted her mother to come up.

Kaylee never thought she would be thinking that way. Her mother did not exactly see eye-to-eye with her lifestyle. It made holidays and visits a little awkward. And although this saddened Kaylee, she refused to bend to her mother's constant negativity.

That night, after Ryan went to bed, she picked up the phone. It had been a few months since she had even talked to her mother. In fact, it was the holidays when they were last in touch. The ringing continued for a few moments before her mother picked up.

"Hello?" her mom answered stoically. Kaylee took a moment to gather her thoughts.

"Hey, mom, how are you?" Kaylee began, not wanting to start off with a showstopper.

"About to go to bed. Why are you calling so late?" Good old mom, never one to deal with pleasantries. At least the conversation would be short.

"I need a favor. I have a great opportunity to travel to L.A. next week for a business contract. Our company has been asked to put together a presentation for a prestigious client, and I've been selected to be part of the team. It could mean a big promotion and better pay." That was all the information that she needed to share: Prestige, money, promotion.

"Next week? That's awfully short notice. Are you sure you just found out about this?" Her mother was always cynical. Kaylee sighed inwardly as the words echoed through her head. *It's a yes or no question, mom.*

"Yes, mom. I only found out today. We leave Monday morning and fly back Friday afternoon. If you could come here, house sit, and spend time with Ryan, it would mean a lot to me." Kaylee continued with the diplomacy, all the while secretly raging inside. Having been retired for nearly three years,

Kaylee knew this was something her mother could easily manage – but the question was, *would* she?

"I'll think about it. I'll call you tomorrow and let you know. Now, I'm going to bed, good night. Love you." With that, her mother hung up the phone before Kaylee could even reply.

Mother had always made her feel inferior. No matter - It wasn't an outright 'no,' so there was still hope. She spent the rest of the night looking over different things to do in L.A.

Tuesday seemed to drag by, and Kaylee felt like she was on pins and needles awaiting her mother's call. She bounced back and forth between nervousness and aggravation. Finally, around lunchtime, the phone rang. Her mother reluctantly agreed and informed her she would be there Sunday morning. After getting off the phone, Kaylee realized that that meant spending an entire day with her mother.

The rest of the week passed at the speed of light. Most of the time was spent on preparation for the trip. In the office, Rose, Kaylee, Alex, Maggie, and Joseph all worked relentlessly to get their presentations in order. At home, Kaylee and Alex spent time packing and determining what they would do together with the little time they had to themselves.

By the time Saturday night rolled around, Kaylee was starting to get nervous; it had been a long time since she was last on a plane. Alex did her best to comfort her without much success. As bedtime neared, Kaylee skittishly approached the subject of her mother.

"Alex, I think it might be best if we don't spend tonight together. You know my mother doesn't agree with my 'lifestyle.' We haven't spoken since Christmas, and I can't risk her changing her mind at the last minute if you're here when she shows up. She's arriving first thing tomorrow. Please don't be mad," Kaylee pleaded.

Alex cupped Kaylee's cheek gently to reassure her.

"I understand. It's a shame that your mother sees it that way, but what can you do? Besides, I'd rather spend one night alone and the next several together, than possibly face this trip without you." With that, she gathered her things and gave Kaylee a kiss goodnight. As Alex shut the front door behind her, Kaylee instantly felt alone. The weekends had been their special time for nearly six months, and now she had to spend the night by herself.

Having a restless night did not bode well for dealing with her mother, who, at 8 AM on a Sunday, showed up at the apartment. She was dressed in her Sunday best, meaning she probably intended to drag Kaylee to church with her. Groaning inwardly, Kaylee got ready and found a local service to attend. Afterwards, they went for brunch.

"Wasn't that nice? How are you enjoying living in the big city?" The pleasant talk seemed to drift in and out of praise and scorn. Her mother was happy she was making something of herself, but she thought Kaylee's passion for fashion was frivolous.

"I love it here, and I enjoy my work. Ryan loves school, and I've, uh, made some good friends." She wanted to talk about Alex, but didn't have a good way to bring her up without causing a commotion. Her mother never really got the whole picture; whether it was due to willful ignorance or that she just didn't understand, Kaylee had stopped trying to figure it out.

"I'm glad to hear you're doing so well. Any luck finding a boyfriend?"

Kaylee sighed. She knew it was coming. The preceding line of questions just seemed to line it up perfectly. Kaylee quickly prepped some safe answers.

"To be honest, mom, with so much going on at work, I've hardly had a chance to be social." That answer felt almost true rolling off her tongue, and her mother seemed to buy it. Thankfully, the food arrived at the right time and they were able to focus on eating. The rest of the meal went by with little discussion.

The remainder of the evening was spent going over Ryan's routine, dinners, and packing. Kaylee had somehow made it through the day without the urge to strangle her mother more than a dozen times. She went to bed early, knowing she had to be up and out of the house by 4:30 in the morning.

CHAPTER 2

Nervousness caused a restless night's sleep and the alarm blared far too early for anybody to be getting out of bed. Grudgingly, she left the house and took a cab to the airport.

Still groggy, she made her way through tickets and security to find herself in the midst of a few cheerful ladies and Joseph, who was sipping a cup of coffee. Everyone was excited about the trip, which made Kaylee smile and join in the merriment, despite feeling sleep-deprived. Even Alex seemed to be in high spirits, especially given her typical cold, professional exterior in the office. Soon they were heading into the belly of the plane and off towards Los Angeles.

The cabin was cramped and everyone seemed in a rush to get to their space. Fortunately, despite the short notice, Alex had managed to book two seats together for them. It didn't look too suspicious on the books, but Alex had talked to Kaylee about the need to be careful. As long as they weren't obvious about their relationship, there wouldn't be any problems.

As soon as the door was closed, anxiety really set in for Kaylee.

"Are you alright, Kay?" Alex asked, easily picking up her nervousness. Alex had taken the window seat to shield Kaylee from the view. "I'm right here with you. Everything will be just fine."

The words seemed to dissolve some of the nerves, but Kaylee still felt dizzy and nauseated. Striking an idea, Alex tossed a blanket over them, holding Kaylee's hand underneath it. Now, to anyone looking, Kaylee was just trying to stay warm. The soothing gesture made her feel safe, and she was able to relax a little.

"I feel like a pair of schoolgirls trying to hide a secret," Kaylee whispered as she smiled at Alex. In response, Alex chuckled and leaned back into her chair. It was still early morning and neither of them had slept very well. Soon the plane roared to life, backing away from the gate. Kaylee tensed a bit, but relaxed and closed her eyes as Alex started gently stroking her hand.

Moments later they were poised for takeoff. Kaylee focused on breathing and the long, gentle strokes across her hand. The softness was nice, especially considering the firm exterior Alex showed in public. Suddenly, they were lurching forward into the early morning sky, set for L.A. Kaylee held her breath, but found herself still very much alive after the turbulent launch.

"There, now. Was that so bad, chica?" Alex cooed and smiled. Kaylee blushed at the pet name and snuggled down into her seat. Soon they were both gently snoozing. Kaylee laid her head against Alex's shoulder and got a surprisingly wonderful sleep – well, as good as it could've been on a cramped airplane.

The flight was more or less uneventful, and they slept most of the morning. Neither of them took note of Rose watching them from a few seats back, or the perplexed look on her face after seeing them sleeping in a rather intimate pose.

After disembarking, they all gathered in a group and went to the baggage claim. Soon after, two rental cars were on their way to the Sheraton. After unloading, they only had an hour to gather supplies and get over to the office complex for a kick-off meeting. Rose and Kaylee drove as a pair, leaving Alex to take care of the other two.

The first thing Kaylee noticed pulling into the parking lot was the sizeable fountain near the main entrance. The compound looked amazing, making her feel small in the grand scheme of things. She was relieved to hear that the others felt equally intimidated. Well, no matter; they had to win this contract, and that is what they intended to do. Resolutely, the group crossed the threshold.

"Thank you everyone for being here today. Rose, thank you for the wonderful correspondence. Do you want to go ahead and start?"

With that cue, Rose stood up and addressed the room. Kaylee sat nearby on her laptop, commanding the presentation. As a team, they nailed the opening proposal. Kaylee felt sure of herself sitting next to

Alexis. Her girl was all business: curt and respectful, calm and collected.

The kick-off only lasted a couple of hours before they were free for the afternoon. The group decided to get an early dinner at a renowned Mexican restaurant and head back to the hotel to prepare the next day's presentations. The aromas wafting from the kitchen reminded Kaylee that she had only eaten airport food all day.

"Good job, Kaylee," Rose said with a smile. "I think we really nailed that first presentation. Alexis, are you ready for the morning?"

Alex was a senior in the company and not usually a part of Rose's team, but this contract was important enough that they had joined forces for the trip. They all sat around nibbling chips and fresh salsa. Maggie turned to Kaylee while the two leaders talked.

"Don't you have a little one at home?" she asked. The question was simple enough, but Kaylee wasn't used to talking about home life.

"Yes. He'll be six in a few months. Do you have any children?" Kaylee was not opposed to talking, but she didn't know Maggie very well.

"Yes, we have two. My husband is taking care of them this week. I was shocked he agreed to do it. Normally it's like pulling teeth to get him to do anything around the house." Maggie chuckled. Kaylee also laughed. "Who's taking care of your little one?"

"My mother came over for the week. It's just me and the tyke, so options were limited." The answer seemed to work well enough, although she heard Joseph mutter something about a deadbeat dad under his breath. The comment kind of threw her for a moment. Suddenly, a gentle hand slipped over her knee under the table. It seemed Alex was paying more attention than she let on.

In fact, everyone at the table had heard his comment. His brash remark set off a bit of an awkward silence that was interrupted only by colorful plates being laid in front of the group. The smells and tastes soon made everyone forget the awkwardness and concentrate on enjoying their meals. Every once in a while, Joseph would mumble another halfhearted statement that the rest of them tried to ignore.

Once back at the hotel, the team went to work, getting ready and rehearsing for the next day's events. They had a full year's worth of wardrobes and accessories to lay out and only three days to do it. They called it a day around seven.

Weary from the travels, Kaylee and Alex returned to Alex's room. As soon as the door shut, Alex spun to Kaylee and kissed her deeply, as if needing her soul. Kaylee returned the fiery kiss with her own weary yet yearning desire.

The passionate kiss quickly turned into a heated battle of tongues, their hands roaming over each other. Alex pressed Kaylee to the wall, giving her hands free access to her prey. The stoic, calm, and collected businesswoman was now out of the public eye and consumed in her passion. Fresh air played across Kaylee's chest as Alex fervently ripped her blouse open. Alex broke the kiss and explored Kaylee's neck and bare bosom with her mouth.

An angry buzz sounded from Kaylee's purse. It was promptly ignored as Kaylee's bra was stripped from her. Alex turned her assault to the light pink peaks of Kaylee's breasts, suckling each in turn. The electricity elicited a moan from Kaylee. In her mind, the buzzing had stopped but was soon replaced by a cacophony of beeps from Alex's cell. A hand found its way to Kaylee's womanhood and had begun teasing it heavily through her cotton panties.

A shrill twang from the room's phone broke the passion. Kaylee panted, still pressed against the wall. The electricity still ravaged her body as Alex moved swiftly across the room, agitated that they had been interrupted yet again.

"Hello?" Alex answered sharply. Kaylee watched, the agony of being interrupted burning inside of her. "Oh, uh, yeah." Alex glanced at Kaylee. "She, um, came to my room to help put together the closing for Thursday." Kaylee suddenly knew she was wanted, but not in the way Alex so fervently desired her. "That really isn't necessary. Uh, okay." Alex had never seemed so out of control and rattled when talking business. Kaylee smiled, knowing it was her who had caused her lover to lose control. "See you in a minute then."

The last words ripped through Kaylee, who quickly returned to reality, realizing her breasts were in the open air and her skirt was hiked around her hips. Frantically they tore around the room, making it seem as if they were working on business. Moments later, with makeup smudged and a faint hint of lovemaking still lingering in the air, Alex opened the door, as if it was completely normal to be holding inter-company business meetings in one's hotel room.

After another hour of work, Kaylee, Alex, and Rose sat exhausted, covering topics that were only meant to be a diversion. Alex said she needed to get ready for bed, and saw both of them out. Kaylee adjourned herself to her room, frustrated and yearning with desire. On the other hand, she was exhausted from the busy day and knew she had another coming up. Sleep came quickly, as Kaylee hugged the pillow and pictured herself in Alex's arms.

***

The following morning passed in a blur of meetings and presentations. By lunchtime, the crew of five were starving and showing signs of wear. They found a small Italian restaurant and gathered around the largest table. Alex sat down, Kaylee next to her, and the other three filtered to their own seats. It was the same process they always followed.

"Do you two always sit together?" Maggie asked with a bit of a chuckle. It was meant as a light joke, but Kaylee almost lost herself in a blush. Nobody seemed to notice as they were getting settled.

"Actually, Kaylee has been working with me over the last few months in a mentorship program," Alex answered crisply, deftly killing any humor or rumors that may have flown south about the two working so closely together. Under the table, Kaylee briefly squeezed Alex's knee in appreciation. The subject quickly returned to the trip at hand. After the meal, the group got back to meetings and outlining the up-and-coming fall line.

After an exhausting day, Alex suggested that the five of them relax and take it easy before dinner. The group dispersed, allowing Alex and Kaylee some much-needed alone time. Alex suggested a swim before dinner, since they were not able to get their normal workout in. Soon the two women found themselves splashing around the indoor pool that seemed abandoned in the middle of the day.

After a few laps, Alex pinned Kaylee in the corner, whispering sweet nothings into her ear. The risk of being seen appeared to bring out a sadistic side of Alex that Kaylee had not yet seen, and she somewhat enjoyed the torment. Kaylee could do nothing as Alex teased and found certain buttons to push while nobody was around. The fires from the night before seemed to be blazing now, making Kaylee rampant with desire.

The duo headed for the hot tub to continue their teasing. The mask of bubbles showed two women relaxing after a hard day. Under the surface, Alex's fingers roamed over Kaylee's torso and hips. Disregarding any caution only drove Alex further. The final straw came when Alex inched her fingers between Kaylee's thighs, pushing them apart. She busied herself with running a slow finger up and down Kaylee's bathing suit, the thin layer of cloth doing little to conceal Kaylee's excitement.

Alex's bold moves had Kaylee panting to keep control in the hot tub. The gentle sliding of Alex's fingers against her sex was leaving her breathless and burning with desire. Alex watched intently as her lover's eyes rolled back with pleasure. Suddenly, a finger slipped under the bathing suit and far into Kaylee. The deep moan that escaped her lips drowned in the frothing bubbles. Alex applied more pressure, drawing Kaylee to tilt her hips towards the surface and almost lose control.

The public setting made Kaylee extremely conscious of the outside world, but she could do little about it as Alex dragged her towards the edge. As quickly as it started, the fingers escaped her gripping tunnel and Alex moved away. Kaylee, already close, groaned in frustration, opening her eyes. Joseph had just walked through the door and was heading to the pool. He casually waved at them as he put his stuff down.

"You. Me. Shower. Now." Alex snapped the order, causing Kaylee to jump in anticipation. The two waved goodbye, excusing themselves to get ready for dinner. Kaylee's body was gasping with desire, weak as jelly with her head dazed and spinning.

As soon as the elevator closed, Alex pulled Kaylee into an embrace, kissing her until a cheery *ding* signaled that the door was about to open. Once inside the hotel room, both stripped from their bathing suits and attacked each other. The phone blared once more. "Get in the shower, I'll be right there." Alex gave a slight spank to Kaylee's bare rump, eliciting a small squeal.

"Hello?" Alex answered the phone as Kaylee turned on the hot water. Steam started filling the bathroom and Kaylee prepared to climb in. Just as she made her move, Kaylee felt the softness of Alex's firm arms wrap around her from behind. "I'm not sure we are ever destined to be alone," she whispered. "Apparently it's time for dinner. Dry off and let's go do our nightly meeting."

Kaylee groaned, her fire still burning from Alex's teasing. Frustrated, she got dressed quickly and headed to the lobby ahead of Alex. Neither wanted to raise any more unwanted questions. By the time both made it downstairs, everyone was waiting. The venue for the evening was an amazing sushi bar that offered a beautiful selection of tantalizing food. *Perfect for date night*, thought Kaylee. The group shared a wonderful meal, but Alex and Kaylee were completely distracted by each other.

The fire between Kaylee's legs refused to be squelched this time. Once back at the hotel, they made a beeline for the elevator. Rose and Maggie were just coming in as the two disappeared into the closing shaft.

"Those two are truly dedicated to our cause it seems." The nonchalant comment from Maggie caused Rose to reflect briefly. She knew the two worked hard, but something was amiss. Deciding to let it rest, the group dispersed into the night.

As everyone made it to their respective rooms, Kaylee was being pushed forcefully onto Alex's bed.

CHAPTER 3

Alex bolted the door, took the phone from the hook, and almost literally tore Kaylee's blouse off. Soon both were completely nude, pressed together in burning need, kissing and exploring each other's silky bodies with abandon. Alex took charge as usual, pressing her thigh between Kaylee's knees while continuing to kiss her. Desire ripped through both of them, bringing out a rougher, power-hungry side of Alex that Kaylee had only briefly experienced before.

Kaylee gasped between kisses and nips on her neck. Alex positioned herself over one of Kaylee's thighs and grinded her sex down against Kaylee. Alex's long black hair cascaded over both of them, blocking out the world. She smiled at Kaylee, and Kaylee lovingly looked into her eyes as two fingers slid deep into her juices. As Kaylee's mouth opened in a moan, Alex swept in for a kiss, her tongue pressing in almost as deeply as her fingers.

Alex deftly worked her art into a rhythm, the heat and passion and frustration burning venomously to a boil. She broke the kiss and moved her attention to Kaylee's collarbone. The succulent nub of bone was an easy target; it wouldn't show the world evidence of their passion. Kaylee felt Alex's teeth nip into her flesh. The sensations quickly started to overwhelm her. She could only lie there and take whatever Alex gave. A low moan escaped her lips as the gentle nip grew into a savage love bite.

The attack continued, Alex driving in a third finger while sucking a hardened nipple into her mouth and pressing Kaylee's throat against the pillow. Writhing and gasping for air, Kaylee felt the earth tumble away as a new wave of electricity ripped through her body. The world exploded in orgasm and Kaylee was tossed into the froth of her passion. Without waiting for Kaylee to come down from her high, Alex switched positions, straddling Kaylee's chest in a sixty-nine.

As Kaylee came down from the first earthquake, she felt the swirl of Alex's tongue reigniting the fire within her and a warm, sweet wetness press against her mouth. *Fair play*, she thought, grabbing at Alex's ass and pulling hard to taste her lover. The two women lapped at each other competitively, each striving to bring the other to the edge first. Both had learned what got them going and the competition was fierce. Kaylee pushed two fingers into Alex, caressing her inside while sweeping her tongue across the studded nub.

Alex moaned, pressing her mouth further into Kaylee and swirling her tongue as deep as she could. Back and forth the two women fought to break the other first. As Alex grew closer, she started to grind herself against Kaylee, using her for her own pleasure. The intensity picked up as each grew closer to the edge. Alex sucked the bud of Kaylee's pleasure into her mouth and applied rhythmic pressure.

The combined sensations rocketed Kaylee back over the edge, driving Alex into wild fits of grinding.

Alex followed soon after, arching her back and flooding Kaylee's mouth with nectar. Panting deeply, Alex repositioned herself, cradling Kaylee. They basked in each other's arms, engulfed in the afterglow of love and lust. Snuggled together, a sweaty, sticky mess, Alex chuckled suddenly.

"We've been trying to do this since the moment we stepped off the plane." The frustration of being without kids but no alone time started to melt away as they shared each other. Alex leaned down and kissed Kaylee, the inferno now reduced to a minor forest fire. The need was still there, but it was no longer as forceful. "You know, we still have chlorine in our hair. That isn't healthy for growing locks."

"Oh, you are so right." Kaylee played coy. "What *ever* should we do about that?" Alex's response was to pull her up and toward the bathroom door. Soon, the shower was running and steam filled the small room. As soon as the curtain closed, Alex turned to Kaylee, pressing her body against the wall while she kissed and nipped at her neck and collar. This time, Alex was gentler, careful not to leave visible marks.

Kaylee panted and writhed, the cool tile wall melding with the heat of the water and the passion between them. Alex tugged at Kaylee's leg, pushing it apart just enough to give access to Kaylee's hub of desire. Kaylee did her best to brace herself on the slippery enamel while Alex slid inside her. The steamy water and Alex focusing on her neck made her knees buckle through the pleasure. Alex refused to let her go, holding her weight with her left arm and pushing Kaylee to yet another shattering orgasm with her right.

Moans echoed around the shower walls as Kaylee rode Alex's fingers into bliss. As the tide receded, she became aware of the water flowing over them. Her eyes fluttered open to see Alex flushed and smiling at her. Alex's wet black hair perfectly framed her face, which now nestled affectionately into Kaylee's breasts. A sudden wave of emotion made Kaylee smile. She knew then that she wanted to spend the rest of her days with the lovely naughtiness of Alexis Raina Carlisle.

After rinsing each other down, they turned the shower off and wrapped up in soft towels. They walked to the bed, pulled down the sheets and snuggled in. The passion they shared made the entire room glow as they lay in each other's arms, legs intertwined. Weightless. Kaylee laid her head on Alex's breast and both of them fell asleep almost instantly.

***

The chime of an intruding alarm clock echoed through the room all too quickly. Alex swiftly reached over and hit the snooze. She moved her arm to gently stroke Kaylee's back. A soft purr was the only response.

"Time to rise and shine, beautiful," Alex gently cooed in Kaylee's ear. Kaylee fought against waking up and continued her deep breathing. Alex rubbed her back a little more insistently.

A mostly-asleep answer came back for her efforts: "Mmm, I love you..." The words made Alex falter. She'd never heard anyone say those words to her, and she wasn't quite sure how she felt about it. Kaylee, on the other hand, didn't seem to realize she'd said anything at all. That would at least give Alex a chance to digest the concept.

"Come on, you," Alex said, a bit more firmly this time. "Before we're late to the meeting."

The snooze alarm blared to life, causing Kaylee to stir at last. After a passionate good morning kiss,

Kaylee snuck back to her room to get ready for the day. She was still glowing from the evening before, unaware of the effect her morning muttering had had on Alex.

CHAPTER 4

With the evening still fresh in her mind, Kaylee felt renewed as the team set forth to tackle the contract presentations. The looks she and Alex shared in the team's temporary office were playful and reminiscent of the night before, fueled further by the thrill of knowing none of the others were aware. The day progressed with presentation after presentation and became so busy that they had lunch delivered in order to save them precious time.

"At the rate we are going, I think we should finish everything up around three. What do you guys think about heading down to Hollywood?" Rose asked through bites of her sandwich.

Everyone looked around at each other. Trips like this were not frequent, and this was the first time Kaylee had been to the west coast.

"I, for one, would love to go see Santa Monica Boulevard," Kaylee answered, the first to speak up. The rest quickly chimed in agreement. Everyone's morale seemed to lift with the suggestion.

"I was hoping you'd all be in. I have made reservations for us at Patrick's Steakhouse. According to Trip Advisor, it's supposed to be really good. I was thinking it could be a bit of a victory dinner. Everyone okay with that?" Rose asked. "Maybe we'll even see a celebrity."

Everyone chuckled and the room buzzed with excitement. The boosted attitude made the rest of the afternoon pass quickly. At the end of the day, they felt that their presentations had been a success. It left only Thursday morning, which was simply a wrap-up meeting, to finish their pitch. *Enough with work*, they all thought.

At the hotel, they all took a few moments to get ready for dinner. Kaylee put on the dress she had brought for the formal night, assuming Hollywood would be a bit formal.

The simple but elegant cobalt-blue dress flowed around her legs as she stepped off the elevator, and the sapphire necklace and earrings matched it perfectly. This was one of the trial ensembles she had designed. The effects of the dress rippled through the hotel lobby, as almost everyone paused to look at her. Suddenly, Kaylee felt like she was showing too much skin at the v-line. Alex, who had her back to her, turned when she saw Rose staring.

"Wow! You look stunning." The words dripped from Alex's jaw-dropped tongue without thought. Rose caught the comment but didn't say anything. Kaylee blushed at the compliment. Soon, everyone was complimenting her, even though *everyone* looked like a million bucks. Alex wore a simple black pencil dress that accentuated her impeccable body. Together, they looked amazing.

The group took two cabs over to Hollywood. Rose and Alex took one, leaving the other three to take their own. It was pleasant company and conversation about fashion all the way to the Boulevard. On arrival, the group took to the streets, casually sightseeing along the Walk of Fame. Cameras flashed, memories were made, and the morale of the group was sky high. Rose kept commending everyone on their performance.

Maggie and Joe found a souvenir store and went in to shop. Rose followed soon after, leaving Alex and Kaylee on the street. Alex put her hand on the small of Kaylee's back, walking with her down the line of stars.

"You're so beautiful you know. I love your dress. I can hardly take my eyes off you." Alex's eyes roamed all over the temptation before her. She was having difficulty restraining her urge to ravage Kaylee in the street. "I wish I could walk arm in arm with you and let everyone know that you're mine."

The words made Kaylee's heart melt, yearning for that very thing. She hoped the next night would be as enchanting. Without warning, Alex quickly leaned in and kissed Kaylee, nothing deep or overly romantic but a kiss in broad daylight nonetheless. It made her feel like the luckiest girl on the planet.

Until the next moment, that is, when Rose showed up.

The two moved quickly away from each other, trying not to be too obvious. If Rose noticed anything, she didn't let on. Soon the group was back together and heading toward their tasty reservation.

The restaurant was a delight of aromas, sights, and music. They were greeted with exuberance and shown to their table almost immediately. Alex made sure to grab her normal spot next to Kaylee and, though they were only together in secret, they looked like the perfect couple.

Rose ordered some wine and appetizers for the table. The waiter was prompt to return with the items and poured a glass for everyone. Dinner was ordered and they discussed the week's events. After the appetizer was cleared away, Rose caught everyone's attention.

"I know that we've had a very busy week. I think we've had a huge success because of the hard work and dedication from our team. You guys have really rocked this." Everyone smiled at the recognition. "I know that we're not technically supposed to be discussing this, but I simply can't hold back my excitement anymore."

The table grew quiet with anticipation. Kaylee watched as Rose turned and pulled something from her purse. She gathered herself and addressed the table one more time.

"First off, I want you all to know, that unofficially officially, we have won this contract." A small round of applause sounded from the table. "Second off, I regret to inform you that Kaylee will no longer be my assistant." The air of the table took a sudden turn. Rose held out a small box to Kaylee.

"Kaylee, we are extending our offer to you to be a full-time designer. You will start as a junior designer and eventually have your own design team. You'll start off with the new client as your designation. Your work over the last six months has been phenomenal, and part of me hates that I'm losing such a wonderful assistant. However, we need your talent on the floor. Do you accept?"

Kaylee had busied herself with opening the box while Rose spoke. Inside, there was a small lapel pin in the shape of a lotus.

"*Yes!*" Kaylee finally squeaked out, not really sure how to respond. "I'm flattered! Thank you so much." As she accepted the offer, everyone at the table congratulated her and clapped. It was not officially on the books yet, however it was all but finalized.

The rest of the meal was alight with delicious food, superb wines, and succulent desserts. Before it was over, everyone was stuffed to the point of misery and a little tipsy. As they left the establishment, they complimented Rose on her choice of designer and congratulated Kaylee on her achievement. Rose and Alex pulled up the rear.

"Kaylee, would you stay behind with Alexis and me?" Rose asked.

Taking their cue, Maggie and Joe hailed a cab and headed back for the hotel. As soon as they were gone, Alex turned to Rose.

"Rose, is there something on your mind?" Alex asked. Rose took a step back from the two of them. She hesitated for a moment, contemplating how she wanted to phrase this.

"I want to let you guys know, er, well. I know that you two are dating." The news shocked both Alex and Kaylee. Kaylee blushed, but Alex kept her cool demeanor. "I know it's against company policy, but you two are, well, cute together. Kaylee, you're no longer my employee, in the technical sense of the term. You have your own team now and you're not directly under me."

Alex softened a bit. Rose knew, but had no intention of getting them in trouble. Kaylee let out a sigh of relief, both mystified to be promoted and excited that Rose was okay with this.

"Rose," Alex said, "thank you for your blessing. You know that I greatly respect you and love my job, but I also want you to know, if it ever came to it, I would leave the company to be with Kaylee."

The words did not pose an idle threat; Alex meant every word. The sentiment made Kaylee blush even more fiercely. To drive the point home, Alex wrapped a protective arm around Kaylee's shoulder.

"I'm sure there will be no need for that, Alexis, and certainly no hostility from me. I cannot say everyone will be enthusiastic about it, but you two are golden in my book. In fact, I only confirmed my suspicions this evening when I saw you kiss. Sorry to intrude." Rose blushed a bit, having mistakenly spied on their intimacy.

"That was her fault," Kaylee grinned, pointing at Alex. "She simply couldn't contain herself to that tough business exterior." The jibe made Alex smile, who leaned in for a quick peck of affection and a playful squeeze.

"It's true. I guess I go so far to maintain my exterior that it's a relief to be able to be myself around someone," Alex confessed, hugging Kaylee tighter.

"Aww, you two are adorable. I know that you have had to keep things hidden this whole week, and probably every day in the office. Would you like me to take a picture of you both on the Walk of Fame?" The offer was heartfelt, and soon Rose was taking several pictures of Kaylee and Alex, each pose and photo a testament to their relationship.

As the evening wound down, the three took a return cab. The conversation turned towards the future and some of the expectations for Kaylee and the up-and-coming contract. As they approached the hotel, Rose turned to them one last time.

"Alexis, I have worked with you for five years. I have tremendous respect for you, and I'm happy to see how content you are with Kaylee. And Kaylee, even though we've only worked together for six months, I am truly happy for the both of you." They all hugged before heading off to their rooms.

***

This time, Alex accompanied Kaylee to her room. A message awaited Kaylee to call home. Kaylee found herself on a Skype call with her mother while Alex waited in the background.

"Mommy!" Ryan crackled over the computer. "I miss you so much! What are you going to bring home for me?" Short and to the point, Ryan got out everything he needed to say. Kaylee was waiting to go souvenir shopping until the end of the trip.

"I can't tell you, or it wouldn't be a surprise," she told him, a broad smile on her face.

After a few minutes with Ryan, Kaylee's mother appeared. She whisked Ryan off to bed, returning a few minutes later to the computer screen.

"He's missed you this week. I guess this is probably the longest you've been away from him. He's doing well, enjoying school, eating right. We've had fun. How's your trip going?" They bounced back and forth, talking about things for a few moments. As the conversation wound down, her mother turned a serious tone.

"Kaylee Anne, I probably should wait until you are home for this, but it's been on my mind all week. Ryan mentioned the woman Alexis, from Christmas, hangs out with you guys all the time. He says she is your girlfriend. You and I have talked about this kind of lifestyle in the past. I do *not* want my grandson exposed to such indecency. When you get home, we're going to have a long talk about this. For now, it's bedtime, and I still love you. Goodnight."

The final sentence was rushed and the screen flicked to black.

Kaylee sat in silence for a few moments, shocked at the tongue-lashing she had just received. It was not the words that hurt – she was used to her mother's viewpoint being shoved down her throat. The upsetting part was the cold, uncaring, brutal suddenness. She knew her mother would not approve, but this was uncalled for. A tear spilled out and trickled down her cheek. Why couldn't her mother just be happy that *she* was happy?

As she blinked away the tears, Alex wrapped her arms protectively around her. The small act sent the floodgates tumbling open and Kaylee turned into Alex, tears streaming down her face. The day had been extremely eventful, and despite the overall amazing outcomes, the sting felt too close to home and too sudden. Alex guided Kaylee to the bed, lowered them both down and held her close. After a while, the tears stopped, and the two slept nestled together.

CHAPTER 5

The next day dawned with a bustle. The team prepared for the final push, feeling confident their efforts were paying off. The half-day of discussions flew by. Everyone broke for lunch in preparation to leave. Overall, the client was more than pleased, the contract had been won, and Kaylee had her promotion. The only thing left was the trip home. Maggie, Joseph, and Rose left for the airport, oblivious to what was going on between Kaylee and Alex.

Alone together, with no kids or busybody coworkers, Alex swept Kaylee into a deep kiss that left her breathless and blushing in the openness of the hotel lobby. The two left to get a spa treatment, including manicures and pedicures. As they went about the routine, they had a chance to talk.

"Kaylee, you have been amazing. I've never felt this way about anyone before," Alex said into the empty sauna. Kaylee could tell it was all pure. No hard-ass businesswoman, no public façade; just Alex. The words made Kaylee blush with happiness.

"I feel the same way." Kaylee felt relieved to start sharing her true feelings. The steam softly hissed around them.

"I know you do. You said it in your sleep the other night," Alex said, looking at her, searching for signals. Kaylee didn't have a response, not knowing how she had already given herself away. "It gave me time to reflect on my feelings," Alex went on. "I'm sure you know already, but I have a problem expressing emotions like this. You're the first person to bring out this tender side of me." Alex chuckled a bit, smiling with slight embarrassment, and kissed Kaylee shyly. "I'd really like to be a proper part of your life, not just the girlfriend with the separate apartment who comes round at weekends. I want us to embark on an adventure together." Alex's words echoed into the heat of the sauna.

"I want that, too," Kaylee told her. "I've never felt this way, but I know I'm ready for the next step with you."

"Before we make that decision, I want you to know something about me. I enjoy everything that we have together, but there's a side of me that I've never really shown you." Alex paused a moment, letting everything sink in. "I have another side, a dominant side. I sometimes like to be a little rougher and controlling than most. There is a lot more to it, but that's the gist."

The air in the room seemed to get thicker as Kaylee turned the words over in her mind. She was unsure exactly what Alex meant, but, as she reflected on the past months, her mind told her that it would all work out.

"Well, I don't have any experience in that sort of thing. I've never so much as read *Fifty Shades*," she giggled. "But I love everything we already have, and I'm willing to try anything at least once with you, Alex. I guess I, erm, submit?" Kaylee chuckled at the last line. Feeling giddy, and finding herself tumbling backwards into Alex's lap, her upturned mouth was quickly met with warm lips kissing her hard and deep. The kiss left Kaylee breathless.

After the sauna, the day continued in a heavenly blur. The manicures, pedicures, and pure indulgence in each other left them both feeling amazing. After the spa, they went to dinner in an upscale seafood restaurant. Kaylee was often spoiled by Alex, and she knew Alex did well in her profession, but the grand scale of the day blew everything else out of the water. The wine and fresh scallops were to die for, and the lobster was almost as succulent as Alex herself. Nothing had ever come close to it.

After a wonderful meal, Alex took Kaylee to a see a musical. They sat hand in hand, watching the characters sing and dance on stage. The entire evening was enchanting. After the show, they stopped for gelato while walking down one of the busy streets. Even with so many people, Kaylee felt as though there was nobody else around but Alex. Throughout the evening, Alex brazenly kissed her, flaunting her like arm candy. Kaylee simply swooned from the attention.

Back at the hotel, Alex took charge while still in the elevator. She dipped Kaylee into a deep kiss that lasted the duration of the ride up. Dizzy and breathless, Alex pulled Kaylee into her room, double-locking the door shut. Alex gently pushed Kaylee to the bed by the small of her back. Once there, Alex swiftly spun her round into a kiss, then stepped back and sat on a chair, pulling Kaylee forward until she had straddled Alex's lap. They continued their heated session of kissing, Alex gliding her hands up and down Kaylee's dress.

Abruptly, Alex grabbed Kaylee's hair and twisted her off the chair and onto the bed, landing between her legs. Kaylee's dress bunched around her hips. Alex's kisses increased in intensity, leaving Kaylee out of breath. Using the handful of hair, she twisted Kaylee's neck to the side, exposing the tender flesh to kisses and nips. This time though, the gentleness went out the door; Kaylee could feel Alex branding her flesh with deep, possessive marks.

The ferocity added to the heat between Kaylee's legs, yearning for more. With her free hand, Alex groped her through the dress. Kaylee felt like a teen again. Driven by pure lust, she was lost to the erotic assault on her body. Alex slid down, kneeling at the bed between Kaylee's legs, stripping Kaylee's lace panties off and tossing them behind her. Kaylee's legs were still clad in stockings and high heels as

Alex hooked her arms around Kaylee's thighs and pulled her to the edge of the bed.

Alex strived to devour Kaylee's womanhood, lapping and sucking every inch of her. The intensity soon had her lover writhing and bucking against the bed. Alex alternated between driving her tongue as deep as she could and sucking the nub of Kaylee's clit. The intensity had Kaylee on the edge in minutes, but Alex seemed to know exactly when to stop to keep Kaylee just a touch away from the brink. Moans echoed through the hotel room.

Higher and higher, the waves of electricity drove Kaylee, and yet not enough to come crashing down. Soon, she was pleading and begging for release. Changing her pattern, Alex slid two fingers deep into Kaylee while her focus shifted to suckling. The movement brought Kaylee teetering to the edge until Alex completely stopped all activity. Kaylee let her held breath whine into a long, frustrated groan. She was so close. She opened her eyes to scold Alex, who was smiling deviously up at her with a raised eyebrow.

"You said you submitted, remember? You know that means you can only get off when I say you can? If you release without permission, you will be punished. Understand?" The words trickled into Kaylee, her heart and womanhood pulsing with desire.

"Yes, whatever you say. Please, just please keep going," Kaylee begged.

Alex only continued to smile, watching Kaylee's legs quiver with anticipation. Instead of returning to Kaylee's exposed sex, she turned to her bag. "You know, I think for tonight, you need to refer to me by a title. Let's keep it simple for now: Ms. Carlisle will do.

"Undress, my love," she commanded. Groaning in frustration, Kaylee quickly stripped her remaining clothes, laying back in the same pose in hopes of continuation. "I want you on all fours for now. Go ahead, lay your head down and get comfortable."

"Okay – I mean, yes, Ms. Carlisle." Kaylee quickly did as she was told. Closing her eyes, she felt cool air drift across her exposed backside. Alex returned, gliding a hand lightly over her flesh. Murmuring mews of approval, Alex slid a finger inside Kaylee, who purred with delight. Kaylee knew what was about to happen. Alex had packed her favorite double dildo, which was more than alright;

Kaylee had grown to love the toy, a strapless strap-on of sorts which regularly drove them both wild.

Meanwhile, Alex continued to slowly tease Kaylee, keeping her near the edge. Kaylee felt Alex shift between her legs, and then the bulbous head pushed into her. Kaylee gasped at the intrusion, filled inch by inch. Alex pushed until the toy disappeared completely, then placed her hands on Kaylee's hips. Kaylee groaned from being so full, and started to moan into the pillow as Alex rocked back and forth, holding the toy inside herself with vice-like grip. The tempo increased quickly. Alex pushed Kaylee's head into the pillow and Kaylee felt the urge of release building more swiftly than before.

"Please, may I release?" Kaylee breathlessly gasped against the pillow as Alex continued to lunge in and out of her. Alex thrust as deep as she could while leaning forward and grabbing Kaylee's hair with a gentle tug.

"May you please release? Are you at a tea party, my love? Is that what you want?"

Kaylee was stuck trying to process what she meant. She knew she had to ask permission; she thought she had just done so. The inferno inside her cried for release, but she wanted desperately to please Alex and do what she was told.

"Please Ma'am – Ms. Carlisle, I need to release," Kaylee pleaded.

Instead of answering, Alex increased her tempo and applied slight pressure to Kaylee's hair. The added adrenaline made holding on next to impossible. "Oh god, please, oh please. I need it. Alex, please!"

"What did you just say?" Alex teased.

"Eh, Ms. Carlisle, oh god, please... I need it, Ms. Carlisle. Ms. Alexis Carlisle." Kaylee was grasping at anything that might work.

"Need what?" Alex was searching for something dirtier; language with some grit.

"Release!" Kaylee begged.

"Not until you stop using that word." Alex's demand seemed distant as Kaylee struggled to hold back her orgasm.

"Please, please. I can't hold it." The response made Alex quicken, clenching hard whilst slamming the phallus in and out of Kaylee. "I need to cum... please, I want to get off... please let me cum." Kaylee was at breaking point. "Please, Alex, fuck me. Fuck me Ms. Carlisle." The edges of reality seemed to blur as Kaylee screamed the words.

"Yes, you may get off, good girl." With the final utterance, Alex groaned, gripped Kaylee's hips and sank home. The other side of the toy had been driving her crazy. She had barely managed to keep grip of its soaking end while she thrust. As Kaylee crashed through wave after wave of orgasm, Alex was awash in her own bliss. The two rode each other to ecstasy, eventually collapsing into a sticky heap. The toy broke their union as the large bulb popped from Alex's soaking wetness. Catching her breath, Kaylee smiled as she came down from her orgasm, her legs still quivering.

A wave of pure desire and need took over Kaylee. She slid herself over Alex' heaving body, straddling her hips. The extended phallus still protruded from Kaylee's body. Slowly, she slipped the bulbous gem back inside Alex. Deliberately and focused, she began grinding; skin on skin as their bodies met flush.

Time swept away as Kaylee peered into Alex's eyes. She smiled down at her lover as they moved together as one, the afterglow of the roughness amplifying the intimate waves of pleasure. Kaylee continued riding on Alex at an easy tempo, sliding their coupled bodies against each other.

Alex slowly glided her hands up Kaylee's silky hips and waist, following with a penetrating gaze. She eventually played cautiously with Kaylee's firm breasts and nipples whilst breathing in every blink of her stare. Alex's body melted to goo, and she pulled Kaylee down into an embrace, kissing her deeply.

"I love you, Kaylee Daniels," Alex whispered, gazing deeply into Kaylee's eyes.

"I love you, too."

Together, they floated in bliss, enjoying the union between them, mind, body, and soul. After the gentle lovemaking, they nestled under the covers, laying with each other, gazing into each other's souls. The night drifted into slumber, limbs and hearts intertwined. No alarms blared the next morning; they were free to awaken naturally with sunlight gently streaming through the curtains.

They leisurely enjoyed breakfast and packed. This time, the trip through the airport was spent as a couple instead of business partners. They walked casually through the terminal, buying souvenirs for everyone, enjoying tea, and making each other laugh. Alex would steal kisses, hold her hand, and make faces at her. It felt wonderful to show themselves for what they were, even if it was only temporary.

CHAPTER 6

Boarding the plane and taking off was not as stressful this time. Alex continued to comfort Kaylee throughout the flight. They discussed the future and what adventures might come, and what the next big step might be. Faster than it should have been, they were touching down in Boston. The magical business trip came to a close as they disembarked the plane. Kaylee felt like her entire life had changed in the course of a week.

She felt contemplative as they walked through the airport. She had been promoted to a full designer, which came with a substantial raise and a new office. The love of her life had confessed she felt the same way about her. She'd made some fantastic memories. All in all, Kaylee felt like she was walking on cloud nine instead of just to baggage claim, hand in hand with Alex. She smiled and gave her one last kiss on the escalator.

"Mommy!" A voice carried across the cavernous space. The young boy tore across the carpet toward his mother. Kaylee bent down and scooped him into her arms, planting kisses and giving him hugs. "What did you get me?"

"Wait and see, little one," Kaylee said, chuckling, and carried him toward baggage claim. The conveyor belt clicked on and bags started dropping onto the rotation. Alex laughed with Ryan and handed him a small airplane as a gift. Kaylee's mother came up to the couple, Ryan still in their midst.

"Welcome home." Her mother's voice was as monotone as ever. "Everything went smoothly here. How was your trip?"

Kaylee turned to face her mom. "It went well, I got a promotion." Kaylee beamed at her mother. "You remember Alexis?"

Alex offered a hand, but Kaylee's mother made no move to take it.

"Great to see you again, ma'am," Alex offered, trying to be diplomatic. The undercurrent of tension seemed to come to a head until Kaylee's mom offered some muttered agreement.

"Mommy, what happened to your neck?" Ryan jerked her scarf out, exposing the trail of love bites from the previous night. Kaylee squirmed, mortified about the public exposure. While she stumbled for answers, Alex just chuckled. Her mother stormed off, not having anything to do with it.

"Nothing, sweetheart. I'm all right." Kaylee let Ryan down, starting to follow her mother. Before she could give chase, Alex gently caught her arm and shook her head.

"Let her go, Kay. She'll come to terms with it sooner or later. Today is not that day, and that's okay. No matter what, we've got each other, and we'll face whatever comes as a team."

Kaylee had been prepared for her mother's negativity this time, and Alex's words added comfort to the situation. Alex gently brought Kaylee into a warm embrace, Ryan joining in. Alex kissed Kaylee once more.

"Mommy, yuck, don't kiss."

Both of them looked down, then to each other and started laughing. They grabbed their bags and started heading for the parking lot. Her mother sent Kaylee a message that she was heading home. Alex loaded the bags into the car and fired up the engine. Soon they were streaking along the highway towards home. Once there, Kaylee handed Ryan a little snowglobe with the Hollywood sign inside.

"This is amazing! Can I have more?" Ryan continually shook the globe to see the glitter bounce.

"I guess we'll just have to wait for the next business trip," Kaylee smirked. She was glad to be home after such a busy week. As busy as it was, she could not have been happier.

E05: EXPLORING

CHAPTER 1

The small coffee pot percolated, wafting fresh brew through the office kitchen. Kaylee rarely drank coffee – she preferred tea – but this morning she needed the pick-me-up. Work had been particularly exhausting. Who said a promotion made life easier? The pay raise was nice, but the increased workload had only become more of a burden. It had been a long week, and the next would be even longer.

The good news was that Blaire from HR had mentioned some promising leads in the hunt to find her an assistant. The thought made Kaylee reminisce about nine months prior, when she herself had first walked through the doors as an assistant. Since then, she had really put in a lot of effort, and it had paid off.

This week had been dragging, though. Thank goodness Friday was finally upon them. Between the stress of the job, the looming Wednesday deadline, and her cycle, Kaylee felt ready to take a personal day.

A gentle touch on her shoulder brought her from her reverie. She turned to face Alex and, recognizing her love, she smiled. Kaylee wanted to hide in her arms, but with company policy as it were, it made any affection difficult. Much to her surprise, Alex did briefly hug her, letting her know it would be okay. Alex didn't normally drop her career mask at the office, so the surprise made Kaylee feel gooey inside.

"What's wrong, Kay?" The emotion was there but muted behind the corporate mask. Kaylee could see it in her eyes: Alex was genuinely concerned for her.

Kaylee put on a smile. "I'm okay, just a little stressed. I have a lot on my plate before Wednesday comes. Not to mention the period from hell."

Kaylee sighed and started making her coffee. Since Alex was there, she made a cup for her, too.

The two cups looked the same, but Kaylee put a ton of cream and sugar into hers.

"You know, it really isn't coffee when you make it like that. Have a little coffee with your sugar," Alex teased as she picked up the warm mug Kaylee had made for her. "I'll tell you what – Tomorrow, we'll have a date day of pampering. My treat. How's that sound?"

"Sounds romantic. Can we start now?" Kaylee asked, tilting her head and raising an eyebrow flirtatiously. They both chuckled as they started heading back to their respective offices. "Wanna meet me after yoga tomorrow?"

Alex confirmed as they parted directions. The warmth of happiness replaced the pains in Kaylee's abdomen. She felt lucky to have her support system just down the hall whenever she needed a boost.

Back in her office, a flurry of emails from her small design team brought Kaylee swiftly back to reality. The half-drank cup of coffee swirled and cooled as she crammed in as much work as she could before lunch. By the time afternoon rolled around, she felt much better.

Friday came and went, and Saturday brought with it a glorious weekend. Ryan exuberantly jumped into the car as Kaylee locked the apartment door. They were heading to their local gym, which was small but a perfect fit for them. Ryan enjoyed playing in the kids' care center while Kaylee got in her workout. It was also reasonably priced and offered a broad selection of classes. Kaylee arrived about ten minutes before the morning yoga session and noticed a new woman had joined the class.

"Good morning. How are you?" The woman was friendly and flashed an infectious smile.

"Good, yourself?" Kaylee began to stretch out nearby. "Is this your first time at this class?"

"Yeah, I just joined the gym. They seem to have great childcare." The woman sat to continue her stretches, the mat flowing beneath her. "I'm Lydia, by the way. Nice to meet you."

"Kaylee, and likewise. That's the reason I joined, too. I have a five-year-old son and he just loves it here."

The two women finished their stretching as the instructor came in. They spent the class chitchatting about various aspects of their lives. Lydia was a stay-at-home mom who painted and crafted on the side for a few extra dollars. Kaylee gathered she had two children and a husband.

Lydia seemed fit and active. She was definitely curvy and had a womanly hourglass figure. Her kinked auburn hair set off her hazel eyes wonderfully.

Kaylee admired her flawless skin and its rich, tanned tone. She blushed, suddenly realizing she was checking out another woman.

After class, they talked all the way back to the locker room. Usually, Kaylee took her clothes and changed in one of the dressing room stalls. But Lydia was clearly not shy; she started yanking her top and sports bra off right in the middle of the locker room. It was mostly empty and so, not wanting to look like a prude, Kaylee started to do the same. Before Kaylee could get her top off, Lydia's supple bosom sprang free of the restricting sports bra. The large D cup breasts bounced, and Kaylee tried not to stare. *Her nipples are pierced!* The thought echoed through Kaylee's head.

Quickly regaining her composure, she finished dressing herself and shortly the two of them were heading towards the childcare area, talking about their kids. When they arrived, most of the children were gone. Ryan and Lydia's son, Toby, seemed to be getting along nicely together. They both laughed as the boys streaked toward them, ready for home.

Alex was waiting at Kaylee's apartment, basking in the gorgeous spring day against the sun-soaked wall. Ryan launched himself from the car, running towards Alex with glee. Kaylee had called the babysitter and expected her any minute. After she got everything out of the car, the three of them went inside.

"What did you bring me, Alex?" The tyke definitely let Alex know what was expected. Alex gently ruffled his hair.

"Do you think I'm going to get you something *every* time I come over here, kiddo?" Alex's words seemed to dampen the boy for a minute. Looking dejected, they walked into the living room together. Alex stealthily put a new Lego pack on the table when Ryan wasn't looking. "What's this here? Who else is bringing you new toys?"

Ryan bounded back into the room, laughing at the trick Alex had played. He quickly took the toy, hugged Alex as a "Thank you" and ran off to his room. Laughing, Kaylee made tea for the two of them while they waited on the sitter.

"I swear, you're going to spoil him if you keep getting him a new toy each week," Kaylee remarked, only half-serious. She placed the cups on the table and sat down.

"Yeah, well, maybe I enjoy spoiling him. I like spoiling him just about as much as I like spoiling his mother."

Kaylee blushed at the thought - Alex truly did spoil her. The doorbell rang, indicating the sitter had arrived.

"Speaking of which," Alex said with a grin, "it's time to spoil her now."

CHAPTER 2

After giving a few instructions to the babysitter, the two of them sailed through the city in Alex's Mazda 6. Kaylee had learned not to ask what their plans were and let Alex take her wherever Alex wanted to go. The conversation took an interesting turn as they got on the highway.

"I've been thinking, Kay, wouldn't it be easier on both of us, and give us more time together, if we were to move in together?" Alex's question seemed to hang in the air for a moment. Kaylee's mind exploded with both joy and anxiety.

"I would love that, Alex, but there are a lot of factors to consider. Our lifestyles are radically different." The potential troubles ran rampant through her mind. Alex did not have children, and for the most part, she only saw the fun and happy times. Kaylee had done a good job shielding her from as much as possible during their time together, for fear of scaring Alex off.

"You're absolutely right. But I think we'll have to live together eventually if we want to make this a long-term thing."

Kaylee pondered Alex's point carefully. The car glided off the highway and onto a main street. It always amused her how matter-of-fact Alex could be, especially around subjects like this.

"What about living with Ryan? I know he adores you, but you've never had to deal with a sick kid before. Are you ready for that?" Kaylee's question seemed to counter the response for the time being. Before Alex could formulate an answer, they had arrived at a chic, expensive-looking spa. "Alex, this will cost a small fortune. You don't have to..."

The look Alex gave Kaylee made her stop. She was not to question how or how much Alex spent on her. Kaylee got out of the car as instructed and followed Alex inside. Cool marble and granite accents covered the posh interior design. The receptionist greeted the two of them warmly. They were both escorted to a changing room before finding themselves next to each other in a couples' massage area.

"I love the little guy. He's fun. Why wouldn't I be up to playing second mommy?" Alex finally replied to Kaylee's question, but the answer seemed almost evasive. Two masseuses came into the room and got busy, ignoring their conversation.

"Alex, I think you would be a great mother. I see how caring you are and how much you love the both of us. I just don't think you fully realize how much of a shift living with a five-year-old will be."

"I know it will be a big change, but I want to be with you. I want to make this work. I'm ready to take that next step and see where it goes." Alex's words made Kaylee's heart swell. It was clear that Alex really did want this, and Kaylee wanted it more than anything too. But beyond Kaylee's happiness, there was fear.

"How would we make the living arrangements work?" Kaylee's new question posed a different set of thoughts.

"Well, you two would move in with me, of course," Alex said with confidence. "I have three bedrooms and more than enough room for all of us." The masseuse started to work on Alex's back, eliciting a soft sigh.

"What are the school systems like over there? How about transportation? Doctors?" Kaylee fired off a few questions, making Alex stumble. The masseuse working on Kaylee quickly eased out the aches that had been running through her body all week.

"Uh, I, well. I don't know, really." Alex fumbled to find an answer. Kaylee knew those were the things Alex had not really thought about. And why would she? Alex was not a parent. "I've never had to consider that kind of stuff. I'm sorry."

"No need to apologize. These are just some of the factors that play into deciding where to live. If we did move to your place, it would be in the summer at the earliest. I can't pull Ryan out of school so close to the end of the year."

Conversation dwindled while they went through the rest of the spa treatments, laughing and talking when they could. As they changed back into their clothes, Kaylee felt more relaxed than she had in years. So far, the day was off to a wonderful start, and now it was time for lunch. A small bistro nearby did the trick nicely.

CHAPTER 3

They sat down together at a small table, idly chitchatting about the past week. Their order was taken, and the delectable aromas from the kitchen only amplified their hunger. While waiting, Kaylee brought up her yoga class.

"I think Ryan made a new friend this morning at the gym. His mom was in my yoga class; she seems like a nice woman. Perhaps I'll invite them out on a playdate next weekend. Would you like to go?" Kaylee took a sip of her drink.

"Maybe. We'll have to see how my schedule goes. How are you liking the yoga thing?" Alex kept fit through running mostly and had never tried yoga, despite Kaylee's insistence that she would love it.

"You should come with me next week and see for yourself." Alex smiled, but shook her head. "I did notice something about Lydia in the changing room that caught my interest." Kaylee's voice had dropped to almost a whisper. "She had her nipples pierced. I always meant to ask you about your clit. I'm curious about it."

"Curious, are you? Curious about what?" A mischievous smile overtook Alex's expression. "Curious as to how it feels when you run your tongue across it?"

The words casually dropped from Alex's mouth like she was having a conversation with her coworkers. Kaylee immediately blossomed red, trying to hide her face. Alex's smile confirmed that that was exactly what she was after.

"Alex! We're in public," Kaylee said under her breath. The reaction only brought a cheeky smirk from Alex though.

"I'm just teasing, my love. I really like it. I have had it for about eight years or so now. I got it when I was in London. It definitely creates a nice stirring, especially when I rub my thighs together." The last line caused Kaylee to turn crimson, not expecting such a graphic description. "What did you want to know about it?"

"Uh..." Kaylee visibly faltered, not sure if she should continue this pursuit, or wait until they were a safe distance from other people. "Well, uh, I guess my first question is, did it hurt?"

"There was a little pain, I suppose, but it was mainly anticipation. It stung for a few seconds after the needle went through, but what I remember most was that almost immediately after, I was on fire. It continuously rubbed me no matter which way I moved. It was like I was masturbating just by walking. There was a heat and dizziness that just added to the euphoria. With hindsight, I was probably quite swollen," Alex continued, speaking as though it was a perfectly normal thing to discuss in public.

Kaylee's mouth hung open. She felt mortified and was now trying to backpedal out of the conversation. Alex chuckled at how much Kaylee squirmed. An older guy in the booth behind Alex laughed out loud, witnessing the conversation and Kaylee's embarrassment. Kaylee slowly sank her head to the table. Maybe she could just crawl under a rock somewhere.

As they finished up their meal and left for pedicures, Kaylee turned towards Alex. Alex had a serene smile on her face, the picture of an angel. The look said, *What did I do?*

"How could you do that to me?" Kaylee went in with an edged tongue. Alex responded by turning and passionately kissing her in the middle of the sidewalk. The world seemed to disappear except for the heated tongue battling for control of her mouth. Kaylee felt Alex's hands pull her close. After the kiss, Alex leaned in to say something.

"I'm really wet for you," Alex whispered, and then turned to keep walking.

Kaylee felt as if the entire world had heard Alex and turned another hue of red. She quickly caught up but couldn't think of anything to say. The embers in her loins were starting to feel heated.

They arrived for their pedicures and switched the topic back to something more socially acceptable. Once again, Alex brought up the topic of moving in together. After they were settled, with their feet soaking, Alex turned to Kaylee.

"So I know there are the issues regarding Ryan to work through. What else are you skeptical about?" Alex's words gave heed to contemplation. Kaylee could think of numerous instances where things would be harder.

"What about my parents and your parents? I know my mother would be furious." Kaylee realized it was a weak ground, but it was an issue they would have to cover.

"You know, your mother is such a wonderful and loving person, I just cannot see how we would *ever* get on without her in our lives." Alex's sarcastic tone said it all.

Kaylee giggled, realizing she had a point: It was none of her mother's concern.

"As far as my parents," Alex went on, "they would be delighted."

"You really think so?" Kaylee and Ryan had spent a full week with Alex's family over Thanksgiving, but Kaylee was still a little new to the concept of supportive parents. "Well, I'd be up for it if you are. Although, remember, if we move to your condo, it will have to wait until summer."

"Would you be up for a trial period now? How about we try this coming week? I can stay at your house, and we can see how it goes."

Alex's idea seemed like a fun adventure. Kaylee took a few minutes of quiet contemplation. The ladies were finishing up with the pedicures and manicures. As they walked out of the door, Kaylee made up her mind.

"I would love that. I'm warning you, though: Parenthood isn't as easy as you might think."

The final words seemed to come across as a grave warning. Alex chuckled at the idea, but realized Kaylee wasn't joking. The chuckle turned into nervous laughter by the time they reached Alex's car. They zoomed off to the next destination, a well-kept park nearby.

***

"Did you see the look on that guy's face earlier?" Alex asked as they walked along the path. The smell of rain loomed in the air, but the rain itself had not yet arrived.

"Which guy?" Kaylee's mind was elsewhere. The trees were coming in nicely and nature was picking up all over the place. Alex reached down and snagged Kaylee's hand as it swung, linking the two of them together as they strolled.

"The guy that was laughing earlier, when we were talking about my clit piercing." Alex knew what she was doing. Kaylee immediately turned red, checking around to see if anyone had heard. They were mostly alone, but Kaylee was not used to such language outside of the bedroom. Although she had definitely become a lot more open to those words since being with Alex, sometimes she felt like Alex pushed buttons just to watch her reaction.

"Oh. Yeah, I saw that guy." Alex started to laugh, but Kaylee fumed. "I'm sure you do that kind of stuff just to watch me cringe."

"Aww, but you're so cute when you blush." Alex had adopted a sarcastic, baby-like tone. The whole thing made her blush even more. "Besides, haven't you ever done anything remotely naughty in public?"

"*Me*? Uh, no. Well, I guess I made out with a girl in a movie theater once." Kaylee blushed as she talked, having never confessed that to anyone. "What have you done in public?"

"You're so naïve. It's really cute." Alex walked to a nearby bench under cover of an enormous oak. She sat down and pulled Kaylee towards her lap. Kaylee resisted slightly, afraid to be caught in public. "Relax, my lovely, and come here."

Reluctantly, Kaylee sat down on Alex's lap and turned to face her. Alex wrapped her arms around Kaylee and pulled her in for a deep kiss. Kaylee tried to fight it, but Alex would have nothing of the sort. For several seconds, the world ignited in passion, the two of them entwined on the park bench. As soon as Alex broke the kiss off, Kaylee bit her lip and looked around to make sure nobody was watching.

"Did you like that?" Alex teased. Kaylee didn't want to admit that she had indeed enjoyed it, so she shook her head. Alex sensed that it wasn't quite the truth and pulled her in for a second kiss. Kaylee blushed even brighter. Alex placed a hand on her hip, rubbing down her thigh. "What about that?" purred Alex.

The fire within Kaylee was fully ignited now, but fear still had a firm grip on her. "I think we should leave the park before we get arrested for public indecency." Kaylee smirked as she stood up. Much to her surprise, Alex ran a hand up her inner thigh for a fraction of a second. The sensual connection was over before Kaylee even knew it had happened. But in its wake, the touch caused her fires to burn even brighter. "I, uh, yeah. So, um, where to next?"

Both of them felt a little flustered as they made their way back to the car. As soon as the car door closed, Alex pulled Kaylee into another kiss. Kaylee was pulled halfway across the middle console as Alex ravished her. Their tongues swirled in blind passion, tuning out the rest of the world. When the kiss broke, Kaylee heard a cheer from outside the car and turned to see two younger guys watching in awe. She wanted to melt into the seat from embarrassment. Alex just chuckled and the Mazda roared to life.

They laughed and joked all the way to the restaurant. Kaylee was a little mortified but also extremely turned on by the thought that someone had been watching them. It was a new experience for her, but not altogether a bad one.

***

The restaurant was a cozy Italian place downtown. The aromas from the street made their mouths water. Soon, they were seated and enjoying a romantic candlelit dinner. Kaylee had a difficult time focusing on the food after the day she had had.

"So, are you sure you want to try a week living with me and the tyke?" Kaylee ventured, wanting to be certain. The waiter brought a second glass of wine while they chatted.

"Absolutely. We'll call it a trial run, to make sure we can go the distance," Alex said between bites. Kaylee's heart melted a little more. "I'll tell you what – Call the sitter and tell her you'll be a few more hours. We'll go to my place, pack up some things, and then head home."

Hearing Alex use the word *home* for her apartment made Kaylee giddy. As they left the restaurant, Kaylee called to tell the babysitter when she would be back. It gave them a few more hours.

The glide through the city took no time, and soon Alex pulled into her driveway and killed the engine.

CHAPTER 4

Kaylee admired the neighborhood and the area that Alex lived in. She started to picture what it would be like to live in an upscale condo here. As they walked into Alex's place, she tried to imagine how Ryan would feel. The neighborhood had a playground and pool she was sure he'd enjoy. Kaylee absentmindedly walked behind Alex as they came to her bedroom.

"You know, we still have a couple of hours alone." Alex's words brought Kaylee from her thoughts. When she looked at Alex, their eyes met with pure desire. Alex closed the distance quickly, hungrily kissing Kaylee. Kaylee felt Alex tugging at her clothing as they battled tongues like teenagers. The dress she wore stood no chance, and was soon yanked over her head. Alex ripped Kaylee's undergarments from her body.

Within moments, both were stripped nude, continuing their heated kiss but easing the pace. Alex wrapped her arms around Kaylee's slight waist, stepping backwards and pulling her toward the bed. She broke the kiss, sliding down Kaylee's body to sit on the crisp white sheets. She took a plump nipple into her mouth, pulling a delighted sigh from Kaylee. Alex's hands roamed over Kaylee's hips and curves as she suckled. The trail of fingertips ended at Kaylee's womanhood, which burned with passion.

"I love when you're so hot and ready," Alex murmured before moving to suckle and nibble other areas. Alex slid a finger slowly down the slit of her desire, looking deep into Kaylee's eyes. "Since we're alone, in my house, would you be up for trying something a little different?"

"Like what?" Kaylee questioned, uncertain. But the inferno in her loins meant she was willing to try almost anything.

"Let me tie you up," Alex replied, gently tracing the outline of Kaylee's nub. The soft and gentle administrations only teased Kaylee further. Alex knew the effect this had and kept pressing buttons. "Well, my lovely, what do you say?"

"I would give it a try for you. Just be gentle, this is all very new to me."

"Of course I'll be gentle, babe. Nothing we haven't done before." Alex grinned as the words tumbled out through heavy breath. She stood up, grabbing Kaylee's hips and drawing her into a kiss. "The only difference is that this time, you'll be constrained a little bit. The feeling will heighten your senses and make everything seem more intense."

Kaylee found herself lying on the bed while Alex retrieved various items from the closet. The first was a long length of silk dyed a vibrant shade of red. Kaylee watched in fascination as Alex got to work on her body.

"If at any point you feel uncomfortable, simply say stop. The silk is smooth, but strong. It will hold fast, no matter how you twist," Alex explained as she circled the bed. "We can stop at any moment if you're not feeling it. Just remember, it's me and I love you. Now, how do you feel about being my prisoner?"

Kaylee simply nodded. Alex cupped Kaylee's face and planted another soft kiss on her lips before continuing.

Alex tied one end of the silk around Kaylee's left ankle as an anchor point. Kaylee admired the stark contrast of the red against her pale skin, fascinated with the feeling of silk against her flesh. The soft light in the room illuminated the vibrant color as Alex wound the tie up her calf and thigh in a spiral.

"I'll keep checking with you to make sure everything's okay," Alex said as she worked. "You need to tell me if it's not. Understood?"

Another quick nod. Kaylee thought that the silk looked pretty, but still was unsure of how this was going to work. Up and around, Alex finally reached Kaylee's hips. The crimson silk coiled its way up the inside of Kaylee's thigh, so close to her heated sex that Alex paused to tease her slightly.

Alex then pulled Kaylee to a seated position. She wrapped the silk around her hips and along the small of her back, then down the other side in the same fashion. Kaylee thought for a moment that she looked like a candy cane, but didn't want to spoil the mood by remarking on it. The flow of fabric against her skin did add an erotic touch to the whole scene.

As Alex reached the other ankle, Kaylee was still unsure as to the purpose of all this. Alex slipped the silk in a way which looked confusing to Kaylee.

"How are you doing?" Alex asked. "Everything okay so far?"

Kaylee nodded at the question, mesmerized by Alex's hands at work. Alex tugged on the silk she had looped through itself and in a split second Kaylee's right leg bent and became bound to itself. Kaylee looked down to see her foot and calf securely tied to her thigh.

She could shift her hips and move her knee sideways, but the leg itself was strung tight. With another few loops, Kaylee realized her left leg was bound in a similar manner. Kaylee was in awe; she had lost all movement and now sat tied to herself. With a few final twists, Kaylee's legs were spread open for whatever Alex wanted.

Alex sat back and smiled at her. "How about now? Want to do more?"

Kaylee contemplated her predicament. She strained her legs against the silk but it refused to budge. She could no longer get up or run away, but she felt safe with Alex. It excited her that Alex now had complete and unrestricted access to her body. Slowly, she nodded, smiling up at Alex.

"Okay, lie back and relax." Alex retrieved another item from outside of Kaylee's view and wrapped a second length of silk around Kaylee's hands. She stretched Kaylee's slender arms above her head and started weaving the silk around them. In short order, Kaylee was bound, arms and legs, in a very compromising position.

"How are you doing with all of this?" Alex asked, positioning herself between Kaylee's legs. Kaylee had become so excited by being bound that a small trickle of nectar flowed freely from her. Alex knelt between her legs and threw Kaylee a mischievous look. "Hmm... It seems you're rather excited, my little Kitty Kay."

Kaylee's blush was almost deep enough to match the crimson ties that laced around her body. She did not want to admit it, but the silk felt luxurious and taught against her skin. The way it gently moved with her when she tried to escape made it that much more delectable. Kaylee smiled through heated cheeks.

"Yes, I'm doing good. I'm really, uh, wet."

Alex chuckled at Kaylee's choice of words. It had been months since she first got Kaylee to use more raunchy vocabulary, but Kaylee still defected to cute phrases to describe her sexuality. With that, Alex leaned down and started lapping at the source of Kaylee's nectar.

Kaylee moaned into the low-lit bedroom, her passion and fire taking off. Kaylee felt the earth shift as she started to quickly build towards climax. The adventures of the day and now being tied in lavish silk had her dripping. Before she could find the edge of her orgasm, Alex stopped and looked up at her.

"Do you want something, my love?"

Kaylee groaned at the games. *Of course* she wanted it. Kaylee knew the words this time.

"Yes, please, make me cum." Kaylee moaned as Alex started gently teasing with her fingers.

"How would you feel about one more item?" Alex held up a shorter silk that matched the others. "A blindfold."

Kaylee looked at the dangling object, slightly perplexed. She knew what it was for, but didn't realize what effect it would have. She quickly nodded her head; at this point she would agree to just about anything if it meant Alex would take her to ecstasy.

The world was enveloped in darkness. She could hear rustling movements and feel the weight of the bed shifting, but she could see nothing.

"What do you think? Everything okay?" Alex's question came from a small distance away as she slipped one of their favorite toys, the double dildo, into position.

Kaylee was a little concerned. She wasn't too sure about the inky darkness that kept her from her love. Kaylee did not want to be a burden though, and kept quiet. She smiled and nodded.

The darkness made things still and dulled. Every sense was on alert, but the world seemed slow and muffled. Suddenly, a warm mouth enveloped her hard nipple. Kaylee gasped at the surprise before moaning into the sensation. She knew it was Alex, but could not see her. A hand snaked its way to her womanhood and two fingers slid easily inside. Kaylee gasped at the familiar feel of Alex entering her and the warm tongue encircling her nipple.

Kaylee felt the bed shift as Alex hovered above her. Given the restraints, the darkness seemed to have a palpable edge. Alex leaned down and kissed her, bringing Kaylee back to the present. Kaylee moaned into Alex's mouth as she felt a hand slide between her captive legs.

"How are you doing, love?" Alex cooed into Kaylee's ear. The break in silence was welcome and it made Kaylee smile to hear the familiar voice. The whisper became suckles and nibbles on Kaylee's neck, once again driving Kaylee close to the edge. Kaylee groaned aloud as the invading fingers slowly slipped from her. The blindfold made for a heightened sense of anticipation. Kaylee desperately needed release.

"Mmm, I want you. Please, make me cum now, Ms. Carlisle." Kaylee used the language she'd been taught, along with the tone and address. To her delight, the plea worked and she felt Alex's phallic extension sink deep into her. Without sight to guide her, she could only focus on the physical drive of the toy thrusting in and out. She could hear Alex start to moan as the other end of the toy drove her crazy.

Kaylee felt Alex place hands on her bound knees to steady herself, riding the toy as it pumped in and out. The relentless rhythm of the assault and heightened acuteness of senses propelled Kaylee faster towards the edge. Alex picked up the tempo and deepened the motion, making Kaylee begin to jolt. Kaylee knew she would be falling into orgasmic abyss at any moment. Alex moaned her name and came in crashing waves. The phallic object in Kaylee kept pounding as Alex came hard.

Kaylee gasped at the edge as she felt the crescendo rush forth from Alex. At the same moment the inky darkness of the blindfold was replaced by an even darker scene. She was no longer coupled with the woman she loved, but a vile replacement. Alex's warm aroma was blackened with stale booze and cheap cigarettes. The plush mattress melted away to thin broken springs that creaked with the weight shifting above her.

Light suddenly hit as the blindfold was stripped off. Nathan's eyes stared at her, his contorted smirk glinting as he pushed into her. Kaylee pulled hard against her restraints, desperate to escape. All the desire had withered away. She blinked, trying to discern reality from memory. Alex slowed her motion, coming down from her high. She looked at Kaylee, smiling. Her face changed as soon as she realized Kaylee was not in a good place.

"Kay, baby, what's wrong?" Alex asked. Her hands deftly untied the silks and she pulled Kaylee into her arms. "Kay, talk to me, my love. What's going on?"

"I'm not sure. I was getting closer and closer, and I could feel you building up to your orgasm," Kaylee confessed, tears threatening to spill down her cheeks. "Then, all of a sudden, I got a blast from the past. It freaked me out."

Alex wrapped her arms protectively around Kaylee and held her tight. "Why didn't you say something? We could have taken the blindfold off. We could have stopped completely." Alex was genuinely concerned. Kaylee was trying to put her mind at ease and the comfort of Alex helped, but she struggled to keep her imagination at bay.

"I didn't want to interrupt your fun... You were in the moment. Plus, it all happened so fast that I wasn't sure what was going on." Kaylee glanced over to the clock on the wall. "Oh shit, it's almost eleven. We have to get home!"

The conversation was put on hold as the two rushed to get dressed, presentable, and pack for a week of living together. They left quickly, speeding through the city, back to Kaylee's apartment. Sitting in the car, Kaylee felt embarrassed about the whole thing and wasn't sure how to bring it up again.

Alex seemed to read her mind. "Kaylee, it's okay not to be okay with something. I always want to make sure you're having a good time. You're completely new to this. Never for a second think that you'll be interrupting my pleasure. I get pleasure by seeing you get off. I want to make sure *you* have a good time." The words comforted Kaylee. "Do you hear me?"

"Yes. I just feel so embarrassed," Kaylee confessed. "I feel like I disappointed you. I know you have much more experience than I do, and I just wanted you to enjoy it."

"I've seen and done a lot of things, Kay, but I was once exactly where you are. Contrary to popular belief, the most important part of kink is not play, nor getting off. The most important parts are communication and safety. If you are not feeling something, or are not in a good head space, you must tell me." Alex's words were a lot to take in.

"I'm sorry for not telling you my feelings about the blindfold. I'll try and work on that." Kaylee felt even more embarrassed at her lack of knowledge. "What kind of experiences have you had?"

Alex ignored her question. "You have nothing to apologize for. Sometimes things happen that we aren't aware of. At those points we stop and talk about it. That's why I kept asking if you were okay." The statement made Kaylee relive what just happened. "I asked to make sure you were having a good time and that everything was okay with you."

Alex glanced at Kaylee as she turned off of the interstate. Kaylee knew they would be home soon.

"Okay," Kaylee said, "from now on, if I'm not feeling a hundred percent about something, I'll tell you. I did enjoy almost everything about today. Those bad feelings, they came out of nowhere, with no warning. How about we stay away from blindfolds for now? I did enjoy being tied up, so long as I could see you," Kaylee told her, feeling it the appropriate thing to say.

"Good. I'm glad that you enjoyed at least part of it. You certainly seemed to be having fun at the time. Perhaps we can continue building your experiences?" They pulled into a parking spot in front of Kaylee's apartment. "Speaking of new experiences, I think I'm about to get mine."

Kaylee laughed at the change in tone, letting the humor dissolve any remaining tension. The babysitter gave a full report as the two walked into their home. Ryan was asleep and had been an angel all day. Alex took out a sum of money and included a tip, bidding farewell to the babysitter. The door swung closed and the two looked at each other for a long moment.

CHAPTER 5

"Welcome home!" Kaylee told Alex, blushing. This was actually happening.

The two felt exhausted from their day-long trip of relaxing. They went to bed and cuddled, neither worried about having to get up and leave.

The next morning came slowly. Ryan was watching TV in the living room when the two women leisurely woke up. After getting ready, they made their way to the kitchen. In normal Sunday fashion, Alex left to retrieve coffee, tea, and bagels while Kaylee cleaned up. When Alex returned, the three of them enjoyed a lazy brunch while making plans for the day.

"So what's on the agenda today, Kay?" Alex asked as they finished up brunch.

"Today is Sunday, so we have grocery shopping, laundry, and the week to prepare for," Kaylee replied nonchalantly. She had a solid system worked out as she disappeared down the hall to start a load of laundry. She came back with pen and paper to make a list.

"That seems awfully busy for a Sunday." Alex's words made Kaylee chuckle. "What's so funny?"

"Well, we spent all day yesterday out, and the work has to be done sometime. When do *you* go shopping and do the laundry?" Kaylee asked, genuinely bewildered that these were not normal things. The differences in lifestyle were already starting to surface.

"Uh, well, I normally... I pay someone to do most of my laundry, to be honest. I may do a load every two weeks just for delicates. As far as grocery shopping, I usually stop on the way home from work and grab something."

Lifestyle differences indeed.

"I'll tell you what, why don't you stay home and relax? Ryan and I will take care of the errands like we normally do, and we'll be home to cook dinner in a few hours." Kaylee had already visualized the day and created a plan in her head. Soon, the two of them were out the door, leaving Alex to familiarize herself with her new surroundings.

After errands were done and meals were made, Ryan's bedtime came and went. The day had progressed smoothly and left a lot of alone time at night. Alex and Kaylee cuddled on the couch to watch a movie, a simple act they had not done many times. Kaylee felt warm and secure nestled with Alex, wondering what the days ahead would hold. They decided to go to bed shortly after the movie to prepare for another long week in the office.

***

The alarmed ripped through the early morning, bringing a tirade from Alex. Kaylee laughed and started her morning routine. She was usually the one who struggled to rise when Alex was around. She already had clothes laid out for both herself and Ryan, so she headed to get washed. Alex staggered into the bathroom as Kaylee jumped into the shower.

"It's way too early for this," Alex grumbled as Kaylee busied herself. "I'm going to go make coffee. Want any?"

"No thanks," Kaylee chimed as she worked through her routine. A thump on the ground echoed down the hall as Ryan dashed from his bed. Kaylee could barely make out the voices.

"Ms. Alex! You're still here. Can we play cars?" The exuberant young child was not aware of how early it was; he just knew that one of his favorite people was still here. Kaylee chuckled from the shower. What a great way to introduce Alex to parenthood.

She finished up and toweled off. Ryan didn't normally get up this early, but it would be an adjustment for them all. Kaylee went to the bedroom, got partially dressed, and started Ryan on his routine. She then went to the bathroom and started her own morning prep.

As Alex finished her shower, they both started to feel a bit pressed for time. Both of their routines started to overlap. The hairdryer ended up tangled with the curling iron cord. Make-up was mixed up.

Flustered, the three of them stumbled out of the door moments before they would be late.

"Alex, if you drive from here you'll be caught in traffic. Do you want to just take the subway with me?" Kaylee asked as they walked briskly towards Ryan's school. Alex hated the subway, and Kaylee knew it. Reluctantly, Alex agreed, the stoic businesswoman starting to appear as they walked. They dropped Ryan off at the school gate and continued. The hectic workday flew by and Alex came to Kaylee's office just as she was preparing to leave.

"Ready for another great subway ride?" The tone was sarcastic, but pleasant. Kaylee was just happy that they were under the same roof for the time being. Once home, the evening really picked up. Kaylee was a flurry of getting dinner on the table, doing simple homework with Ryan, and tidying the house up. Alex watched almost as if a bystander. She tried to help where she could but looked awed by Kaylee's control over it all.

The second morning worked infinitely better. Alex and Kaylee started to work the kinks out in their system, taking turns in the small bathroom to ensure everyone was ready on time. They managed to beat the clock and get out the door before they were late. The day passed with little event until they got home.

"Is Ms. Alex living with us now?" Ryan jumped up and down as he asked.

Kaylee turned to her son, smiling. "Would you like her to?"

Ryan screamed something she thought was yes and bounded down the hall. Kaylee turned to put the finishing touches on the fish she had prepared. With the table set and dinner ready, Ryan was still a ball of energy. "Ryan, please sit down and eat."

"Alex, let's play airplanes!" Ryan zoomed around the room, launching a small model plane at Alex. Chuckling, she returned the toy, but kept eating. "Please, please, please. Play with me!"

"Not now, kiddo. Why don't you sit down and eat so we can play after?" Alex tried to bargain with the scamp. Ryan agreed and ate three bites before rushing off to his bedroom. "Wow. He certainly has a lot of energy tonight."

"He likes you and he's happy to have you here. It may take him some time to adjust to the fact that you'll be around more often." The Ryan-copter zoomed through the dining room once more. Both of them laughed at his antics. After dinner came bath and bedtime. No matter what Kaylee did or said, Ryan would not settle. Each time she tried to tuck him in, he bounded from his bed and back to Alex.

"What if I agree to read you a story? Would you go to bed then?" Alex asked, trying anything as the evening wore on. Ryan leapt from the couch, pulling Alex by the hand. After twenty minutes and two stories, Ryan finally nestled into bed.

When Alex returned from his bedroom, she collapsed onto the couch beside Kaylee. "This is a lot more work than I thought it would be! And there are two of us taking care of him. I can't imagine doing all of this on your own." Alex blanched at the thought. "I have a meeting first thing, so I need to be up and out a bit earlier than normal."

They decided to call it an early night and recharge for the next day.

***

The blare in the darkness meant it was time to get up; this time Alex was alert and on the move. *So career-driven*, Kaylee thought to herself. Ryan awoke with the same excitement and kept buzzing around Alex, begging her to play with him. He couldn't understand her rush. When it came time to go, Ryan started in on a tantrum, saying he wanted to stay home and play with Ms. Alex. Alex visibly started to panic as the minutes ticked by.

"Go ahead, I'll catch up," Kaylee called from the hallway where Ryan was thrashing in the throes of his tantrum. As soon as she was gone, Kaylee did her best to wind Ryan down. Eventually, they compromised on doing something fun before dinner and were finally off to school. Kaylee was not able to catch up to Alex until lunch time, since both women were so busy.

"I'm sorry about this morning," Kaylee started as they shared lunch. "You know, he's really taken a shine to you."

"I noticed. How do you do this every single day?" Alex's normal stoic disposition was gone, a sign she was exhausted. "I love the scamp and all, but what a handful."

"You're telling me," Kaylee said, chuckling. "He's never had anyone other than me at the house. It's a whole new world for him. Plus, you're the one who's always bringing him new toys and playing rowdy."

Alex was chagrinned at the statement and smiled wryly. The rest of the afternoon flew by and before they knew it, they were picking up Ryan from school. As they arrived home, Ryan demanded to know what fun thing they would do.

"How about you help me make dinner?" Alex chimed, with a confident look on her face.

Kaylee could only stare. In the several months they had been dating, she had not seen Alex cook, nor had she ever volunteered for such a colossal task as teaching a child to cook. Kaylee almost opened her mouth but bit her words back, deciding it would be fun to watch. Besides, she thought, how complicated could broiled fish and salad be?

She watched from a safe distance as Alex busied herself alongside the five-year-old. She explained what she was doing at each step of the process. At last, she popped the broiling pan into the oven and turned to make the salad. Alex asked Ryan to add each ingredient as she cut it up. In no time, they had crafted a wonderful salad.

"Can I add the dressing now, Ms. Alex?" the five-year-old asked, bouncing back up on the chair.

Alex turned to check on the fish. As she opened the door, a plume of black smoke washed over her. Stepping back, the fire alarm screamed, causing Ryan to drop the dressing jar into the salad. In his distress, he knocked the bowl from the counter, sending the salad and an arc of dressing across the floor. Alex dumped the smoking fish into the sink and ran from the kitchen.

"Think we should get take-out tonight?" Kaylee asked with the calmest, straightest face she could muster. With a glare, Alex grabbed her keys and marched to the door. "I love you," Kaylee called after her. "Drive safe!"

Kaylee turned to the horrendous mess that was her kitchen. By the time Alex returned with tacos, the oven and floor were spotless. Kaylee could tell that Alex was a ball of nerves and so avoided giving her too much grief over the accident.

"That was really fun, Ms. Alex. Can we do it again tomorrow?" Ryan did not quite understand the subtleties of people yet. Kaylee did her best not to laugh and simply smiled at the child. Soon after, it was bath and bed time. After Ryan was down, Kaylee found Alex frazzled on the couch.

"Are you okay, my love?" Kaylee asked gingerly. Alex looked exasperated, sipping a cup of tea. Another cup steamed next to her. Kaylee took her spot and grabbed the warm drink.

"I really made a mess of things tonight. I'm sorry." Alex seemed distraught as she spoke. She was definitely not her normal, in-control self. "Kay, I've barely even touched the surface of the things you do on a day-to-day basis and I feel like I'm already getting my butt kicked."

"You'll get used to it. You learn to roll with the punches." Kaylee laughed, putting her arms around Alex and kissing her on the head. "How about a nice hot shower to help you relax?"

Alex narrowed her eyes over the cup of steaming tea. A devilish grin stole over her face.

CHAPTER 6

The two left the tea and stripped down on their way to the bathroom. They had spent the week together, but it had been a busy week with no personal time. The steam billowed through the small room as they stepped into the tub and pulled the shower curtain closed. Alex dipped under the running water, soaking her long black hair. The refreshing downpour seemed to melt away the stress of the week.

Kaylee took her turn under the coursing water, both of them relaxing in heated silence. When she opened her eyes, Alex was staring at her intently. Kaylee got an idea and decided to go for it. She started by slowly inching her way forward until her lips met with Alex's. Instead of the powerful kisses Alex always bestowed, Kaylee softly explored Alex's mouth. Alex seemed to concede control for the moment.

Kaylee slowly pushed Alex against the tiled wall, causing her to gasp at the sharp contrast of hot and cold. She left glistening kisses in a trail down Alex's neck and along her collarbone. Again, Kaylee was soft and sensual, each movement measured. Her hands started to glide over Alex's torso and hips, the water adding an edge of sensuality. She continued to kiss down her breasts, and ever-so-gently took one of Alex's nipples into her mouth.

Kaylee wrapped one arm around Alex's waist while placing the other hand on her thigh. She focused on overwhelming Alex, taking advantage of the rare moment when *she* was in control. After a few more moments of teasing, she switched to the other breast, slowly matching the speed of her tongue with the drone of the water. As her mouth enveloped Alex's other nipple, she heard an audible gasp through the din, which made her smile. Kaylee slid her body sensually up Alex, letting her hardened nipples tease Alex's slick and perfect skin.

Kaylee wrapped an arm around Alex's neck and pulled her down for a passionate kiss. As the two explored each other's mouth, Kaylee let her hand trail into the V of Alex's legs. With her ring finger, Kaylee slipped between juicy, swollen lips. Alex moaned into Kaylee's kiss this time, as if letting go of her stress entirely. Kaylee withdrew and slid the digit in small circles around Alex's clit while tugging gently on her piercing. When Kaylee released the sensual kiss, Alex straightened against the wall, gasping for breath.

Kaylee slid slowly down Alex's curves, sucking in the residual water droplets. She got on her knees, putting her at eye level with the object of her desire. She gently parted Alex's legs with her hand. Alex immediately responded by propping her leg on the edge of the tub. The angle put Kaylee slightly lower, so she leaned in and ran her tongue over the protruding lips. Alex groaned and pressed her head back against the tiles as Kaylee slowly and delectably devoured her.

Kaylee lapped and circled her tongue at just the right speed to make Alex's heart pound. She pulled and teased the piercing in Alex's nub. For a split second, she thought of making her beg for a change, but decided against it. Sensing her lover was growing anxious, she snaked her tongue deep inside of Alex. As she withdrew, she pushed two fingers in to replace it and encircled Alex's piercing with her mouth. She applied a slight sucking action, gently moving her fingers back and forth.

Alex gasped and raked her fingers heavily through Kaylee's wet hair. She started to grind against Kaylee, who kept up the pace, pushing firmly against her lover. Within moments, Alex crashed hard against the wall of her orgasm and began shuddering. Wave after wave shook her body as the slow build of her orgasm toppled over her. When she came around, she let her leg fall and slid to the floor of the tub. She dared not try to stand while the world still spun. Alex closed her eyes and enjoyed the bliss and relaxation of the steam.

Kaylee pressed a bubbly soap puff against Alex and gently bathed her. Alex melted; she had never been bathed by a lover before. Kaylee spent time and effort making sure every piece of Alex's perfect flesh was attended to. As she rinsed off, Alex pulled her in for a long, passionate kiss. The water started to grow cold, so they at last got out and toweled each other off. Alex took Kaylee by the hand to the bed and laid her down.

Their slightly damp bodies pressed together as Alex positioned herself between Kaylee's legs, kissing her with deep, longing desire. Alex was in an odd mood, full of passion and emotion; Kaylee could feel raw hunger and adoration emanating from her. The attention made Kaylee's heart well up. Alex then dipped and slid her tongue across Kaylee's womanhood. The electrical storm of pleasure sent a bolt through her. Alex started lapping at Kaylee with urgency and need.

Kaylee found herself grasping at the sheets, her moans echoing through the bedroom. Alex circled her tongue around Kaylee's clit, driving her further towards the cliff of orgasm. Three fingers buried inside to accompany the swirling tongue. Kaylee felt full and quickly tumbled towards release as Alex deftly pulsated her fingers. Alex shifted positions and straddled one of Kaylee's legs, leaving her fingers deep inside.

Alex leaned up, encapsulating Kaylee in another passionate kiss. Kaylee burned with aches of desire and adoration as she pulled her lover close. Kaylee could feel Alex grinding her clit ring into her thigh and lifted her leg slightly to push harder. They gyrated in unison, driving each other closer to the brink of orgasm. The two women rasped and panted as they edged closer with one another.

"Cum with me, please," Alex whimpered into Kaylee's ear. Kaylee drove her knee up further, pushing the piercing against Alex's tender nub. In the same breath, Alex scooped her fingers deep into Kaylee. The women reached their crescendo together and rode the waves of their orgasm to bliss. Alex laid her head on Kaylee's shoulder as they throbbed, breathing deeply. She eventually rolled off to the side as they came down from their high and murmured a gentle, "I love you." Sleep came quickly.

***

The alarm sang its song, rousing the two from slumber. Some of the tension they had felt throughout the week still lingered, but at least Alex had a smile on her face and a spring to her step. By now, the morning routine was starting to come together nicely. They even had time to sit for breakfast while Ryan finished getting ready. Soon, the trio was out the door and heading to drop Ryan off.

As they left the school, Alex walked slower than usual. Her normal pace usually kept Kaylee clipping at her heels. Alex seemed to be in a deep, contemplative mood. Kaylee slid her hand into Alex's as they walked, which was met with enthusiasm.

"What are you thinking about?"

Alex seemed to stir from her reverie at Kaylee's words. The cool morning smelt as though it might rain at any moment.

"Everything. Being with you. This last week." Alex took a breath to gather her thoughts. "It's given me a lot to think about. You bring out a side of me that I've never really acknowledged or known." Kaylee blushed, realizing she was talking about the emotional charge of the previous night. "And despite this week being extremely hectic, I've enjoyed myself, and I'm glad we decided to try this little experiment."

"And may I ask what you think of this little experiment?" Kaylee asked as they walked along.

"To be honest, I'm still wracking my brain about it. I've never dealt with kids before. In fact, the only kids I know aside from Ryan are my brother's, and they're spoiled little brats. You were right about it being a radical lifestyle change for me." Alex brought the point to the forefront. "I realize that being a parent is a full time job — more than a full time job! You never stop."

"True enough," Kaylee chuckled. "But for all the sleepless nights, the sicknesses, and the tantrums, it's been an amazing journey for me. And so far, I've faced the majority of the last five years alone."

"I can only imagine how difficult that must have been, raising a child by yourself." Alex seemed truly amazed. "I'm still a bit shell-shocked about this last week, and I'm sure we only scratched the surface."

"That's very true." Kaylee smiled at the sentiment. "Look at the bright side: We're past the point of having to change diapers. But you gotta stop buying him stuff or he'll turn into one of your brother's spoiled brats!"

Alex chuckled as they hit the subway station. Once they boarded the train and found seats, she spoke again. "If you don't mind, I think I need a few nights in my own place to unwind and reflect." Kaylee had guessed this would happen. "You were right: Taking on a family is quite a bit more of a commitment than just dating. I think I need to break into this a little more slowly."

Kaylee smiled. "I know, love. No worries. I'm not upset that you asked. Being a parent is no easy commitment. Even if we only scratched the surface, I think you coped really well with all the challenges that came up." Alex beamed back at her in return. "I just need to be up front and say that if we're going to be long-term, Ryan is part of the package."

"I know that, Kay, and I love the scamp. I would never think about it any other way." Alex grasped Kaylee's hand. "I'm still up for the challenge, especially with you there to help me through it."

"I'm here for you, absolutely, in every way I can be. You can stay over any night you want. In fact, I look forward to it. Especially if we can repeat last night," Kaylee added, blushing.

Alex chuckled, proud that her shy woman was becoming a little bolder. The train pulled into their station and they got off.

"Did you just make a sassy comment like that in *public*, Miss Daniels? You're going to have me all hot and bothered before I even start work!"

Kaylee turned an even deeper shade of red from the thought. "I'm definitely looking forward to several repeats of last night, except maybe the part where my kitchen blew up."

They both laughed, thinking of the mess that was made, and turned the corner to enter their office building. They made lunch plans and quickly headed to their respective areas. Kaylee reflected on their conversation and the last week. It had felt amazing to have help around the house. It also made her heart swim at how well Alex got along with Ryan.

For now, they would wait and see about moving in together. They had plenty of time to decide since Ryan still had a month left of school and the summer break. Her thoughts attempted to drift off into daydreams, but she pulled them back to her current task.

Thank God it was Friday.

GAY PRIDE

The bright sun cast tiny shadows under everyone milling about the square. Kaylee kept a close eye on Ryan as he dashed through the crowd. The parade was due to start any moment. Alex's parents, Robert and Julia, had come to visit for the weekend, and they joined Alex and Kaylee for the parade. Gay Pride was a big event in Boston, and the parade was fun for the whole family. It was also one of the few times Kaylee felt safe to truly be herself in public.

Robert spent most of the time playing with Ryan and some other boys at the parade. Kaylee was excited to see a positive male influence in Ryan's life. Alex excused herself, leaving Julia and Kaylee alone to chat. From their vantage point, everyone heard the music rolling down the buildings. Soon an array of rainbows would line the street. Kaylee fought to keep her nerves under control, especially because Alex was not around.

"Kaylee, I have a proposition for you. How would you feel about Robert and I taking Ryan tonight?" Julia inquired. Kaylee looked at her, stunned. It was not every day that they got a babysitter, and this was essentially one for free. Overnight, no less.

"Really? You would do that?" Kaylee said, more out of surprise than anything. Drums sounded and a cheer rose from the crowd. Robert and the boys all sprinted over to see what was going on.

"Absolutely, I know that this is a special day for you and Alexis. Perhaps you can go on a date?" Julia smiled as she explained her intentions. "Plus, it will allow me to spend some time with my grandson, and it takes twenty years off my husband." She chuckled, looking over at Robert playing with Ryan and a group of kids.

Kaylee hugged Julia in appreciation. She felt elated by the news of having a free babysitter and a night with Alex. It was the last bit that sent her over the moon, though. They already considered Kaylee and Ryan as part of the family, even calling Ryan *theirs*. The simple gesture made her heart melt. She adored Alex's parents.

A giant wisp of cotton candy approached them. "Boys!" Alex held the treat aloft. The girls all started to dig in as Ryan and Robert came running over. Within minutes, the cotton candy was reduced to a cardboard spiral. "Well that didn't last long."

"Did you really expect it to?" Kaylee chuckled. Ryan and Robert headed back to their spots as the first floats started to move through the square. The rest of the adults headed over to join them. Alex slowed a bit, dragging Kaylee into a deep kiss. On any other day, Kaylee would be skeptical to kiss in public; today she kissed back with enthusiasm, despite Alex's parents being nearby. Together, they walked toward the crowd.

"What was that hug about?" Alex asked as they came close, a look of apprehension coming across her face. Kaylee noticed, but was too enthralled with the parade to say anything.

"Well, great news, actually." Kaylee smiled. "Your mom volunteered to keep Ryan overnight at their hotel so we can have a special date. She says there are slides in the pool. He'll love it."

"Really? Like seriously? That's amazing of her. Guess I should give her a hug too!" Alex said, laughing, her temporary apprehension vanishing entirely. The parade was in full swing as they got to the line. Candy flew into the crowds, people marched and waved, and a myriad of music filled the air. Kaylee loved seeing all of the rainbows and vibrant outfits.

As the crowds filtered in, Alex slipped behind Kaylee and wrapped her arms protectively around her. Despite the large turnout, Kaylee felt safe and warm. As the different floats moved by, Alex swayed Kaylee to the music, dancing in place and being a little bit silly. The whole ordeal made Kaylee laugh. Looking around, she could see other couples together, laughing and enjoying the day. She truly felt that love was in the air, and she was happy to be a part of it.

At various intervals, the crowd would cheer at the passing floats. On more than one occasion, the group was showered with candy, which Ryan and the other kids scooped up as quickly as possible. Kaylee even caught a small pack of skittles to share with Alex. Julia moved to join Robert a short distance away, watching over Ryan. Alex moved her head slightly to nuzzle Kaylee's neck.

"What are you thinking about, my love?" Alex asked quietly in Kaylee's ear. Kaylee smiled as if she had been caught red-handed.

"I was just thinking about how beautiful this is. How we're free to do what we want here. Everyone is celebrating that equality, that love. I want it to be like this all the time," Kaylee said thoughtfully. "What about you?"

"Pretty much the same thing. It's nice to know that we're among friends; that I can hold you in public, claim you as my own, and not have to deal with stupid people." Alex's answer was a lot more confident and personal. "Plus, I can do this."

Alex leaned Kaylee back into her, kissing her deeply. In that moment, the parade and thousands of cheering people disappeared. It was just Kaylee and Alex. As the kiss ended, the balloons and confetti returned, the music blared, and crowd came back into focus. Kaylee smiled up at Alex before turning to watch the parade again.

Everything about the day was wonderful; it was amazing to see such a diverse mix of people out in support of the community. After a few hours, things began to dwindle and the group started their trek toward the cars. Alex walked hand in hand with Kaylee. Ryan and Robert dashed about. At one point, the young boy was close enough to stop.

"Ryan, I have a question for you," Kaylee said in a motherly tone, trying not to sound excited. Her son stopped dead in his tracks and fell in next to Kaylee as if something was wrong. "How would you feel about spending the night with Mrs. Julia and Mr. Robert?"

It took a few moments for the concept to process, but then he realized they would be able to play more. His whole face lit up and he nodded vigorously.

"Can I really?" Ryan asked exuberantly. At a single nod from Kaylee, he dashed off to play with Robert. Julia had been walking close by and saw the whole thing unfold. They smiled at his youth.

"Thank you so much for offering this up," Kaylee said warmly. "It means a lot to us."

"Oh, no worries at all," Julia replied. "We're happy to have him. It's not every day that we get to play with children. Plus, with the way this is working out, he's already pretty much a grandson."

"Mom!" Alex exclaimed, turning a bright shade of pink. Kaylee had never seen Alex blush before.

"Thank you. Should we bring him over later?" Kaylee asked, not entirely sure about this kind of protocol.

"Actually, why don't we all go back to your apartment and then head out," Julia stated plainly.

"Yeah, then we can stop for some pizza on the way to the hotel. It will be a grand time!" Robert said as he walked up to the group. "I mean, the tyke just needs some pajamas and maybe a few toys. Oh, and a swimsuit. They have that indoor play area."

"Well, if you guys are sure, that would be amazing. Thank you so much!" Kaylee exclaimed. Alex stepped forward, drawing some cash out of her wallet.

"Here Dad, this should cover dinner for everyone," she said, holding out the cash.

"Alex, put your money away," Robert intervened. "We want the chance to spoil the boy as much as you have."

Kaylee laughed out loud; Robert had hit the nail on the head, Alex regularly spoilt Ryan rotten. Reluctantly, Alex stuffed the bills back into her wallet and shouldered her purse. The group set off for Kaylee's home. Ryan and Kaylee quickly gathered everything he needed. After a quick round of goodbyes, hugs, and kisses, the group bid farewell and parted ways.

***

"This is amazing. So nice of them," Alex said as they got into her Mazda. "Well, beautiful, what would you like to do?"

"I read that there was a great little film on at the Wilbur Theatre tonight. Perhaps we could go to dinner, then go see it?" Kaylee tossed out the suggestion, not used to being the planner. Generally, Alex took care of everything.

"Perfect. What do you want for dinner?" Alex asked.

"Uh, well, I don't know. Why are you asking me?" Kaylee questioned.

"I thought you might want to decide for a change," Alex reassured her. Kaylee had found that she quite enjoyed not having to make the plans. She was perfectly happy to leave the decisions up to Alex.

"Well, hmmm. How about sushi?" Kaylee ventured. "We haven't done anything like that in a while."

"Sushi it is," Alex confirmed, and the two started off.

"So how come I'm the one making the decisions today?" Kaylee asked while they started through the city. "You normally call the shots."

"Do you remember the shower we had together last week?" Alex mentioned casually as she turned a corner. "You took charge; you were in control. How did that feel?"

Kaylee hadn't given it much thought. Reflecting on it, she had enjoyed the power and the change of pace, but wouldn't want to do it all the time.

Then it hit her: "You gave up control because you wanted a different experience." Kaylee beamed a smile. "So letting me make the plans every once in a while adds a thrill to the whole thing."

"Precisely. It's just like the rope play a couple of weeks ago. Actually, I wanted to talk to you about that." Alex parked the car at the restaurant and the two started into the building. "I know you're really new to this, so I wanted to illustrate something very important."

The restaurant had large aquariums of fish swimming around, sleek and modern decorations, and very friendly staff. They were seated quickly. Alex ordered a small bottle of filtered *sake* and then turned back to Kaylee.

"All right, so what about it?" Kaylee asked, perplexed at this point.

"Well if you recall, I asked you several times where your head was." Alex took on a serious tone.

"I would ask how you were doing, what you were feeling, and if everything was okay."

"Yeah, I remember. Vividly, I might add," Kaylee said with a smile. The response got a chuckle from Alex. "What about it?"

"Well, I was checking your head space. I wanted to make sure you were okay with everything. In the event that you were not okay with it, we could've stopped to discuss. Remember, my biggest concern is your wellbeing. Safety first, and all that." The sake arrived and the two women placed their order.

"Yes, I remember. I still feel bad about freaking out though," Kaylee confessed, still worrying about the incident.

"That's one of my points, Kaylee. You shouldn't feel bad. I think it's time we implemented a basic system," Alex offered. "For instance, a common one is green, yellow, red."

"I'm going to guess green is go, red is stop," Kaylee said, smirking. The two women took their shot of *sake* together, and the sushi arrived at the table shortly after.

"Right, in ways. It deals with head space though. So red means that there's something really wrong. It's generally a trigger," Alex tried to explain. Kaylee wasn't sure she understood. "For instance, the blindfold brought back a bad memory."

"Right," Kaylee said.

"Well, let's say that the memory was so bad that it gave you a flashback or a panic attack," Alex laid out. "Instead of just a bad memory, you relived it. That would be a red. That's a situation we never want to happen."

"So red isn't just 'stop,' it's something we should never get to," Kaylee explained in her own words as she grasped it. "That must mean yellow is like the traffic light and means slow down."

"Yes, again, in ways. In the case we just talked about, yellow would definitely be a slow down. It means we need to evaluate why there's a snag." Alex was pleased Kaylee understood. "Or in cases where there's pain involved, yellow could mean 'not so hard.'"

"Okay. So, uh, kind of like, there's the hard line and I'm getting close to it," Kaylee said. "For whatever reason that is."

"Precisely. For *us*, when we get to a yellow, we should stop and discuss, even if it breaks the scene or mood. The most important part is that we communicate." Alex smiled as things came together. "I will always make sure that we stop at a yellow."

"Okay," Kaylee confirmed, smiling back to Alex. The two women began to eat their delicious meal. Their conversation turned back to light tones as they ate. Afterwards, they walked down the street to the theatre. The show was pleasant enough, but not exactly thrilling. Kaylee enjoyed it because it was a Pride event, so nobody batted an eye as they cuddled throughout the film.

***

With no reason to go back to Kaylee's apartment, the two decided to stay in Alex's condo for the night. When they arrived, Kaylee sat on the couch while Alex went to change. For several long moments, Kaylee sat waiting in silence, the hum of the air conditioner her only companion. At last, the door opened. Alex stepped into the low lighting and stood in front of Kaylee in a sexy pose. Her body was wrapped in a sheer lingerie nightgown cut to accentuate her curves. Kaylee was enamored with the look. It was regal and seductive.

"Ms. Carlisle, how may I serve you?" Kaylee said wantonly and without hesitation. Alex smiled at the title and how easily Kaylee fell into the role.

"You have an outfit on the bed. I want you to go change and then come to me," Alex said steadily, her hips swaying as she crossed the thick carpet to the couch. Kaylee rushed to the bedroom, a want and desire to fulfill Alex's request already burning inside her. The outfit in question was akin to a French maid's outfit. The only difference was the cut and volume of cloth that appeared to be missing. Kaylee was sure she would be showing less skin if she were nude.

She felt exposed and slightly embarrassed, but the desire to please was building. She shuffled to the door and peered out at her Alex.

Alex was sitting on the couch, staring at her, smiling. She knew that this would be a little on edge for Kaylee.

"Come, my little maid. I want to see you," Alex coaxed. She sat with both legs folded under her. Kaylee stepped into the light, the short ruffles undulating with her hips. She tried to be seductive without looking foolish. "Mmm, perfect. Go fetch me a glass of wine, Kitten, and come to the bedroom. You may get yourself a glass, too."

Kaylee did as she was told and followed Alex into the bedroom. Candles were lit around the room and soft music played. Kaylee set the wine down and smiled. Alex picked up her glass and took a sip.

"Perfect. What is your color?" Alex asked. She sat her glass down and shifted back on the bed.

"Positively verdant, Ms. Carlisle," Kaylee answered demurely. "Please let me serve you."

The evening began with a simple request from Kaylee to serve. Alex answered with a smile and started by giving small tasks. Kaylee would jump to refill wine glasses and fetch small items. As the night progressed, the tasks became more sexual in nature. Kaylee's pride swelled with each compliment and coo. She felt that she could get used to this. Their clothing gradually disappeared, a reward for good service. The bed became sprawled with discarded cloth. The game did not stop when they lay together nude.

Kaylee found herself staring into Alex's soulful eyes, captivated as Alex took control of her. With each caress and movement of hand, Kaylee fell under Alex's seduction. The fervent desire to please became an unquenchable thirst. Whatever Alex requested became hers. At one point, Kaylee was required to please herself while Alex watched. Kaylee jumped to do her bidding. Their bodies writhed together, passion swirling between them.

Each moan and gasp from Alex elated Kaylee, her sole purpose dedicated to pleasing Alex any way she could. The symphony of noises blended with the crescendo of passion. Their movements became less directed and the commands stopped coming. The night undulated between control and unbridled chaos, command and seduction. With each climax, the focus shifted, each desiring to push the other to their limit.

Kaylee's mind drifted in euphoria. She found herself panting Alex's name more times than she could remember, with Ms. Carlisle all the while demanding Kaylee to voice her wants and desires. In equal measure, she lost track of how her body swayed and pulsed with orgasm. Pleasure washed over her, time and time again as small touches caressed and kissed her skin. The actions blended into the night, dancing together in ecstasy. With each electrical burst of pleasure, Kaylee strived to please Alex.

Alex seemed the puppet master, guiding the actions, setting the scene. At first, each small request carried such little weight and feeling. Then the requests quickly brought rushing waves of desire that swept away inhibitions. Kaylee swayed to her bidding, driven to please, submitting to Alex without naming it as such. Their bodies writhed as one. Their hearts beat together.

Their bodies slick, their minds floating on cloud nine, the two women pleased each other in every way they could think of. The hours that passed only served to deepen their connection. As much as their nerves quivered with pleasure, their hearts swelled with love and desire. Kaylee felt fulfilled, awash with the experience of submission.

Their night stretched into the wee hours of the morning, having no need to return home, nor pay for a sitter, nor look after a child. Kaylee lay spent, her body convulsing with passion. Alex pulled her close, their bodies drained and draped across each other. Their lovemaking hung thick in the air. Trying to catch their breath, they smiled at each other. Exhaustion threatened to overwhelm their physical bodies. They laid close, resting and staring into each other's eyes.

Alex left small kisses over Kaylee's face, her hand gently cupping Kaylee's cheek. Kaylee's heart swelled once more, elated and warm from the wonderful evening. Kaylee had no guess as to the time, but she felt complete. She felt safe and sated. Her mind began to drift off into the blissful aftermath of orgasm, threatening to fall into slumber. A kiss made her open her eyes. She smiled at Alex.

"So how tired are you, Kitty?" Alex whispered devilishly.

Kaylee's eyes snapped back into focus. "What are you proposing, Ms. Carlisle?"

E06: JEALOUSY

CHAPTER 1

The soft mat under Kaylee's palms and heels squished as she shifted her weight. The light music in the background filtered through her concentration, soothing her mind. After a few moments, the instructor changed positions and the class followed. Kaylee loved her weekly yoga classes; she got a workout and felt tranquil afterwards. Plus, she made a new friend, something she had sorely missed having ever since she moved to Boston.

The last ten minutes of class were spent in quiet meditation, reflecting on the week ahead and evoking positive vibes. Kaylee felt that the whole experience recharged her from the past week and gave her a fresh outlook for the weekend. The instructor ended class with *Namaste* and, while everyone started to filter out of the small gym room, Lydia caught up with her.

"What a great class. How are you doing, Kaylee?" Lydia asked, smiling.

"I'm doing pretty good," Kaylee said, returning the smile. "Stressful workweek. It's hard to be stressed after yoga, though. How are you?"

"I understand that. Brent is out of town this week. It's been a nice break, if you know what I mean, but it's also left me alone with Toby and Zack," Lydia said, half laughing.

Kaylee raised an eyebrow at the break comment. "Some kinks to work out between the two of you?" she asked as she pushed the dressing room door open.

"I don't know if I would say that. He just acts like a kid a lot. It's nice when I only have *two* children to take care of, rather than three. How are you, and uh, Alex, right?" Lydia didn't seem to mind that Kaylee and Alex were gay, but it still felt like a grey area for public conversation.

"We're doing well. We even talked about moving in together," Kaylee said as she changed.

Lydia was still not worried about getting dressed in font of everyone, so Kaylee had somewhat picked up the habit. "In fact, we had a trial run a few weeks ago. That was interesting."

"That's great. I hope it works out for you two. What does Ryan think of it all? I mean, if that's not too forward a question." Lydia gave pause for a moment, not sure if she crossed a line. To busy herself, she started to pull off her clothing. Lydia knew Kaylee was gay, but held no reservations about stripping in front of her. It actually made Kaylee feel good that Lydia was comfortable with it.

"Ryan has only ever known me to be with women and they get along really well. Alex acts like a big kid too, sometimes. They're fun to watch," Kaylee said with a smile, remembering the fun they all had. "In fact, Alex and I were going to meet over by the park to let Ryan burn off some energy. Would you like to join us?"

"Well I don't have to rush off for anything. And I'm sure the kids would love to continue playing for a while. Sure, why not!"

The two women finished changing and started toward the daycare area. Upon their arrival, Ryan ran to the gate.

"Momma, are you ready to go to the park? You said we're meeting Alex there, right?" Ryan's exuberance could never be curbed, it seemed. Kaylee chuckled and nodded.

"Yes, we are. What would you think about Toby and Zack joining us?" Kaylee asked. Ryan took a moment to process and then leapt away, yelling to the boys. The two adults laughed while gathering everything up. In short order, everyone arrived at the park. The kids all ran to the play area, the women following at the rear. As they neared some benches, Kaylee's phone rang.

"Hey, Alex... Oh, no problem... Yeah, that will be all right... Okay, bye. Love you!" The conversation lasted for just a few seconds. Kaylee turned to Lydia. "Alex is just a few minutes away."

"Right on. I'm excited to meet her," Lydia said as she sat down on a bench. The boys were busy running all over the park. "What does she do again?"

"She works in the marketing, branding, and advertising division of the company. So basically, I design the clothes, and she sells them." Kaylee joined Lydia on the bench. "How's the crafting business going? What kind of things do you craft?"

"Well, I like to sew and knit, though I've tried a lot of different things over the years. Quilting was boring and time consuming. I really liked jewelry-making and glass etching." Lydia pulled up her necklace as she was talking. The pendant was beautiful glass, swirled with glitter and multiple colors. "This is one of my favorite pieces."

"You *made* that? It's amazing. Do you make other kinds of jewelry?" Kaylee was fascinated by the whole process. *How awesome would it be to have a fashion designer and a jewelry maker team up*, she thought.

"Well, I have tried a lot of things. I even had an attempt at specialty adult jewelry," she chuckled, "but that gets expensive really quickly." Lydia seemed like she wasn't hesitant to talk about any topic; she shared that trait with Alex. It fazed Kaylee a lot less now than it would have done six months ago.

"That's right. Don't you have your nipples pierced?"

Lydia smiled. "I do. I guess you probably noticed in the dressing room. I got them done, gosh, probably eight years ago. It was well before any thoughts of a second child. We thought Zack was it, so we had them done after I was through breastfeeding." Lydia had no qualms discussing personal matters.

"Did they hurt? Do you like them? How long did they take to heal?" Questions gushed forth from Kaylee. Perhaps she was more interested in getting them done herself than she thought.

"Well to be honest, yes, they did hurt, and the second one a lot more than the first. I love them, but they took some time to get used to. As far as healing time goes, I think mine were pretty okay in about six weeks, although it can take much longer. The first few days are definitely the most painful. Are you thinking of getting them done?"

"Well, the thought has crossed my mind quite a bit recently. My mother was never one for tattoos, or piercing anything beyond your ears," Kaylee explained. "I got my little butterfly done out of rebellion more than anything else." She smiled at the memory. Ryan came dashing over, followed by the other two.

"Momma, can I have a drink?" Kaylee pulled her water bottle out and handed it to her son. "Alex!"

Like a bolt, Ryan forgot his request and took off across the park toward the parking lot. Toby and Zack hung back to quench their thirst. Alex fought her way over, pulled by Ryan. She laughed and tickled him, freeing herself from her would-be captor as she walked over to the bench.

"Hey babe," Alex said cheerily as she slowed down. She put her hand on Kaylee's back and gave her a quick peck on the cheek.

"Alex, meet Lydia. Lydia, this is Alex. Lydia is in my yoga class and her son Toby is in Ryan's class at school." She introduced them. The boys all quickly said hello and then fled from the adults.

"Nice to meet you, Lydia. How are you?" Alex seemed to slip instantly from the fun-loving child-tickler to her business self. Kaylee thought it was odd, but maybe Alex just needed a bit of time to warm up to Lydia.

"I'm great. We were just killing time here at the park. Yourself?" Lydia did not seem to notice the change in personality. They shifted to make room for Alex on the bench.

"Actually, I'll stand. I've been sitting all day. I'm doing well, just finished up a few extra hours at the office." Alex smiled down at Kaylee. "Had a few things to get cleared up for Rose before Monday."

"Why, what's happening on Monday?" Kaylee was bewildered. Normally Rose kept her in the loop pretty well.

"It's not my place to tell you – That's Rose's job. It's all good, though, nothing to worry about. But I'm famished. Have you had lunch?"

The question made Kaylee look at her phone; it was already almost one. "Wow, where did the time go? Yeah, I'm pretty hungry. Would you like to join us, Lydia?" Kaylee asked while turning to her friend.

"Oh, I don't think so. Three young boys in a restaurant sounds like a recipe for disaster. Besides, with Brent away, I have the afternoon to myself. I think it's time to get some projects done. Thanks for the invite, though. We'll let you three get to it." Lydia started to gather up her items as she spoke. "Come on, boys. Time to go home!"

Alex and Kaylee followed suit. They packed into their vehicles and set out to lunch. The venue was a nearby bistro for a light meal. Kaylee was ravenous and the aromas from the kitchen only intensified her hunger.

"It was nice to meet your friend," Alex said after the waiter left with their order. "But do you think you could give me a heads-up next time?" Kaylee felt the statement come across as a bit tense.

"Uh, sure. I meant to tell you on the phone, but you were off before I could say anything," Kaylee said evenly, trying to smooth over the ripple. "Besides, Lydia is nice. I thought you two would really get along."

"We might. I'm just not a fan of surprise guests, I suppose." Lunch arrived and the subject was forgotten. Ryan attacked his chicken fingers while the adults enjoyed a superfood salad. "What would you like to do tonight?"

"I don't know. Movie?" Kaylee offered between mouthfuls.

"Nothing really out at the moment. I have a suggestion but not sure if you'd be up for it." Alex paused to take a bite before continuing. "There's this great club called The Machine. They're hosting a lesbian night tonight, if you're interested."

"A club? Like music-dancing-drinks club?" Kaylee asked, chuckling.

"No, a book club," Alex quipped. "Of course, drinking and dancing. So, what do you think?"

"Well, to be honest, the idea of being in a dark room packed with people and loud music isn't the most appealing. And I can't dance." Kaylee fumbled on words, trying to come up with reasons not to go. "Maybe we could just do a quiet dinner?"

"Come on, when was the last time you went to a club? I know it's been years for me. I'll stay with you the whole time, promise." Alex tried her hand at persuasion. Kaylee struggled with it for a moment, pretending to focus on her salad. "Plus, we had a great time at Pride. It'll be the same kind of crowd."

"Okay," Kaylee said finally. "I'll give it a go. Just for you though."

The group finished their meal and headed in separate directions. Kaylee and Ryan went home to clean up and get ready for the babysitter, while Alex headed to her condo to get ready for their night out. As Kaylee looked through her wardrobe, she felt the beginnings of butterflies in her stomach. She was nervous, but Alex really wanted to go.

CHAPTER 2

The dim thump of music and a crowd of people outside the club's door made Kaylee's butterflies try to escape. The music seemed upbeat and the people friendly, but Kaylee was way outside of her comfort zone, even after Alex pulled her close. Kaylee felt like she was stepping back into college and her anxieties started to flare.

Once inside, Alex led them to a small table that was out of the way. Kaylee settled a bit; it was still early in the evening and not overwhelmingly crowded. Alex disappeared and came back with drinks a few minutes later.

"What do you think?" Alex asked, trying to feel out Kaylee's mood. She took a sip of her drink before setting it on the table.

"I really like the music, and there aren't too many people here at the moment. So far so good, I guess." Kaylee smiled as she lifted the yellow and orange cocktail. She hadn't really drunk this type of beverage in a long time. She could taste the sweet blend of juices, with only a small bite of alcohol. "This isn't bad at all. What is it?"

"A tequila sunrise. I guess you never really had a chance to get out and experience this side of life too much. The night is young. We can stay here as long as you're comfortable. No pressure," Alex reassured Kaylee. "Perhaps we can even try some dancing in a bit?"

"Yeah, that sounds good. Alex, there's something I wanted to ask you." Kaylee paused for a moment to take a drink before continuing. "Do you recall me asking about your piercing, and mentioning Lydia's nipple piercings?"

Kaylee felt odd talking about something so private in a public setting. She tried to ignore the thought that everyone was listening. She really wanted to get all of this out before the evening was over, and perhaps now would be the right time.

Alex nodded slowly, taking a moment to remember.

"Well, I think I've finally decided that I want to get it done." Kaylee blushed a little at her confession. "I want to get mine pierced."

"You want to get your nipples pierced?" Alex didn't pull any punches or show any tact about the subject. Kaylee's eyes popped open in surprise as Alex casually announced it to the world. After a second, she realized that nobody was paying attention and nodded her head, blushing slightly. "Perfect, we can set up an appointment! What about next week?"

"Well, I'm not sure I'd ever have the nerve to actually go and do something like that. Not unless I have some, uh, liquid courage. Which I might just have by the end of tonight." Kaylee smiled, trying to crack a joke.

She was met with a stern face. Alex leaned in with a look of concern. "Kay, I can understand where you're coming from, but this is not a light decision to make. It's something you definitely shouldn't decide while drinking, nevermind actually get done."

"I'm not deciding now, though. I made the decision before we even got here. I just wanted to tell you about it now. I thought that, since I've made up my mind about it, we could go after the club when I have more nerve. Besides, we haven't even finished one drink yet," Kaylee offered in defense.

"Well, we can think about it. How about we go dance for a bit?"

The two women went to the dance floor. Kaylee tried her best not to appear foolish, usually letting Alex guide her. After several songs, the pair went back to the table. Alex excused herself to the restroom, leaving Kaylee alone to order the next round.

"Christine?" A voice from behind Kaylee made her jump. "Hey it's me, Rachel.... Oh, you're not Christine."

Kaylee turned to face this Rachel with confusion sprawled over her face. She froze. "No, I'm not. I'm Kaylee. Are you, uh, missing your friend?"

The woman paused for a moment, wobbling slightly and squinting through the haze. "Not at all.

You just look like a friend I used to know. So, uh... Do you live around here?"

"Yeah, I moved here about ten months ago." Kaylee wasn't exactly sure what to do, and the girl wasn't making any move to leave. "What about you?"

"Oh, I've lived here most of my life. Love it here. Great place. Have you ever been to Salty Dog's? I work over that way. You should stop by and see me sometime, cutie." The girl slurred her words out, leaning against the table.

"Um." Uncomfortable, Kaylee tried to drop a hint. "Sure, maybe my girlfriend and I can come by sometime." The woman took another moment to process the words, and then realized she had no chance. She smiled at Kaylee and walked away without another word.

"Who was that?" Alex asked as she came back to the table. "It sounded like a great conversation."

"Someone who has probably had a bit too much to drink. She thought I was one of her friends and then asked me out. It was odd. Does this stuff normally happen in clubs?" Kaylee asked with a chuckle as the drinks arrived at the table.

"Yeah. It's one of the many fun things you have to deal with in the club scene: Random people butting in where they don't belong." Alex huffed, not appreciating the humor of the situation.

"I'm sure she's just drunk and meant no harm. She left as soon as I mentioned you. Want to go dance some more?"

Alex nodded, but she still seemed tense as they danced. After several more songs, Kaylee felt the call of nature and started working her way through the dance floor. Alex cut her way back to the table. As Kaylee approached the stairs, a woman stepped in front of her.

"Care for a dance, you beautiful woman, you?" The woman stood taller than Kaylee, with shoulder-length blonde hair and a lascivious smile.

"Uh, no, thanks. I'm just heading to the restroom. Then I'll be getting back to my girlfriend." Kaylee tried to keep it concise and casual. The woman frowned and allowed her to pass. After a quick trip to the restroom, Kaylee successfully navigated her way back to the table, pleased at how quickly she managed to deflect that one.

"Another friend?" Alex asked, an edge in her tone. Kaylee wasn't really enjoying the scene anymore, and Alex seemed irritated.

"No, some woman who wanted to dance with me. I told her I was on my way back to you." Kaylee felt a bit confused at Alex's reaction, but was more concerned with her anxiety. "I think I'm done with this place. I really enjoyed the dancing, but I'm starting to get overwhelmed."

The words seemed to jolt Alex back to herself. Visibly softening, Alex embraced Kaylee. They gathered their things and started for the door. Once they were on the street, Kaylee felt instantly better. The growing crowd had played a number on her during the latter part of the evening, and Alex's odd mood had only fueled her anxiety.

"Are you okay, Alex?" Kaylee felt a little out of place in the situation. She knew Alex kept most things inside, but tonight she didn't seem herself.

Alex tried to pass it off while they walked. "I'm fine. Just feeling a bit off, I guess. What would you like to do now?"

CHAPTER 3

The cocktails had been strong and, as the cool air hit, Kaylee started to really feel the effect. She was pretty sure she only had a few drinks, but to be honest, she hadn't counted. Kaylee felt relaxed and buzzed, but she didn't know what she wanted to do next. Then, an idea burst into her mind.

"You said you would take me to get my nipples pierced!" Kaylee blurted out, despite people being around. When she realized others were watching, she turned crimson.

Alex chuckled, feeling a little lighter being outside. "Yeah, but not tonight babe. Let's wait and go next week, or even tomorrow."

"I thought you said it would be hot to see my nipples pierced," Kaylee countered in a low voice. She was definitely feeling very buzzed, and teasing Alex was fun. "I mean, wouldn't you like to play with them?"

"Oh, I'm not saying it wouldn't be hot. I'm just saying that perhaps you should think about it a bit more." Alex evaded the second question entirely.

"I should think about it? I *have* thought about it, a lot. I think about your tongue swirling around them, how sensitive they would be." Kaylee leaned forward, purposely pressing her breasts into Alex's arm. "Just thinking about it has me a little turned on. What do you think?"

"I don't know, Kay, you've had a few drinks. You really shouldn't. Are you sure you don't want to wait?" Alex seemed to have an edge of concern in her voice, but the pleading and teasing was tempting her. It was a rare occasion for Kaylee to act so provocatively, especially outside of the bedroom.

Kaylee nodded. "Yes, I really want them done now."

"All right. I'll call to see if they can take you. Just a warning though, they'll have you sign a form that states you haven't been drinking. If they can tell you've had a few, they won't touch you."

***

Kaylee's nerves kicked in as they entered the tattoo parlor. Various artworks adorned the walls while a woman sat at the front desk, directing customers. Before she knew it, Kaylee was sitting on a high-backed surgical chair in a sterile room. A man walked in and headed straight for the counter.

"Good evening, ladies," the man said as he started to sanitize himself. He turned and smiled. "I'm Derek. What can I do for you?"

"Uh, Alex, I don't think I can do this anymore." Kaylee squirmed a bit. The liquid courage had worn off and she wasn't feeling so comfortable anymore.

"You said you wanted to do this, and this is your chance." Alex grinned at her. "You're welcome to back out, but I think these new piercings will look *very* hot."

The encouragement bolstered Kaylee up a bit. "Uh, I want to have my nipples pierced," Kaylee finally blurted out.

The man turned and opened a drawer upon the request. "Great choice. Before we start, please read and sign these forms." Derek handed Kaylee a tray and clipboard. "They cover things like health, consent, and liability. The second sheet is yours; it's about aftercare. Once you sign, please go ahead and take your shirt and bra off." Derek continued his preparation, laying out several torturous-looking devices. "Have you ever had any piercings before? How long have you been considering this?"

"Well, um, no I haven't, not anything other than my ears," Kaylee explained, reading over the forms. "I've wanted it for a month or so I guess, but really it's been a lot longer than that. I just, never, uh, really considered it properly until recently." After reading over everything, she signed the form and took a deep breath. Kaylee fidgeted on her seat, hesitant to undress in front of a stranger.

"Well, I can tell you that this is one of the more popular piercings..." The man halted, seeing that Kaylee had not started undressing. "Ma'am, I'm not really sure how you expect this to happen without taking your top off."

"She's just shy. Kay, he has a point." Alex was there as the voice of reason. "I'm right here. We can leave now if you want, but if you want them done, you'll need to undress."

Kaylee hesitated for a moment, fighting herself.

This man has probably seen thousands of breasts, Kaylee told herself.

Yeah, but this is a private part of me only shared with Alex, she countered.

You want this, so go out there and live a little Kaylee argued back.

As her inner voices finished their closing arguments, Kaylee finally removed her bra and felt cool air on her breasts.

"Hmm, ma'am, your nipples are on the smaller side. I'm not sure they'll hold..." Derek had been busy looking through various needles and up until that moment, had not paid any attention to her breasts. "Alright, so this is how it's going to work. I'm going to put a small clamp over the nipple to reduce blood flow. Then I'll lift them up and put markers where the piercing will go. Your nipples will need to be hard to show where the rings will be. Are you okay with this?"

"Uh, sure?" Kaylee was a bit confused, but she was already bare and resolved that she might as well go through with it. Derek reached out and placed a hand on her left nipple, rubbing it back and forth. "What—What do you think you're doing?"

"I'm sorry, didn't you just tell me I could do this? I need to make sure your post will hold." Derek had a puzzled look on his face. Kaylee wasn't so sure about this. She looked to Alex for guidance, who was watching intently. "All right, with your nipple hard like this, you can expect a barbell to be your best bet. You could probably go with a small ring, instead, if you want."

Derek held up one ring to her nipple, showing Kaylee with a mirror. He then held up a small barbell. Kaylee realized this was really about to happen and began to get a little nervous. She pointed to the small ring. Derek turned to the table and began to get several pieces of equipment ready and sterilized.

He turned to her with a small felt pen and marked the spots, again, getting confirmation with the mirror. The last step was the cold clamp. "Last chance, ma'am: Are you sure?"

"Yes, I'm sure," Kaylee said to Derek. Alex put her hand on Kaylee's shoulder to comfort her. Kaylee watched as Derek put a small needle towards her breast.

"Alright, close your eyes, take a deep breath..." Derek instructed. "Three... two... one..."

Kaylee yelped at the needle's pinch and saw stars as the small ring was inserted into her nipple. She sucked in a breath at the pain, tears welling up in her eyes. She hadn't expected that. Any semblance of her buzz from earlier was most definitely gone.

"Oh, man. Oh, that hurt." Kaylee moved to instinctively cover her breasts. The tender flesh pulsed at her touch. Derek was busy preparing the second ring. "Wait, uh, can I have a moment? I'm not sure on the second one, please. Uh, Alex?"

"You're doing great, Kay. Just one more moment and we'll be done. Then we can go home and get some rest. Besides, one is already done. Do you really want to be lopsided?" Alex's gentle encouragement helped her get through the distress. Derek followed the exact same procedure. *Three*... Kaylee screwed her eyes shut. *Two*... Breathe in. *One*.... Breathe ou—

"Ouch!" Kaylee bucked against the chair, pain ripping through her left breast. The searing flesh throbbed on her chest as Kaylee felt the metal invading her body.

"And you're done! They look great. How about checking them out?" Derek smiled to ease the mood and pointed Kaylee to the full-length mirror. Kaylee loved the look of the two small rings protruding from her nipples the moment she saw them. She turned proudly to show off for Alex, forgetting that Derek was watching.

"What do you think?" Kaylee said proudly, buzzing once again with excitement.

"That you're hot as hell and I want to have my wicked way with you," Alex said smoothly. Kaylee blushed at Alex's bold statement. Derek also blushed, having been unaware that they were a couple. He quickly covered the necessary aftercare information and excused himself, leaving Kaylee to get dressed again.

"Truly, they look amazing. Now let's get you home so we can celebrate."

CHAPTER 4

As soon as the babysitter was gone, Alex turned to Kaylee. The look in her eyes sent a chill down Kaylee's spine. She knew that it was a Ms. Carlisle night tonight. After checking in on Ryan, they went straight to the bedroom. Alex was already sitting at the edge of the bed when Kaylee walked in.

"Strip, my pet," Ms. Carlisle said crisply. "I want to see your new jewelry."

Kaylee rushed to see to her command as swiftly as she could. The throbbing pain in her nipples made clothing very uncomfortable. Her skirt and panties were tossed to the side and Kaylee stood nude before her lover.

"Gorgeous, my little Kitty. Come closer so I can look at you."

Kaylee seductively crossed the room until her bare breasts were at eye level with Alex. The new piercings felt sexy, even if they were still tender. Once she crossed the room, Kaylee did a slow spin, showing off her curves and shifting her body.

"I thought you said you couldn't dance," Alex smirked. "Were you telling me a lie, my pet?"

The false pretense almost made Kaylee break character and smile. She knew that that would not bode well, so she fumbled with a way to come back clean.

"No, ma'am. I would never lie to you. I simply do not believe I can dance." Kaylee fidgeted flirtatiously in front of Ms. Carlisle.

"I think you *can* dance, and you just proved it. I think that constitutes a lie and deserves punishment. Perhaps you need a spanking." Alex had a solid, steady tone to her voice, with just a hint of wickedness. Kaylee swayed her hips and turned.

"A spanking? But..." Kaylee began, a bit concerned with where this was going.

"Are you questioning me, my pet?" Alex was firmly locked in her role, and expected Kaylee to fall into hers.

"No, ma'am, I'm not. I, uh, well..." Kaylee stammered out.

Alex reached out a hand, tracing a finger along Kaylee's hipbones. The finger trailed up her stomach to her fresh piercings. Alex made sure not to touch the tender flesh, but she spent several moments admiring them. The soft, gentle strokes made Kaylee coo.

"As gorgeous as these are, you need to go and get a sports bra," Alex said, breaking character momentarily. "I want to have my way with you, but I don't want you to be in pain or damage your newest accessories because of it."

Kaylee jumped to do what she was told. She returned to find Alex positioned on the edge of the bed, her legs spread open, ready for Kaylee.

Without a word, Kaylee dropped to her knees and began rubbing Alex's thighs softly. Alex watched Kaylee in silence. Their eyes met, sparking that burning desire. Kaylee felt a stirring deep within her, but it wasn't simply lust or desire. It traveled deeper, an aching sense that she needed to be submissive. The hungry look in Alex's eyes illustrated the beauty of their power roles.

Ms. Carlisle gave a slight nod of her head, granting permission. Kaylee didn't just feel an obligation to do as she was told – She felt the sense of pride of a job well-done. She wanted, *yearned* for that approval. She needed to hear Alex call her name and tell her what a good kitty she was. These tumultuous emotions raged within Kaylee as she leaned into Alex.

Alex kept her eyes locked with Kaylee, feeling Kaylee's breath on her exposed sex. Kaylee slowly drew her tongue across the velvety folds, sending a shiver down Alex's spine. Alex sighed with delight and smiled. That smile drew on Kaylee's inner need to please, and she started lapping away, trying to elicit a stronger reaction from Ms. Carlisle.

"Mmm, what a good kitty you are," Alex panted, running a hand through Kaylee's wavy locks. The words rushed over Kaylee. The pleasure of knowing how well she satisfied her Alex burned deep. Redoubling her efforts, she drove her tongue deep into Alex, striving to push her over the edge. Alex let out a moan of approval.

The hand on Kaylee's head applied pressure as Alex started to grind her womanhood against Kaylee's tongue. Kaylee slid out of Alex and focused on her clit. In the same fluid motion, she pushed two fingers deep inside. A groan of ecstasy filled the tiny room – Kaylee knew she had Alex close. The burning desire raged in both of them, but Kaylee's *need* was only to please Alex.

With a few more swirls of her tongue, Kaylee felt Alex's grip pull hard. Alex's body convulsed and shuttered with a powerful orgasm. Kaylee gradually let up as Alex came down. Alex lay back on the bed, her body still twitching. Kaylee felt satisfied with her work, but she waited, kneeling. She knew Ms. Carlisle wasn't done, and would soon give further instructions.

"Mmm, that was amazing, my Kitty Kay. Now it's your turn. I want you to lie down on your stomach on the bed," Alex directed as she recovered. "Be careful with your new piercings." Kaylee jumped to comply, while Alex walked into the living room. "Close your eyes. I bought some things and do not want you to see."

"Yes, Ms. Carlisle." Kaylee snapped her eyes closed and turned her head to the far wall. Her bare form lay face down on the bed with nothing but a bra on to protect her newest accessories. She could feel Alex moving through the room, but couldn't tell where. Kaylee waited in anticipation with building excitement as the silence drew into an eternity.

A light sensation raced up the back of her thigh. Kaylee wiggled her bottom in response, not knowing what to expect. The line being traced followed her leg, then her butt, and then her back. It traced an arc before racing down the other side. The feeling was so light that it almost tickled. It made Kaylee squirm and wonder what was about to happen.

"My pet, do you recall the red, yellow, green system?" Alex questioned, Kaylee nodded. "Good. We're going to employ that system tonight. If it gets to be too much, you know the drill."

"Yes, I... I remember, Ms. Carlisle." Kaylee nodded her head again, yet nothing else came. The room was silent. Kaylee could not feel the slightest shift of weight nor hear the faint rustling of cloth to determine where Alex stood. Without warning, Kaylee felt a small slap on her backside, causing her to jump in surprise. There was no pain, but it startled her nonetheless.

Another *thwap* struck her cheeks, this time more firmly. Kaylee still felt no pain but rather excitement about the unknown. The third strike came more quickly than before and focused on one cheek. This one stung ever-so-slightly. Kaylee had never been spanked like this before. She had heard about it but had never been sure why people would willingly want to experience it.

"What is your color, Kitty?" Mrs. Carlisle's voice rang out.

"Green, Ma'am," Kaylee answered quickly. As soon as the sound of Kaylee's voiced died out, it was replaced with the sound of the leather strap slapping human flesh. This one stung, causing a small groan to escape Kaylee's lips.

Kaylee had expected to feel silly, even joking about the topic. The real reaction was far from a laughing matter. She was not only starting to anticipate the swings, but she wanted them.

Mrs. Carlisle picked up the tempo. Kaylee could feel her flesh glowing with light heat after the short session. The pain intermingled with pleasure, creating rushes of excitement. A part of Kaylee did not want to admit it, but her body had responded very positively to the activity.

"Are you ready for your punishment?" Alex said suddenly, between spanks. Kaylee's head swam with intoxicating thoughts and feelings. The words took a moment before they sank in, and she spoke out of turn.

"Punishment for what?" Kaylee blurted out before remembering character. "Uh – Ms. Carlisle."

"For lying about dancing earlier," Alex quipped. "You know lying is not good." Kaylee had thought the dancing comment was made in jest, but now doubted the humor. "I think ten lashes should cover it."

"Uh, yes. Yes, ma'am." Kaylee sucked in air, not knowing what to expect. The first slap was brusquer than the playful taps from earlier. Kaylee's nerve endings danced with heat radiating from the impact. The second and third were spread out, causing Kaylee to twist and buck. Four and five brought forth a deep moan from Kaylee's open mouth.

Kaylee could feel the warmth emanating from her backside. The tender flesh caused her to writhe with each strike. She knew the worst part was that her body betrayed her: She was enjoying this. The excitement Kaylee felt caused her nectar to flow and leak down her leg. At last, the tenth spank came, causing Kaylee to buck and almost climax. She felt elated, giddy and swimming with heated emotion.

Alex knelt on the bed over Kaylee, running her hands lightly down the tender flesh. The sensation gave Kaylee chills. Alex straddled one of Kaylee's legs, forcing them open slightly. Kaylee felt something cool slide between her thighs. She could not see, but the texture felt different than anything she had ever played with. The toy found her opening and pressed firmly into her. Kaylee gasped at the fullness. The rigid object had no give, but her nectar allowed it to enter easily.

Alex focused on moving the toy in and out. The firm object drove Kaylee's already-heated body quickly toward the edge. Within minutes, Kaylee felt herself nearly fall from the cliff and into the abyss of orgasm. As her body clung to the edge, she relived the heat and intensity of the spankings. She felt a sense of pride in her service. She had been a good kitty, and this was her reward. Kaylee let go and allowed herself to fall into ecstasy, her juices gushing from her body in a moment of pure bliss.

Alex continued her ministrations until Kaylee came down, and then pulled her into a protective embrace. At last, she revealed the toys: A small leather crop and a pretty glass dildo. Kaylee struggled to focus through glazed eyes. Alex could feel the euphoria and heat radiating through Kaylee's skin and focused on giving loving, soft touches. Both women lay together in a bubble of contentment.

"What did you think?" Alex whispered into the dimly lit room.

Kaylee's mind fluttered around, trying to come up with an answer, trying to be honest with herself. This all-consuming, euphoric afterglow she was floating around in defied all logic.

"I don't know what to say," Kaylee started, as she focused on the undulating currents of emotion within her. "I'm lost for words. I've never had that done to me, I-I thought it was bit of a joke at first."

"Do you still think that?" Alex countered, bemused by Kaylee's headspace.

"No. I... I don't know. I'm still shaking. Thank you," Kaylee said as she snuggled closer.

"I assure you, it was my pleasure." Alex nuzzled and kissed Kaylee. "Try and get some rest. I love you."

"I love you, too," Kaylee answered, her mind drifting off into euphoria. Both women fell into a warm sleep, cuddled together.

CHAPTER 5

Monday morning came all too soon, ushering in another week. Rose and Kaylee had a meeting first thing. Kaylee liked Rose, but these early meetings generally made for a busier week. While Rose worked on the projector, Alex walked in carrying a round of coffee and tea for everyone. Kaylee was a little surprised; Alex didn't normally come to design meetings. That probably meant something big was about to happen.

"Alexis, thank you for the coffee. Hope you had a great weekend," Rose said in her normal cheery tone.

Kaylee thought about the weekend and noted how her nipples were still throbbing against her bra. She blushed momentarily, recalling the sound of the leather as it met her skin and the warm, fuzzy afterglow that had not yet fully dissipated. Looking up, Kaylee's eyes met with Alex's for a brief second, echoing and amplifying every thought.

Rose was still speaking. "I think we can go ahead and begin once Blaire gets in."

Why would Blaire need to be here? Kaylee's mind stopped focusing on everything non-work-related and snapped into the conversation. Just then, a door opened and two women walked in. Blaire was the hiring manager that had brought Kaylee into the fold almost a year ago. Behind her was a woman roughly the same height as Alex and strikingly pretty. She had blond hair and captivating blue eyes.

"Good morning, everyone. I wanted to bring Megan by before we get her set up in the office." Blaire continued in her slightly-nasal voice. "Megan, this is Alexis, Rose, and Kaylee. Alexis and Rose are the managers of their respective departments, and Kaylee is one of our clothing designers."

"Nice to meet you all. I'm Megan." Megan's voice was silky and clear, but soft-spoken. She stepped toward the head of the conference table to shake hands with everyone. Alex stood up and met the woman with her normal, stoic business veneer. Rose was next, then Kaylee stood to greet her.

"Nice to meet you. Are you new here?" It was nice to have a new office member, considering the increased workload they had had since starting their latest contract.

"You could say that," Blaire said. "I take it you haven't told her?"

"Told her? It's nine-fifteen. We haven't even made it to coffee yet," Rose joked. "Kaylee, Megan is starting an internship with us. She will be your assistant."

The news hit Kaylee like a sack of bricks. She had received the promotion just a few months ago, and now she would have her own assistant. Her head swam for a moment trying to process the idea. She looked over at Rose and then to Alex, who sat smiling behind her cup of coffee. She realized now that Alex had known about it.

"Well, that sounds great. I look forward to working with you, Megan," Kaylee said at last, not wanting to appear lost. Megan smiled.

Blaire started towards the door. "Well, Megan, let's go. I better show you around." Blaire was never one for chitchatting when there were things to do. The two women gave a quick goodbye as they left the conference room. Kaylee stared at Rose and Alex intently, waiting for one of them to break the silence.

"Well, surprise! We didn't mean for it to go quite like that, but it worked out well." Rose chuckled. "Congrats, Kaylee. You earned it."

"The look on your face was priceless," Alex laughed, breaking her mask for just a moment. She seemed much more at ease in Rose's presence after the business trip. The three women covered some base topics before returning to their respective offices. Alex joined Kaylee before heading off.

"This is crazy," Kaylee said. "I've never managed anyone before, not even in a fast-food restaurant. What am I supposed to do?"

"Relax. Managing people is a breeze. You tell them what to do, they do it. Done." Alex made the whole thing seem easy. A knock at the door paused the conversation. Without waiting, Megan barged into the room with some folders.

"Oh, uh, hi. Sorry to interrupt," Megan said, smiling at Kaylee. "I was wondering, uh, what you'd like me to do?"

"Oh, you're not interrupting anything at all," Alex cut in, rolling her eyes at Kaylee.

"Okay, cool, so um, should I just wait on you then?" Megan seemed unaware of Alex's biting remark. She shuffled her feet for a moment.

"Yeah, I'll be out in a few minutes," Kaylee told her quickly. She didn't want Megan to feel uncomfortable because of Alex. "Go ahead and start setting up your email and everything."

"How do I do that?" Megan asked. Kaylee wasn't sure if she was joking or not.

"Open up Outlook and bam! E-mail." Alex seemed to be in a bit of a mood, but Megan still ignored her.

"Tell you what, why not just work up some outfit sketches until I get there?" Kaylee didn't know what was going on with Alex, but Megan seemed to accept the answer and left the room. "What was that about, Alex? That wasn't like you."

"I think she's a walking stereotype, to be honest. She rubs me the wrong way. I'm not sure I like her." Alex's face had her business mask back on. "Good luck training that one. Well, I'd better get back to it, and you have quite a task ahead of you."

"Oh, come on. Give her a chance. You've only just met her."

"Technically speaking, I met her a few weeks ago during a very painful interview," Alex confessed. "However, the final decision wasn't up to me."

"You didn't like her then?" Kaylee asked, now even more confused.

"Like I said, I'm not overly fond of her, and I don't think she'll catch on very quickly. She seems more of a free spirit than a corporate climber." Alex's words weren't exactly cutting, but it gave a clear portrayal of how she saw Megan. "Maybe she's a nice girl, but her personality is just too airy for me."

After Alex left, Kaylee took a moment to reflect. She had never known Alex to voice such dislike. *But I have an assistant*, Kaylee's mind squealed in delight. The fact that she was moving up in the company sank in. That news flooded almost everything else and the thought of Alex's dislike for Megan was lost.

The rest of the afternoon was spent giving a company introduction to Megan. To Alex's credit, she did have the woman pegged. Even computer basics escaped Megan, and Kaylee soon felt frustrated with trying to teach her. On the other hand, Kaylee saw real potential in Megan's designs and enjoyed her personality.

"Megan," Kaylee finally said. "You seem to be struggling with a few things. Is everything okay?" Kaylee was alarmed that someone didn't know how to use Microsoft Office in this day and age. Megan was only a few years younger than Kaylee, and their generation grew up with computers.

"Well, to be honest, my parents never vested much interest in the technological advancements of the world. They were, uh, kind of hippies. Couple that with not buying into corporate America, and they were also pretty poor. We were a pen-and-paper kinda family."

Megan's explanation made sense, but left a lot of questions unanswered. "I suppose there's always time to learn, and you'll need to if you want to advance your career," Kaylee said thoughtfully.

"Hopefully we can get you up to speed during your time here. This stuff is all pretty easy once you get into it."

The rest of the week seemed to follow the same schedule. Kaylee put her own tasks on hold, trying to get Megan up to speed. Megan's jokes and easygoing demeanor made the time pass quickly, despite her difficulties on the technology front.

By Friday, Kaylee felt like Megan was making some improvement. She invited her out to lunch with her and Alex. Kaylee hoped that if the two of them got to know each other better, they would get along.

"I invited Megan to come along with us for lunch," Kaylee told Alex when they met in the hallway. Alex stood stunned for a moment as Megan smiled and waved at her.

"Oh, uh, great. Nice to have you along, Megan." Alex remained diplomatic, having cooled off from Monday's encounter.

The three of them set off to one of the local sandwich shops. The walk passed quickly on the gorgeous day, although Alex had little to add to any of the conversation.

"I really dig Boston. It's one of my favorite cities. It's so nice this time of year," Megan commented as they crossed the street.

"I've really grown to enjoy it, too," Kaylee said. "I moved here about ten months ago. In fact, Alex took me out to lunch on my first day." She was trying to draw Alex into the conversation, but not having much luck.

When Alex didn't offer a reply, Megan continued. "Far out. So, what brought you to Boston then?"

"Well, I was offered a position here, so I moved. Pretty much like you did, I guess." Kaylee contemplated for a moment. "Where did you move here from?"

"I've lived all over Chicago and most of Illinois, and some other towns throughout the Midwest. My parents were like gypsies, I swear," Megan laughed as she entered the shop.

Kaylee hung back, holding the door for Alex.

"Well that explains a lot," Alex said under her breath. Kaylee chuckled and shook her head at Alex before they started in behind Megan.

"At least try, love. You might like her," Kaylee whispered in light amusement as they headed to the register and placed their orders. Kaylee felt that it was her duty to step up and pay for lunch, since Megan was *her* assistant. A wave of pride washed over Kaylee as she handed her card to the cashier. This was a moment to remember.

"Thank you so much for buying me lunch. It means a lot to me," Megan started in as they all sat down. "This is a really nice place. Do you come here a lot?"

"Generally, Kaylee and I have lunch together every Friday." Alex seemed defensive for some reason, but Kaylee tried to keep it pleasant. The conversation through the rest of lunch was awkward and broken.

As five o'clock hit, Kaylee was more than ready to end the week and looked forward to going home.

CHAPTER 6

The car was mostly silent as the Mazda whipped through the city. Alex and Kaylee were heading to dinner for their date night. Conversation seemed detached. Kaylee felt like something might be wrong with Alex, but she kept getting mixed signals. The restaurant was an upscale Japanese steakhouse where the chef put on a show.

"Alex, are you alright?" Kaylee asked as they were seated. A few people sat across the long table and more were on their way.

"I'm great. Hungry, though, and tired after a long week. Why?" Alex spoke in her business manner. There was something different about her, though; Alex seemed to be internally struggling with something.

"No reason, I suppose. You just seem a little on edge tonight. I was wondering if something was on your mind." Kaylee kept trying to get words out, but nothing seemed to flow. Then realization struck: They were surrounded by people. Alex wouldn't open up in such a public setting.

A stout man pulled a cart onto the would-be stage and started his show. As the fire blazed and the chef performed small parlor tricks, Kaylee kept the conversation light and civil. The food ended up being delicious, but the evening as a whole was not so satisfying. The lack of personal conversation left Kaylee feeling confused about Alex's standpoint. As they returned home, nothing had really changed in Alex's demeanor.

***

The apartment was quiet when they got home. Kaylee checked in on Ryan to make sure he was asleep. Before heading to bed, she locked up and went through her nightly routine. When she got to the bedroom, Alex was waiting for her. Kaylee was rather shocked at the sight. Alex stood in a corset and black leather boots, her strap-on pointing proudly at Kaylee. For a split second, Kaylee was not sure if she should laugh, leave, or bow down.

"Strip, young lady," Alex snipped, setting the demeanor for the scene. Kaylee immediately did as she was told, despite feeling conflicted. On one hand, she had really enjoyed their role-play sessions and the concept of submitting. On the other hand, the tone of the night already seemed dark.

Alex strode to Kaylee, her hips swaying seductively as she approached. Kaylee thought Alex looked delicious with a dash of danger. Alex ran her hands over Kaylee's body, along her hips, her back, and her breasts. Kaylee felt like she was a piece of meat being sized and assessed. Alex worked her way around Kaylee until she was breathing on Kaylee's neck. The light tickling sensation gave Kaylee goosebumps across her skin.

"Are you nervous?" Alex whispered into Kaylee's ear. Again the lightness of her touch seemed to shoot electricity through Kaylee. "Maybe you should be."

"Yes, Ms. Carlisle," Kaylee said obediently, falling instantly into the role she was meant to play. Kaylee could feel the silicone phallus pressing against her. The night already seemed surreal.

"Lay on your back," Alex whispered although it felt like a command not to be trifled with. Kaylee rushed to do as she was told. Alex watched intently. As soon as Kaylee was on the bed, Alex joined her, straddling Kaylee's face as if to get into a sixty-nine position. "Eat me, Kitten."

Before Kaylee could give a verbal confirmation, Alex pressed herself onto Kaylee's mouth. Kaylee complied, feeling that surge of need and want to please Alex. *The mood may be different, but I want to please her*, Kaylee thought to herself. She lapped at Alex's nectar, causing Alex to sigh and moan as she traced her fingertips across Kaylee's abdomen in swirling patterns.

Kaylee tried to focus hard on her task. Alex continued to lightly tease Kaylee, even moving her hands along Kaylee's breasts. A sudden tweak of the nipple caused Kaylee to buck against the bed in pain. Her concentration broken, Kaylee shoved Alex to where she could speak.

"Alex, that hurt!" she scolded. "They're still tender from last week." She slowly returned to her place, working herself back into the mood.

"That is Ms. Carlisle. I will leave them alone for now," Alex's said in an authoritative tone. Alex leaned forward onto one hand, freeing the other to roam over Kaylee's lower body. Fingers traced lines along her hips and thighs, occasionally dipping down to tease her juices. Kaylee started to enjoy the caresses and got back to work.

"Mmm, that's good!" Alex purred while shifting forward. The change pushed Alex's clit further into Kaylee's mouth. Taking the hint, Kaylee lightly sucked Alex's nub while reaching around to push a finger into her. The angle made the strap-on press uncomfortably against Kaylee's throat. Kaylee didn't want to say anything, so she tried to focus on the goal of getting Alex off as quickly as possible.

Three fingers suddenly entered Kaylee's depths, filling her completely. Kaylee moaned into Alex, not able to move her mouth anywhere else. Alex started a slow and steady grind with her hips, matching the rocking motion with her fingers. It was harder to breathe now, but Kaylee wasn't sure she wanted to stop yet. She was very much enjoying what Alex was doing at the other end.

Alex suddenly removed her fingers and climbed off of Kaylee, who struggled to appear like she was breathing normally. Once Alex had moved, she traced her fingers along Kaylee, as if trying to decide what she would do with her.

"On your knees, Kitten." The tone was still assertive, yet seductive. Kaylee swirled with emotion, simultaneously wanting to please Alex, to be pleased, and to ease up on the scene. She did as she was told, pushing her backside into the air on all fours. Alex knelt behind her and drove her tongue deep into Kaylee. Kaylee gasped at the sudden onslaught, moaning into the sheets.

Alex was not being gentle, but Kaylee felt excited by the roughness. Now that she was on the receiving end and could breathe, her worries dulled. Kaylee gripped the sheets in both hands as Alex pushed her closer and closer to the edge. Kaylee could feel the dam about to burst when Alex stopped and leaned up.

"Not yet!" Alex smirked as she traced a line with her fingertip along Kaylee's back. Kaylee groaned and released the built up anticipation in a huff.

"Aww, that was frustrating, Alex."

"That is '*Ms. Carlisle*,'" Alex quickly retorted. "Keep that in mind, or you may indeed end the night frustrated."

Kaylee felt conflicted once more. The raging fires within her cried for release, but there was something about Alex's attitude that made this scene less appealing. Kaylee had little time to contemplate, though. Alex slid her body up Kaylee until she could feel the silicone toy press against her. As soon as the bulbous head touched Kaylee's entrance, Alex thrust deep into her, forcing a moan from Kaylee's lips. Alex immediately pulled back and lunged forward again.

Alex gripped Kaylee's hips roughly as she continued to thrust back and forth. Soon both women were panting at the rough play. Alex would not let up on the onslaught, pounding into Kaylee from behind. The intensity and heated passion overwhelmed Kaylee until her mind could focus only on what was being done to her.

"F-uck! Oh *fuck*," Kaylee gasped, moaning into the pillows in an attempt to keep quiet.

Kaylee could hear Alex talking dirty to her, but her mind was too wrapped up in what was going on to comprehend the words. Alex was being rough – not just with the thrusting, but spanking her butt with one hand, gripping her hips hard, and even pulling her hair a few times. Kaylee was awash in a sea of conflicting emotions. Her mind kept fighting to understand where this roughness was coming from, but the continual stimulation drew her attention back, keeping her close to the edge of orgasm and pulsing with desire.

Panting for breath, Kaylee did her best to withstand the storm. She could feel Alex's thrusts coming in ragged succession. Kaylee knew Alex was close. She too was about to explode. Alex picked up the pace, determined to ride Kaylee to delicious release. Suddenly the intensity became too much for Kaylee to bear; the spankings too rough, the nails too deep, the darkness too dark.

"Yellow!" Kaylee felt disappointed to throw in the towel, but the scene was overwhelming her. Alex must not have heard; she surged into Kaylee. Alex gripped her hips, driving the hard phallus as deep as it would go. "Alex, please. Yellow!"

Kaylee's words became little more than a whisper to Alex's grunts. Finally, Alex moaned in ecstasy and slowed down, her body convulsing from the intense orgasm. With one final thrust, she buried the silicone toy in Kaylee and knelt triumphantly behind her. As the world came back into focus, she realized Kaylee was not in the same euphoric state.

"Kay, are you okay?" Alex said, the first hint of normalcy returning to her. Alex pulled out of Kaylee with a squelch, and sat back on her ankles. "Kay?"

Kaylee felt empty. She could tell it was over, but her mind still worked to process everything. She had enjoyed many aspects of the scene, but not all of it. Kaylee felt conflicted about whatever had just happened. Her body felt sore from the spanking and rough play. The session was intense, and part of her was happy she could share it with Alex. But part of her felt like it was a different side of Alex, something she hadn't seen before.

Kaylee knew that Alex had said something, but her head hadn't gotten around to processing it yet. Kaylee felt like she couldn't make her mind work. She knew that Alex had had an extremely intense orgasm, but Kaylee felt cheated. She knew that the scene was over, and her body ached from it. She was no longer in the mood, but by the same token, she desired release.

"Kaylee?" Alex said softly into the silence. "I'm sorry."

Kaylee could feel the bed creaking as Alex moved off to get undressed. Kaylee shifted her body to lie down. Alex came to bed and snuggled behind her. Kaylee didn't know what to say. She felt the warm embrace and enjoyed the closeness; yet, part of her wanted to break down but felt too numb to react.

"Kay, I didn't mean to go that far. I..." Alex seemed almost as much at a loss for words as Kaylee was. Kaylee wanted to say something, wanted to explain the feelings silently raging inside of her. Nothing came, though. "Please talk to me, Kay."

Alex's hand softly stroked up and down Kaylee's arm. The gentle touch reminded Kaylee of so many great times. Now those memories felt overshadowed by the rawness of what had just happened. Kaylee felt confused and unsure of what to say, so she just lay there. She felt Alex give up on trying to talk it out. A single tear rolled down Kaylee's cheek as they drifted off into fitful sleep.

CHAPTER 7

Kaylee's week passed by quickly, most of it spent with Megan. By Friday, Kaylee had her working unaided at her own station, allowing Kaylee to finally get back to her own tasks.

The week had been busy and decidedly awkward with Alex, even if Alex had kept mostly to herself. At eleven-thirty, she popped into Kaylee's office. Her normal business demeanor seemed slightly off.

"Would you like to go to lunch? Just the two of us," Alex said softly. Kaylee stopped what she was doing and nodded. The two of them set off towards one of Kaylee's favorite places, a small Thai restaurant. "I'm sorry I've been quiet this week. I've been doing a lot of thinking."

"I'm sorry, too. I've been so busy with Megan," Kaylee answered, not exactly sure what to say. The walk was quieter than normal. They didn't hold hands.

"You have nothing to apologize for, Kay. This is my fault," Alex explained. "I... Well, I... Look, I've had these pent-up emotions that I don't understand. I don't know how to deal with them."

The floodgates seemed to be opening up. Kaylee had kept everything to herself over the past week, and it seemed Alex had, too. Kaylee stopped on the sidewalk and looked at Alex. She gazed into Alex's piercing green eyes, now clouded with regret and guilt.

"This is all so new to me. I've never felt this before for anyone, and I feel like I'm screwing it up." Alex took in a heady pause before continuing. "I don't know what to do about it and it's tearing me apart. I've never floundered with anything before, not in school, not in my career – hell, not even with other women. You're different, though."

"Alex, tell me what's wrong. What has you so flustered?" Kaylee had guessed wrong. She thought this was all about their last date night. Now it seemed to go much deeper. Kaylee put her thoughts and feelings on the back burner, now only concerned for Alex. Alex turned and started walking slowly again.

"Well, I don't know really. A bunch of small, stupid things." Alex's business mask seemed to have been forgotten.

"Tell me, babe. What's wrong? What small things?" Kaylee was almost pleading now. "I can't help you if you don't let me in."

"You're right," Alex blurted out, as if an epiphany had overcome her. "I guess it boils down to jealousy, but it seems like so much more than that. I was angry that you invited Megan to our lunch last week. Jealous over those women at the club. Even kind of miffed about Lydia and her kids at the park. But I never thought I was a jealous person."

Kaylee reflected over the last few weeks and realized that those actions had impacted Alex in ways she had not considered. The whole confession shocked Kaylee. They got to the restaurant and were seated quickly. Kaylee contemplated everything Alex had said while food was served.

"Is anything else bothering you?" Kaylee ventured. She wanted to get everything out on the table.

"Well, yeah. I guess our trial run last month gave me a lot of doubts about myself." Alex tried to gather her thoughts. "I know I want you to be that special person in my life, but I'm not sure I could be a good mom. There's so much to being a parent. I completely failed."

"Alex, I love you. We can work through all of this. I think you'd make a great mom, and Ryan already thinks you're awesome." Then Kaylee added, "I also think that we can get through anything together, but only if we talk about it." She looked to Alex and smiled. "I believe those were your wise words."

"You're right. I'm sorry." Alex seemed unsure of herself. "I'm just not sure how to express what I'm feeling. Especially not in the middle of a restaurant."

"Yeah, maybe we need to set aside some private time just to sit and talk. To be honest, I've had some stuff on my mind, too."

"It's about last Saturday, isn't it?" Alex said, throwing a quick glance at Kaylee before returning her eyes to the table. "That's really been on my mind a lot too. I've been beating myself up all week for my recent behavior. I'm so sorry, Kay.

"Yeah, that is a big part of it. Don't get me wrong, I really enjoyed most of it. And everything we've done together has blown me away. I just felt like—" Kaylee paused, not exactly sure what to say.

"Felt like I was being selfish and domineering, like you were just there for me. Like I wasn't listening. Like I used you," Alex said with a tone of finality. Alex knew what Kaylee was feeling; she had seen the pain in her eyes. "Kay, I pushed too hard and too fast. My mind was clouded. I wasn't listening properly and I regret all of it."

"Yeah, that's pretty much it, I guess," Kaylee timidly ventured. "It just seemed like you weren't, well, you. You seemed distant that entire week. And then, Saturday night..."

"You're right, I was distant and not my usual self. I was kicking myself for not being able to deal with my emotions." Alex stared at the table as she confessed. "For taking you to get your nipples pierced when you'd been drinking. Hell, for even being upset about you making friends."

"Alex, you could have told me. We could have talked about it." Kaylee's voice was tiny, almost nonexistent. "Instead, you took it out on me; you made me bleed with how rough you were."

Alex paused. The words took a moment to sink in. She had taken her emotional turmoil and turned it on the one she loved instead of working through it. *Some fucking girlfriend.*

They ate in silence, the last statement veiling thick between them.

"Kay, I really fucked up," Alex finally mumbled, aghast at herself and the realization that had truly sat in. "I don't want to lose you. I don't want to hurt you. Please, I'm so sorry. Let me try to make it up to you."

Kaylee looked up to see tears stinging Alex's eyes – in public, no less. Kaylee had gone over and over how to broach this topic. Could she really be with someone who could hurt her like that? Someone who didn't even *understand* that she was hurting her?

"I said 'yellow'. I thought that was supposed to mean something," Kaylee started to break down, tears threatening to spill down her cheeks. "I didn't know what I'd done to make you so angry."

"Kay—" Alex floundered for words. She knew that it was her fault this was happening. *She* had caused this. "You did nothing. It was all me. Yes, yellow means something, and I'm disgusted with myself. I don't know what's going on. This isn't me. Please let me try to fix it." Alex reached across the table to take her hand. "Kay?"

THANK YOU FOR READING

If you enjoyed *Branding Her* would you do me a favor and leave a review on Amazon? Even a very short review helps immensely and would *really* mean a lot to me. Thanks!

For free updates and stories please sign up to my mailing list at www.ALEXBPORTER.com

And if you'd like to be social, connect on Twitter @lesficAlex or tweet using #BrandingHer.

THANKS

A massive thanks to everyone involved in the
making of this series.

Edited by Haley Torboli.

BRANDING HER
OTHER BOOKS IN THE SERIES

BY ALEX B PORTER
WWW.ALEXBPORTER.COM

CPSIA information can be obtained
at www.ICGtesting.com
Printed in the USA
LVOW10s1509170717
541644LV00011B/187/P